ONE

Beulah Price's body looked like a hotdog that had been left on the grill too long. Charred skin stretched taut over her ribcage and collar bones. A wisp of hair clung to her scorched skull. Baked into her right pinky was a garnet ring that had belonged to my grandmother.

The entire museum had sustained damage before we could control the fire, but the area around her body was the worst. A kerosene heater lay on its side between Beulah's remains and a set of stairs leading up to the clock tower.

Harold Seeton, the Fire Chief, had taken one look at Beulah's body and dropped with a heart attack. The ambulance standing by hauled him down to Riverton Memorial Hospital and left me in charge.

When I was convinced to accept the position of Assistant Chief, I was promised that the responsibilities were minimal and that nothing ever happened except an occasional chimney fire and the odd drunk tossing liquor bottles on a bonfire. And car crashes. There were frequently car crashes out on the highway. Looking back, I should have realized there was a reason no one else volunteered. It wasn't that I was a good leader or well organized. It was definitely not that the department, exclusively staffed by men, was eager to jump on the equal rights wagon. It was that the job entailed a lot of paperwork and get your ducks in a row crap they knew enough to avoid.

I wanted to run out of the building and puke behind a tree, but I already had enough problems being taken seriously by the other firefighters. Respect doesn't come easy when you're forty-seven years old and look like a slightly overweight Shirley Temple. I'm cursed with sandy sausage curls, big brown eyes and dimples you could lose a truck in. Add to that the fact that the oldest guys on the crew could remember when I wore dresses with pinafores and tights with ruffles across the seat. The only thing going for me was a willingness to hand over the whole thing to the State Fire Marshal's investigator as soon as he could find his way to Winslow Falls.

We'd been working steadily for three hours, pulling down plaster and checking for hot spots, and it didn't look as though there was much left to do but wait for the coroner and the guy from the state. I trudged outside, tugged off my turnout coat and settled on the fire engine's running board. I took stock of the museum. Much of the roofline had been eaten away by flames. A full white moon hung over the sodden stump that had been the clock tower. Nothing at all was left of the giant wooden hand ornament that decorated its steeple. And, as much as I didn't like to think of it, there wasn't much left of Beulah either.

The cold air felt good, and it was a relief to take a break. I wished for a cup of coffee and a shower. I wished I'd never volunteered for the fire department.

"Whadaya got on?" Clive Merrill rounded the corner of the truck reeling up a hose in time to get an eyeful.

I glanced down and remembered I was wearing my pajamas. They were flannel, printed with sushi rolls and takeout boxes. I received them in the mail that morning from my son, Owen, since he wouldn't be able to make it home for Christmas. His card said that they represented the extent of my abilities in the kitchen: raw foods or takeout.

"No one expects you to recognize lingerie when you see it, Clive." Winston Turcotte spat a gob of tobacco into a used paper coffee cup, pushed back his helmet and scratched his bald head.

"It's not lingerie. Don't start saying I showed up in the middle of the street in lingerie."

Ray Twombley, the police chief, turned his camera on me just before I pulled my coat back on. "It's not my idea of lingerie." Ray pressed a button on the camera with a hairy forefinger.

"Ray, why don't you put that thing to good use and take photos of the fire scene instead?" I crammed my helmet onto my springy curls and stomped back into the museum. Winston and Clive clomped up the stairs after me. I surveyed the sooty, clammy space wondering what to do next. Everywhere my eye landed there were puddles and filth. In light of the clean-up ahead of us, I could see Harold lucked out by having a heart attack. I was thinking of what to tackle next when Winston came up with a suggestion.

"Maybe we oughta move the body," he said, burying a plug of chew between his ruddy cheek and his yellowed dentures.

"I think we'd better wait for the state investigator." I wondered again how long it was going to be before he showed up.

"She looked pretty well baked on. Ya think any of her'll stick?" Clive stuffed a piece of gum into his mouth and began blowing droopy bubbles. I felt the wave of heat in my body that comes with nausea and tugged off my coat again. Credibility be damned, my supper was on its way back up. I tore out the door and barely made it down the front steps before the roiling became uncontrollable. The icy December wind stung my face as I heaved.

"Are you all right?" asked a voice. I shook my head and heaved some more.

"Feeling better?" asked a man I didn't recognize.

"Not even close." I wiped my mouth on my sleeve, tipped my head back and looked him in the face. At only five foot three myself everyone appears tall, but I was certain he was just under seven feet tall. His mustache and beard were such flaming red I had a fleeting thought of turning a fire hose on his face.

"Sorry to bother you. I'm looking for the Fire Chief."

"Then you'll have to head to the hospital in Riverton," I said. "Harold had a heart attack when he saw the body."

"If it was that bad, I'm not surprised you needed a little air," he said. "So who is in charge?"

"Gwen Fifield." I stuck out my hand. "I'm the Acting Chief until Harold gets back on his feet."

"Hugh Larsen with the Fire Marshal's office." Hugh grasped my hand with his enormous paw. If I had to guess, I'd have said he left a Viking ship docked out front instead of a pickup or SUV.

"You can't imagine how glad I am to see you."

"Are you feeling up to heading back inside?" he asked, releasing his grip.

"I'll never hear the end of it if the guys think I shirked my duties." I led the way back toward the museum. "Besides, I don't think I've got anything left in my stomach."

"So what is this place?" Hugh reached out for the door and held it open for me. I glanced around at the museum. The first floor remained standing, but every surface was wet. As the door slammed behind us, a chunk of plaster fell from the ceiling and landed at my feet. At least the place was wet instead of gutted. Considering all the flammable items in the building, it was surprising we weren't staring at a cellar hole.

"It's a museum the victim started as a pet project about fifty years ago. The Historical Society uses it for their meetings. Most of the displays are of local interest."

"Do they get much business?" Hugh glanced around at soot-smeared castoffs from nearby homes.

"Not really. There isn't much to see unless your taste runs to old canning equipment and arthritic typewriters."

"Hey, buddy, this is a restricted area." Ray

scowled at us. "Did you let him in, Gwen?"

"This is Hugh Larsen, from the Fire Marshal's office," I said.

"Did Harold authorize this?" Ray asked.

"Harold was too busy receiving CPR to give orders," I said.

"State law mandates that the Fire Marshal's office investigate whenever a body is found in a fire," Hugh said, "but Acting Chief Fifield is officially in charge. No one else has jurisdiction until she releases the scene." Ray grunted and turned back to his camera. My stomach turned over again at the thought of being in charge. This was a lot more complicated than drunks at a bonfire.

Winston and Clive stood in front of a display of model trains that had been the museum's most popular exhibit. Clive bent low over the track and patted a tiny fake fir tree with a bony finger. Scale model houses and tunnels were grimy and wet. The miniature village looked like an industrial town that had never been visited by the EPA. Both men shook their heads, then turned back to the clean-up.

"I need to take a look at the body. Are you up to showing me the way?" Hugh asked. I nodded and headed for the stairs to the second floor. I stopped just short of the clock tower room at the front of the building. I didn't want to see what was left of Beulah again. I always expected she would keel over in the museum one day, just not like this. I kept my eyes fixed on the tower window and focused on the way a street light lit up the dumpster behind the general store.

"So tell me," Hugh squatted next to the body. "What do you think happened?"

"It looks like she fell down the clock tower stairs," I said. "Then the kerosene heater tipped over and started a fire."

"How can you be sure the victim was the museum founder?"

"It's got to be Beulah Price. She wore that ring every day."

"That's not much to go on. Are you sure about identifying the ring? Could someone else be wearing it?"

"She and my grandmother were best friends for most of their adult lives. When my grandmother died, she left the ring to Beulah. Once we settled up my grandmother's estate I took it to her myself. As far as I know, she wore it every day for the last eleven years." I wiped an unprofessional tear on my pajama sleeve and hoped he hadn't noticed.

"Okay. We'll work from the assumption it's her until we get an ID from the coroner."

"There's something I should mention." I said. "We've had a rash of fires in the village over the last few weeks, and they've been escalating in damage. This could be one more of them."

"Okay." Hugh stood, pulled a small notebook out of his coat pocket and clicked open a pen. "What else was torched?"

"It started eight weeks ago," I said, "with an abandoned chicken coop. The next week there was a fire in a stack of green lumber at the sawmill. The coop was no big loss, and the lumber just steamed and smoked. No real damage was done."

"Anything else?" Hugh jotted an entry in his notebook.

"Unfortunately, yes." I began pacing the floor, stamping my feet to get the circulation flowing. Now that the flames were out, the building was bitterly cold. "Someone tossed something flammable under the porch of an empty house. Most of the porch burned before we could put it out. Then a garage caught on fire. A few days later an old camp down by the river burned to the ground. Last week a house was badly damaged, but we managed to save most of it."

"That's quite a list in such a short time span," said Hugh. "What does your Fire Chief have to say about it?"

"He thinks it's carelessly tossed cigarettes or faulty wiring. I wanted to call you guys in when the camp burned, but Harold wouldn't hear of it."

"It does seem like a lot of calls for such a small community," Hugh said. "Do you usually have so many?"

"I've lived here my entire life except for college." I stopped pacing and craned my neck to look Hugh in the face. "We've never had anything like this happen in all that time."

"This is the first time someone was in the building when the fire started?"

"Yes. All of the other fires occurred in out-buildings or unoccupied homes. I guess we've been lucky no one was hurt before now."

"Should the museum have been unoccupied?"

"It was after hours, and no meetings were scheduled. There's no reason I can see that Beulah should have been here." I breathed on my hands and rubbed them together. I could hear Clive and Ray down on the first floor, arguing about who was going to get to stay overnight in front of the building in case of a flare-up.

"Six months ago she hired someone to take over the daily operations of the museum because she'd had a hip replacement and the stairs had gotten to be too much for her. What would have made her come out here tonight?"

"Maybe she missed being at the museum," Hugh said. "Maybe she left her favorite sweater here the last time she was in."

"She was ninety-one years old. With her mobility problems, she wouldn't have run out for a sweater. It would have been faster for her to knit a new one."

"It doesn't sound likely." Hugh inclined his helmet toward the steps. "Would anyone have wanted to do this to her?"

"Beulah was elected Honorary Mayor for most of the last thirty years. She baked cookies for neighborhood kids and took casseroles to the bereaved."

"Do you have a suspect in mind for the arsons?" asked Hugh. "Anyone at all?" I stared out the window, mulling over village gossip. Accusations toward an immigrant family had been flying since the first fire broke out. New Hampshire is a typical New England state. Generally, citizens are leery of people from away. Even people from neighboring Massachusetts are suspect, and Brazil is about as away as you could get.

Through the window, toward the back of the building, I saw movement. In the darkness I could just barely make out Diego DaSilva glancing up at me before darting off through the trees. I hoped that he was just a curious kid wanting to see what all the excitement was about. The DaSilvas were making it easy for someone to suggest that they were responsible. It just wasn't going to be me. I turned back toward Hugh.

"I could give you plenty of suspects if Ethel, the woman who took over the museum, was lying there instead of Beulah. A lot of people in the village would be happy to light the museum on fire if they could be sure Ethel would be in it."

"You think someone set this fire to kill the museum curator?" Hugh cocked an overgrown russet eyebrow at me in surprise.

"She's the human equivalent of a canker sore." I crossed my arms over my chest. "Nursing mothers avoid her to keep from curdling their milk."

"If someone wanted to kill the curator, there are simpler ways to do it," Hugh said.

"You asked for suspects. More people would be tempted to get rid of Ethel than Beulah, and it makes more sense that she would have been in the building."

"Were you one of those people?" Hugh pulled his

notebook back out of his pocket.

"You think I did this? I'm a firefighter." Who did this guy think he was? I thought he was supposed to be helping me, not accusing me.

"More fires are started by firefighters than I'd like to admit." Hugh said. "Where were you this evening when it started?"

"At home. I'd already gotten ready for bed."

"So I see." Hugh nodded toward my pajama top.

"I dashed out when I got the call." I gnawed on my thumbnail. "Changing into street clothes wasn't my priority."

"Can anyone verify that you were home?"

"No," I said. "You'll have to take my word for it." Hugh jotted something else in his notebook and gave me a long look.

"Any family?"

"Two sons," I said. "One's graduated, the other's still in college."

"You don't have any plans to go out of town for the holidays, do you?"

"I'm the postmistress." I shook my head. "We don't get vacation time at Christmas. It's our busiest season." Winston stopped to add his two cents as he passed by carrying a push broom.

"Gwen doesn't go on vacation," Winston said. "We count on her to keep everyone up-to-date on all the goings on around here."

Postmistresses have a reputation of being busybodies. It's been my experience that the average postal employee in a small town is on the receiving end of a lot more information than she asks for. I know about the hangnails, root canals and ailing aunts of the majority of my customers, and by and large, I haven't solicited that information. I have never, to my recollection, asked what someone thought of the current president, the quality of the pie at the last Grange supper or whether anyone thought that the pastor was a bit long winded the previous Sunday morning.

I don't even think of myself as a good listener, but when people see me standing behind that window, they see an audience for the story of their lives. They don't hand it out all in one day, but over the years a picture of each of them builds up. I don't mind, really, it's just the reputation of being a gossip is irksome considering I never wanted to know any of it to begin with.

"She seems like she's right in the thick of things. Since you're the head of the information bureau, is there anyone who should be informed of the victim's death?" Hugh asked.

"Good Lord," I said. "I've got to call Augusta."

TWO

"Whadaya think, Gwen?" asked Winston Turcotte the next morning, leaning on the post office counter as he sorted his junk mail. "Is this one of them cases of spontaneous human combustion like you see on the TV? Or is it related to all the other fires?"

"All that television watching is melting your brain," I said. Winston's discovered a whole new world since he got Clara to loosen up the purse strings and they installed a satellite dish.

"Of course the fires are related." Clive Merrill tugged on a fishing lure dangling from his favorite hat. "We all know it's them Silver kids."

"DaSilva kids," I said, "and no, we don't know it's them. You can't accuse people for no reason. Even Ray knows better than that." Ray Twombley, the Police Chief, is not known for his mental abilities. He sticks out his tongue when he ties his shoes.

"Ethel was hollering at them boys yesterday." Winston lobbed a balled-up piece of mail toward the recycling bin and missed. "They'd picked up Jasper and were lugging him off someplace. I don't know what she thought they wanted with her damn cat, but she was all het up."

"Voodoo sacrifice." Clive leaned in, eyes bulging with the excitement. "If that ain't what they were up to, I'll eat my hat." Clive touched his lucky fishing hat. Lures hung from every square inch of the green canvas. I'd never seen him anywhere without it perched up on top of his egg-shaped head except at a fire scene. Even then, I wouldn't be surprised to discover he had just stuck a fire helmet on top of it. I would have given a lot to watch him try to choke the thing down.

"They're Catholic," I said. "I'm pretty sure Catholics don't practice voodoo."

"Some of 'em do. That was on television, too. One of them haunting shows in New Orleans. Some big black woman with a head scarf was selling rosaries and little bags of dried chicken feet and parsley with a curse written on a recipe card stuck to the outside," Clive said.

"Sounds like something from Gwen's kitchen." Winston laughed. "She's been known to near poison people with her chicken soup."

"How'd you know they're Catholic?" asked Clive.

"Luisa was in the post office last week asking if there was a Catholic church nearby," I said. "She wanted to attend mass with her kids."

"Ah ha." Clive's lures jangled as he nodded. "She or one of her kids has something to confess."

"Taking your family to church isn't a crime," I said, "or the admission of one. She seems nice."

"Nice or not, there were no fires to speak of around here until they showed up," Clive said. "Well, except chimney fires."

"And that brush fire you let get outta control last year," Winston said. "And the year before. And I think the year before that. Who keeps authorizing your burn permits, Clive?"

"He snuck a pad of them off Harold's desk when he thought no one was looking." I said. "Come to think of it, maybe he's been setting the fires."

"I bet you're right," Winston said.

"You keep throwing accusations like that around," said Clive, "and I'll tell Clara where you've been spending Wednesday nights."

"Where have you been spending your Wednesday nights?" I peered at Winston. His wife Clara is known for her jealous streak. I've no idea why since Winston never turns a lustful eye toward anything besides homemade dessert.

"Would ya look at the time," Winston said. "I've gotta get over to the dump and open up 'fore angry taxpayers start rattling the gates." I watched Winston as he hitched up his belt and hurried out the door. I wondered why he hadn't answered my question.

Ray was late coming in, but knowing him, he had spent the morning at the general store repeating gruesome aspects of the fire to anyone who would listen. Gossip goes down best with a tasty doughnut. On her good days, Dinah's doughnuts are worth the calories. On a bad day, you could use them to fill gaps in a stone wall. Her raised doughnuts were responsible for at least ten of the extra twenty pounds

I'm lugging around.

"What brings you by this morning, Ray? Police business or just the mail?"

"I want to talk to you about that state investigator, Lou something."

"His name is Hugh. What about him?"

"Just because we've got to put up with him doesn't mean you have to make him feel too welcome."

"What does that mean?" I asked. "Too welcome? Like buying him a fruit basket?"

"No, like making his job easier for him."

"How would I do that?"

"I just don't want you to offer help to the wrong guy." He leaned on the counter and winked.

"Are you implying that you're Mr. Right?" My social calendar may have been as empty as the church on Super Bowl Sunday, but if I ever chose to date again I wouldn't be searching for someone whose biggest mental challenge each day is verifying that his socks match.

"Let's just say," Ray leaned in close enough for me to smell his doughnut breath, "I can make sure that you never need to take another sobriety test like the one last year."

"I swerved to avoid hitting a deer." I slapped the counter with my mug, splashing coffee everywhere. "That's why I'd gone over the yellow line, and you know it." He'd been hiding behind a clump of hemlocks with his radar gun. Drunks are bigger game than speeders so he made me walk the white line while patting my head and rubbing my belly. The episode occurred on the main drag out of town and caused a lot of rubbernecking. To this day there are people in town who pull over to let me pass when they see me in their rearview mirrors.

"This is my first chance at solving a real case like one on TV." Ray fingered his gun holster.

"This isn't about your fantasy life." It was difficult to imagine Ray solving anything more challenging than a crossword puzzle on a children's menu at a chain restaurant. "Beulah died last night."

"Come on, help me out for old time's sake." Ray winked again.

"Our old times involve you storing your leech collection in my wading pool and giving me chicken pox on purpose." Ray and I'd known each other since the first grade. The only time he had ever been nice to me was the summer he discovered girls. He kept stopping by my house to ask me to go fishing just to catch a glimpse of my older sister Augusta.

"You hear things all day at the post office. I'm just asking you to keep your ears open, and if anyone seems to know anything, you could pass the information along to me instead of that other guy."

"You want me to eavesdrop on my customers?" I wiped up the coffee with the tail of my denim shirt.

"Don't get all worked up," Ray said. "I thought you'd be flattered. Think of it as being deputized."

"Deputized? Why don't you flatter Winston? Or Dinah? They hear all sorts of things at the dump and the store."

"Well, I figured that they're always busy at work and wouldn't have the time you do to chat people up."

"Are you saying," I said, "that I'm not as busy as the guy who watches people sort their trash into the correct bins?"

"There you go getting huffy, as usual. I just meant that you can stand around talking with people, and no one will think anything of it."

"For someone who wants a favor, you sure are going about it the wrong way." I slammed the window shut.

"Think about what I said," Ray called through the closed window. "Remember, I can administer as many sobriety tests as I like."

I slipped out the back door and hurried toward the general store. Dinah makes great Italian sandwiches, and arguments always make me run for comfort food. Besides, I was expecting Augusta to swoosh into town around lunchtime, and she wouldn't be willing to eat anything I cooked.

Like most towns around us, Winslow Falls is an architectural free-for-all. Protective covenants go against New Hampshire's "Live Free or Die" motto. There is no bad part of the village. Conversely, there is no part considered exclusive either.

I skittered down the icy sidewalk past the Marshalls' small tan trailer. A tiny deck clung to the front of it more by wishful thinking than sound construction techniques. On it a ripped black trash bag, raided by wildlife the night before, squatted beside a turkey fryer and a rusted washing machine. The machine had been left on the curb months ago by the neighbor down the street. Six Marshall family members had swooped down on it with hopes of never setting foot in the Suds Your Duds Laundromat ever again. They got the thing as far as the deck before they thought to check if it would fit through the door.

Next door to the Marshalls is Freda Jerold's Victorian. She paints it in a new color scheme every five years. No one else paints anything other than their nails any more frequently than every ten. Two years ago, she had it redone in a hot pink with turquoise trim and orange shutters. Her own front stoop is bare except for a welcome mat and a cast iron boot scraper shaped like a sheep. Most people say that Freda has flair. My son Josh says she must have a family history of mental illness.

A bacon fog hung in the air as I pushed open the door of the general store. Winston straddled the stool closest to the TV, his cracked leather belt losing a tug-of-war match with gravity. He propped both elbows on the counter, coarse-knuckled hands wrapped around a burger squirting ketchup like a punctured artery. Clive perched his flat behind on a stool in the middle, not missing a thing. Ray was down at the far end talking with Hugh. He must have been in some kind of a hurry to get to Dinah's before me.

"Are ya here for lunch?" Winston glanced up from his burger. "I thought you musta caught a stomach bug the way you were carrying on last night." Little bits of ketchup clung to his gray stubble.

"Don't pay him any attention, Gwen." Dinah wiped her plump, red hands on a dishtowel and tossed it onto her broad shoulder. "What'll you have?"

"Two Italian sandwiches with hots and oil," I said. "Has anyone heard how Harold's doing?"

"I rung up Bernadette this morning," Winston said. "Looks like he'll prob'ly need his tubes cleared out with one of them balloon contraptions." Winston eyed a blob of fat that dripped from his burger and splattered a spot about where his own heart lay. He paused, then gulped down another greasy mouthful.

"Of course he will." Dinah thumped a plate of fish and chips in front of Clive. "That man eats his weight in doughnuts every week."

"I hope he enjoyed it while it lasted," I said. "Bernadette won't let him get away with that anymore."

"Harold's not the only one overeating. Two sandwiches? You're never gonna catch a new man that way." Clive wagged a French fry at me before cramming it into his mouth.

"I'm expecting my sister today, and I thought that we would call on Dinah to cater our lunch. Not that my private life or the size of my backside is any of your business." The villager geezers started harping on my non-existent love life a couple of years after my husband Peter died. Usually, it didn't get a rise out of me, but I felt a hot flush creeping up my cheeks as I sneaked a peek in Hugh's direction.

"Augusta's here?" Clive pulled an inhaler from a fishing vest pocket and took a deep drag. Ray cupped his hand in front of his mouth and checked his breath. Winston reached for a napkin and dabbed at the grease spot on his shirt. Augusta has that effect on most men.

"She will be. She's the executrix for Beulah's estate," I said. The bells jingled again, and as if on cue, Augusta stepped through the door.

"There you are, Gwen." Augusta swept across the floor and enfolded me in a perfumed embrace. She deposited a lipstick smear on each of my cheeks before turning her attention to the rest of the room. "I went to the house, but you weren't there, and now I can see why you would have preferred to stop in here. Do any of these fine-looking gentlemen belong to you, or is it an open field?" Augusta asked, pulling off a glove and smoothing her streaming blond hair. She's always gotten right to the point. Women in my family are known for speaking their minds, but from the time that Augusta could string a sentence together she was schooling her elders in forthrightness.

"Winston's still spoken for by his lovely wife Clara. Ray's been purchased and returned to the store by three different wives, and Clive's still new in the box. I'm not in the market, so feel free to help yourself," I said.

Where she had come from I had no idea. She's moved house so often she stopped bothering to get a phone installed, relying on her cell phone instead. Augusta usually changes her order three times in a restaurant before settling on something. As for her different men, I'd given up trying to keep them straight years ago. My sister has sexual attention deficit disorder.

Some people had been surprised when Beulah appointed Augusta as the executrix of her estate, but I wasn't one of them. Augusta was always Beulah's favorite. I think she admired Augusta's life even if she didn't understand it or think it was right. The last I knew, Beulah had left her little Cape Cod house to my sister in her will.

If Augusta was in mourning she was hiding it well. Her blue eyes sparkled. Her perfect porcelain nose wasn't red or raw. Her outfit did little to suggest she was feeling heavy hearted. It was, however, perfect for traveling by plane. With the way her green dress clung to her curves, airport security wouldn't have needed an x-ray machine to spot any guns or explosives hidden under there. As a matter of fact, her most frequently used weapons bobbed front and center like a pair of creamy buoys above the deep vee of her neckline.

Dinah keeps charcoal briquettes on hand year round for the times the power goes out and someone wants to cook supper on the grill. Augusta appeared out of place standing there next to them. I imagined that I fit right in, slightly dusty and suitable for everyday use.

Clive seemed to agree and jumped off his stool. He brushed some crumbs off the seat with his fishing hat, nodded his head in her direction, and gestured she should sit. Clive Merrill wouldn't hold a door open for his own elderly mother if she was holding the Christ Child in one hand and the cure for AIDS in the other. Winston choked so hard on his coffee you would have thought the cup was full of fish bones. Augusta noticed none of this as she shimmied over and flashed Clive a smile. He quivered and stood in attendance slightly behind her.

"I don't know what I'd do to thank the man who fetched me a strong cup of coffee." Augusta slowly draped one long leg over the other and moved her hemline out of the realm of public decency. She swiveled her head and laid waste all the men in the store with her high beam smile. Winston and Clive dove for the coffee station at the same time. Clive emerged triumphant, being five years younger and not encumbered by a belly the size of a laundry basket.

"Now where might a girl find some sugar?" she leaned so far toward Clive that her buoys threatened to drift out into the open ocean. If I were her, I would have put a napkin over the darn things to soak up the drool that trickled out of the corners of Clive's narrow mouth.

"Why don't you just stick your finger in that coffee and stir. I'm sure that would sweeten it up just right." Ray swaggered up and placed a hairy hand on her arm. She spun her stool toward him. Clive grabbed his plate and slunk down the counter toward Hugh.

"You always were just the cleverest thing," Augusta said. Winston started choking again. Dinah slapped him on the back. I was rapidly losing my appetite.

I glanced back down the counter, and Hugh waved me over with his notebook in his hand. I wondered if he'd Super Glued it to himself by accident.

"I thought you said you had no suspects in the arsons," said Hugh.

"I remember," I answered. "What's the problem?"

"This gentleman says there are a bunch of suspects," Hugh said, "strong suspects. Why would you tell me otherwise?" Clive shook his head, making the fishing lures on his hat dance a jig.

"I didn't," I said. "You asked if there was anyone I thought was a suspect. You didn't ask what Clive thought."

"That's shaving things close." Hugh said, his massive hand wrapped around a silver pen.

"Let me guess." I glanced at Clive, who was rooting around in his left nostril with a ratty blue handkerchief. "He mentioned the DaSilva kids."

"Of course I did." Clive inspected his handkerchief. "You should have too. Who else could it be?"

"Good question," I said. "I didn't mention them because I don't believe they were involved."

"That oldest one was seen lurking around the museum just before the fire call came in." Clive stuffed his handkerchief into his back pocket.

"I saw you coming out of the museum earlier that evening, too," I said. "Does that mean you set the fire?"

"Don't be ridiculous," Clive said. "I'm a firefighter."

"So am I," I said, "but Hugh put me on the suspect list last night, too. Isn't that right, Hugh?" He flipped back through his notebook to verify our conversation.

"Yes," he said. "I did ask about a motive. It seemed prudent after you mentioned the curdled milk."

"How thorough of you," I said. "Have you asked Clive about his reasons for being at the museum? As a Museum Trustee, I happen to know it was closed and no meetings were scheduled."

"It was personal." Clive spewed bits of food as he spoke.

"More personal than the details of your prostate surgery? I remember you being eager to talk about that with everyone that came into the post office."

"Clive's not the only one to mention the DaSilvas. I'd like to check them out," Hugh said. "I thought since you're local you'd be helpful in making contact."

"I won't be finished at the post office until five-thirty," I said.

"I've got to do some more work at the fire site anyway. How about if I pick you up there when you close?"

"Does this mean I'm not a suspect anymore?" I asked.

"No, it does not," Hugh strode toward the door. "See you this evening."

THREE

Trina burst into the post office ten minutes late. I'd hired her to help with the extra holiday mail. I need an extra set of hands to deal with Christmas cards alone. Too bad she spends most of her time checking her manicure and calling her kids to make sure they haven't killed each other.

She yanked her hat off a tangled blond mess I suspected hadn't seen a hairbrush that morning. She exhaled forcefully as if practicing Lamaze breathing and dropped a canvas tote bag in the corner of the back room.

"Why is that children can sense when you are in a hurry, and they slow down to half speed?"

"Sounds like Owen and Josh when they were kids. If we were running behind for an appointment, one of them usually managed to give the other a head wound that would bleed all over both of them. You don't want to be the woman who habitually turns up at church or the dentist with bloody children."

"I came close to giving Kyle and Krystal head wounds this morning myself. Krystal had a tantrum because her favorite leggings were in the wash. Then Kyle drew a mustache above her upper lip in purple permanent marker while I was making their lunches. I scrubbed her face until I wore off a dime-sized patch of skin. Tonight they're having their photos taken for our Christmas cards."

"The best thing to do with kids is to maintain a sense of humor."

"The closest thing to a sense of humor I've had lately is a Good Humor Bar. My thighs are spreading like the contents of an overflowed toilet."

"You look about the same to me."

"Thanks a lot. Next you'll be telling me I've always had these wrinkles." Trina leaned toward me and opened her eyes wider than they looked like they ought to go. Her perfectly groomed eyebrows arched up to an unnatural level. She pointed at the corner of the left one with her finger. She had lost a nail tip recently. Trina is the only woman I know who uses nail tips. Most other women in the village don't even wear polish on their natural nails. Trina was a transplant from somewhere out west and hadn't adjusted to the fact that most women here cultivated a life based more on function than form.

"Wrinkles break a face in. With jeans you pay more for them looking a bit worn. Why complain if you get it done to your face for free?" I asked. Trina burst into tears.

"Do you have anyone who will fill in for a couple of days so that I can schedule a Botox appointment?" Trina tugged a tissue out of the box I handed her and dabbed at the mascara running down her cheeks.

"You're the person who fills in so that other

people can schedule appointments. Besides, I can't help you to immobilize parts of your face. I have to look at it too often for that. How old are you?"

"Thirty-four this coming July."

"Good Lord. Put the money away in a college fund for the kids."

"I know I seem shallow, but I can't help feeling like Chris just isn't interested in me anymore. He comes home late, flops on the couch with dinner on a tray, and falls asleep in front of the television."

"Sounds like a lot of other men. Is he busier than usual at work?" I knew that Chris was a contractor and had a lot going on with the housing boom hitting the area. He was up to his ears in renovations and waterfront spec houses.

"I think he's worried about money."

"Then dropping a bundle on a cosmetic procedure isn't going to help." I shifted my attention to the door as Ethel Smalley glided into the post office like a ship carefully docking. She sailed at me ramrod straight with her formidable bosom at full mast. It served as a sort of bumper against the edge of the counter as she cruised to a stop and stretched back her magenta lips into her best recruitment smile.

"So glad I managed to catch you in, Gwen" she said, as if I was usually negligent in my manning of the post office.

"Are you here for your mail, Ethel?" I asked with all the hope of a death row prisoner strapped down and staring at the red phone.

"I'll grab it in a minute. What I really wanted was

to talk to you about the museum." As soon as Ethel had taken over as museum curator, she had noticed leaks in the roof that the other trustees and I had the good sense to ignore. Immediately she had spearheaded a fundraising effort to pay for the repairs. Anyone in Ethel's path had been drafted into service, and I'd been trapped behind the window at the post office when she had come in hunting for recruits. The Historical Society had settled on hosting a pancake breakfast the morning of the annual Groundhog Day ice fishing derby. The one good thing that could have come of the fire was to have put a stop to the fundraising efforts permanently.

"And?" I folded my arms across my chest.

"And I've scheduled a joint meeting of the Museum Fundraising Committee and the Museum Trustees for tonight."

'Why? There isn't much of a roof left to fix. It was Beulah's museum, and now she isn't even around to enjoy it," I said.

"I'm surprised at you. Keeping the museum running is the best way to honor Beulah."

"I've got a mountain of paperwork to do for the fire investigation."

"Leave it for the man from the state. You don't know what you're doing anyway."

"This isn't because you are worried about being out of a job, is it?"

"My finances have never been better. Working at the museum was a kind of public service. With what it pays, it's practically volunteerism. Which brings me back to tonight's meeting."

"I'm even busier than usual now that I'm filling in for Harold."

"I've already told Gene and the others you would feel it your duty to participate. It's the least you can do to make amends for not stopping that foreign family from terrorizing the rest of us. They ought to slither back to whichever Third World hole they crawled out of and stay there. I've half a mind to call Immigration." Ethel drummed her fat fingers on the counter. Sweat was beginning to run down my back. That always happened to me when I was being barked at by strange dogs, being dive-bombed by bats, and speaking with Ethel Smalley. In my experience it's easier to reason with the dogs and bats. I gave it one more try.

"It's my busiest season at work. My son's coming for the holidays, and I need to get ready for his visit. I don't have time for anything else right now."

"Poor Beulah's life's work is moldering," Ethel said. "I'll expect you at my house at seven." She slammed the door behind her as she stomped out into the cold.

Luisa DaSilva stood in the doorway of her sagging trailer, her high-heeled sandals at odds with the snow neatly cleared away from the steps.

"I have papers," she said.

"We aren't from Immigration," I said. "This is Hugh Larsen of the Fire Marshal's office. He needs to ask your sons where they were when the fires around town were started."

"My sons are good boys. They don't make trouble. We have papers." She stood shivering in the doorway, her silky red tank top rippling in the breeze.

"We must speak with them," Hugh said. "May we come in?" She left the door open, and we entered the trailer. The spongy floor bounced under the weight of the three of us. Hugh quietly fought the door into place in its twisted frame. A child about two years old played with building blocks in the middle of the floor. He ogled us silently, then turned back to his toys.

"Please, sit." She pointed to a clinically depressed sofa. "I get my sons." She glided off down a narrow hallway toward the noise of children. I sat carefully on one end of the sofa, and Hugh lowered himself onto the other.

"Think it will hold us both?" he asked.

"I hope so," I said. "I doubt redecorating is in the budget." Children's paintings were thumbtacked to the paneled walls. The blue curtains hanging in the windows were cleaner than the ones at my house. Nothing was new, but nothing was dirty either. Luisa returned with three miniature versions of herself, shiny black hair, large dark eyes and white, even teeth.

"These are my sons, Diego, Tulio and Ronaldo."

"Hi, guys," Hugh said. "I'm a fire investigator, and I want to ask you kids some questions about the fires around town. Have you heard about the one last night at the museum?" They all looked at their mother.

"Why you ask us?" Luisa asked. "We know nothing."

"When did you move to Winslow Falls?" Hugh asked.

"We live here four months." Luisa tapped her pretty little foot, sending more spasms through the floor.

"Why did you come to Winslow Falls? For a job?" Hugh settled himself against the sofa back and stretched out his long legs as if he had all day to conduct this interview. A garlicky smell drifted toward us from the kitchen, and it reminded me it was suppertime. Hopefully, his posture was an interrogation technique designed to speed things up.

"I have papers." Luisa tapped some more. "I have papers for work." She crossed her arms over her chest.

"I understand," Hugh said. "Do you have a job?"

"I clean houses," Luisa said. "I work for Beulah. I clean the store of Gene Ramsey. At night I clean for Dinah and the library. Sometimes for other peoples, too."

"So sometimes you work at night?" Hugh leaned forward. "At the store and library?"

"Yes." Luisa stared at Hugh warily.

"Who takes care of your sons when you are at work?" Hugh asked.

"I say to you, my sons are good boys." She bent to pick up the toddler who'd been burying its face against her legs and taking peeks at me through spread fingers.

"Where were they last night?" Hugh asked.

"We were here," said the tallest boy. "We watched television." He looked at his brothers, and they nodded.

"See," said Luisa, "good boys."

"Did you ever work at the museum?" Hugh asked.

"Yes. I say to you I work for Beulah." Luisa kept her eyes glued to the floor.

"Did you like her?" asked Hugh.

"She was good lady." Luisa bit her lip. "She was helping me with English, and she liked my baby."

"Did she like all of your sons?" Hugh asked. "Some people in town are saying the older ones are troublemakers."

"I no say more. My sons are good boys." Diego stepped toward his mother and placed a hand on her back.

"We will say no more," Diego said.

"I need to know where you all were when each fire occurred," Hugh said.

"We will say nothing," Diego said. "We know nothing."

"You go now." Luisa hustled to the door and yanked it open with a slim hand. Hugh stood and reached into his wallet. He pulled out a business card and extended it to Diego.

'Since you're the spokesman, give me a call if you think of anything you want to say to us." We retreated down the wobbling wooden steps as Luisa slammed the door.

Hugh crossed the tiny yard in three long strides and held open the door of his truck for me, waiting until I was settled in before closing it. No one had held the car door for me since my husband's funeral. As he draped his arm over my seat to turn and back down the driveway I caught a whiff of his cologne. Seven years of celibacy is a long time.

"How well do you know that family?" he asked.

"Probably a little better than most people in town. Like Luisa said, they moved here about four months ago. I met her when she rented a post office box. I think she's lonely. She chats with me at the post office when she comes in."

"What about a husband?" Hugh fiddled with the heater.

"I've never heard of one."

"Do you think one of them started the fire at the museum?"

"No, I don't. For one thing, their mother is out of a job. It looks like money is tight enough without cutting out steady income."

"They're definitely not telling all they know though," Hugh said.

"I'll ask if anyone saw them at the scene of any of the other fires." I'd ask, but I wouldn't necessarily pass along what I heard. Eyewitnesses can be unreliable, especially when it comes to seeing favorite scapegoats at a crime scene.

FOUR

Ethel's house was less than a quarter of a mile away, but we were already late, so I decided to take the car. Besides, it was cold and dark, and an arsonist could be roaming the streets.

Pulling up to Ethel's I caught sight of Gene Ramsey's station wagon and Clara Turcotte's sedan, each pressed against the snow banks. Pauline's Ford Escort stuck into the street, reducing the road to one lane.

"I can't believe you talked me into this." Augusta rolled her eyes at me and reached for her door handle. "Committee meetings in Winslow Falls are one of the lower rings of hell."

"Then I must be kippered by all the fire and brimstone. Sometimes I think all I do is attend committee meetings." I opened my door and stepped out of the car before I could change my mind.

"That's what that smell is. I thought it was just your woodstove seeping into all your clothing." Augusta slammed her door and started for the walkway. Ethel yanked her front door open and scanned the street for latecomers.

"Nice of you to join us." She beckoned us into the

house with a plump hand, cocktail rings flashing like fireflies. Entering the living room, I saw the other museum trustees and historical society members perched on a new living room set. The smell of fresh foam filled the air. Pauline and Clara sat bolt upright on the gingham checked sofa. Augusta sauntered over and draped herself between them. She fluttered her fingers at Gene, who sat in a recliner upholstered in a pastel kitten pattern.

Coy ceramic kittens frolicked on every horizontal surface in the room. The top of a console television, the molding over the windows and doors, even a metal tray table was crowded with feline bric-a-brac. Ethel has an I Brake for Yard Sales bumper sticker on her car. Now I knew what she shopped for.

The scent of a real litter box filled the room. White hairs clung to the legs of Gene's dark trousers. I wasn't sure if they were domestic or imported, but I wasn't eager to acquire my own set. I hate cats. Who wants to look like they need to shave their pant legs? I have a hard enough time remembering to remove my own leg fuzz, and I'm allergic to the little beasts. Whenever I'm around one my eyes feel like I've fallen face first in a salt pile. My cheeks started to burn like a redhead at the beach.

I saw a wooden chair in the corner and dragged it over to the end of the sofa. Using a crumpled napkin from my pocket I wiped off the seat as discreetly as possible. I sat down and let my eyes wander the room. In the corner sat a wingback chair with more pet hairs covering the seat.

Ethel plopped herself down on the cat hairs and swung her little feet back and forth as they dangled above the floor by a good four inches. Pulling a mitten I was knitting from my bag, I settled in for what promised to be a long evening.

"Now that Gwen's finally gotten here we can begin the meeting," Ethel looked at me and shook her head. I flicked my eyes up at the clock on the wall. Its little black paws pointed to two minutes past seven. "The purpose tonight is to discuss fundraising to repair the museum."

"Who says the museum should be repaired?" Pauline slid forward on the sofa.

"I assumed it would go without saying that the museum will reopen." Ethel leaned toward the group and glared.

"Has anyone checked into the museum's insurance?" I asked, hoping to get a baseline for discussion and to delay hostilities. Ethel could start an argument with a dead man.

"Of course I have." Ethel reached toward a heaped-up table and grabbed a file folder. "The museum has coverage, but there is a hefty deductible."

"Pauline is prudent in asking about closing the museum," Gene said. "Without Beulah, I'm not sure there is sufficient interest to enable it to continue."

"Beulah could hardly have been considered the driving force behind the museum lately." Clara polished her glasses with a tissue and slid them back onto her nose. "We knew the day was coming soon when Beulah would not be with us. We were always going to have to decide about the museum's future."

"How much is it going to cost for repairs?" I asked. "Can we raise enough money to do it, or will the museum be closing whether we want it to or not?"

"We need to raise a considerable amount of money to remain open." Gene said. "As Ethel said, the deductible is high, and there is a great deal of damage to the building and the exhibits. We would need to come up with an extraordinarily lucrative fundraiser."

"Like what?" I shifted in my seat to get more comfortable. Fundraiser talk was never speedy.

"What about calendars with ladies who pose nude?" Augusta winked at Gene.

"That's hardly appropriate for a museum fundraiser," Clara said. Augusta smiled at her and crossed her legs.

"Bake sales are popular," Pauline offered.

"I've sampled your baked goods. You couldn't raise enough money to build a doll house, let alone repair a life-sized building. I'd have divorced you after the first meal. Not that divorce is off the table, with the way your husband's been flirting with that foreign woman," Ethel said.

"If I wasn't concerned about the Museum I wouldn't be caught dead in the same room with you." Pauline glared at our hostess. The two haven't gotten along well ever since Ethel moved to town eight years ago. Relations haven't gotten easier since they both applied for the job of museum curator.

"Isn't it strange that with your concern about the

museum as well as the favors you and your husband did for Beulah, she gave me the curator job instead of you? Could it be that she thought you were not capable of doing the job? Or was it something else? Didn't Beulah trust you?" Ethel pursed her magenta lips as she scanned the room, watching her words sink in.

Feeling the tension in the room made me wonder again whether the fire was as simple as it seemed. Enough animosity existed between Pauline and Ethel to have fueled a raging fire. I could picture Pauline hating Ethel enough to kill her. Had she killed Beulah by accident? Or was it something else after all? Beulah choosing Ethel for the curator job over Pauline had started a lot of speculation.

"What about you? You bent over backwards to make Beulah like you. Everyone knows it isn't in your nature to be nice, let alone for no reason. What were you up to?" Pauline made a good point. Ethel didn't douse her cereal with the milk of human kindness. So why had she tried so hard to charm Beulah?

"Let's return to the topic of the meeting. I'm sure we've all got more to attend to this evening than listening to unfounded accusations." Gene said.

"What about a First Night Winslow Falls celebration?" suggested Clara.

"That's a great idea. You could charge a ticket price for admission and have a bake sale and an auction. Maybe even a sleigh ride," Augusta said.

"The Historical Society could make a presentation about the steeple and the history of the museum to make the case for repairs stronger," I said.

"That makes more sense than lewd calendars," said Ethel, staring at Augusta again. "I've got a bunch of photos and clippings at the museum you could use, Gwen. Stop by tomorrow and pick them up. I'll be meeting the insurance appraiser there at noon."

"You be careful Ethel. It would be a real shame if the building was structurally unsound and you had an accident," said Pauline.

"I'll talk to Winston about flooding the Hartwell Church parking lot for a skating rink," said Clara before Ethel could respond to Pauline and drag the meeting out longer with their quarreling.

"You do that. Any other suggestions?" Ethel glowered at Gene who could usually be counted on for anything that brought business into the community.

"I could run the auction, I suppose," he said. "Still, I remain unconvinced it wouldn't be wiser to simply close."

"That's settled then. We've got less than two weeks to get everything taken care of. I expect all of you to rise to the challenge no matter what other obligations you think you have. Gwen, you can start by helping me with the refreshment tray." Ethel wriggled forward in her chair and heaved herself up from its cushy depths. Glad to stretch my legs, I followed at a safe distance. If her swinging hips were going to knock anything over, I didn't want to be blamed for it. Never let it be said that I sent any yard sale kittens to an early grave.

The air in the kitchen was fresh and frigid. It made me think of those TV ghost hunting programs where true believers describe atmospheric changes when a ghost is present. No ghosts appeared, but I noticed a disassembled window that solved the mystery. Someone had covered it with plastic wrap anchored by duct tape. That bit of Yankee ingenuity held out the wind pumping the plastic like a bellows but did little for the cold.

"It's a bad time of year for replacement windows, Ethel. You didn't fall prey to one of those companies that took your money and didn't finish the job, did you?" One had gotten away with scamming a new couple out on Mill Street just a few weeks ago.

"No. It was those damn DaSilva kids. Chris said he'd fix it for me, but it's one of those old ones with the pulleys. It doesn't stay open without something to prop it, so I asked him if he could repair it, too. Apparently, the weight fell down in between the walls, and he figured that getting a replacement from somewhere else would be easier than fishing it out. Now that he's finally found the part, he hasn't the time to fix the darn thing. Kids these days," Ethel said.

"Maybe you should leave town until he gets it fixed," Pauline suggested from the doorway.

"I manage okay except for when I get up to take my pills in the night. Then it really is miserable," Ethel said.

"Glad to hear it." Pauline slammed the kitchen door behind her as she left.

"What makes you so sure it was the DaSilva

kids?" I asked.

"Who else would it be? We all know they're up to no good, always sneaking around." Ethel pressed her knuckles on her fleshy hips.

"Sneaking around?" I asked.

"That oldest one, Diego, I think his name is. He was at the museum fire. I saw him hanging around beside the building. Clive said he was at the fire at the lumberyard, too."

'When did Clive say that?" I hadn't heard him mention it, and it's been my experience that if he thinks something is even remotely interesting, he will repeat it until your ears fall off.

"Well, I don't remember when exactly. Sometime recently. Now what was it we came in here for?"

"The refreshment tray," I said. Ethel glanced toward the Formica table on the far side of the room. Packaged cookies fanned out on a plate in the center of the tray. A white cat sprawled on top of them, helping itself to cream from a crystal pitcher.

"Oh, Jasper, aren't you a little dickens?" Ethel lifted it off the tray, nuzzled noses with it, then blew the cat hairs off the cookies. She restacked them and added more cream to the pitcher. "You can go ahead and carry that out now."

"No way. You want to serve your guests hairy food, feel free, but I want nothing to do with it. My reputation as a cook is bad enough without people saying I messed up store bought cookies."

"Suit yourself." Ethel shoved Jasper straight into my chest. I automatically grabbed him and felt my throat constrict. My eyes began to water. I should have brought an emergency inhaler. Jasper rubbed his whiskers across my neck before I could drop him. Sneezing and gasping, I staggered back to the living room and scouted for a box of tissues. I spotted a three-dimensional cat worked in plastic canvas. A tissue poked out the bottom like a tail. Lord, have mercy.

Clara dug into the cookies with a will. I thought about giving Gene and Augusta a signal that they should give the refreshments a miss, but they were too busy flirting to pay any attention. They stirred cat spit cream into their coffee without noticing a thing. Clara stopped eating long enough to pick a cat hair off her tongue. I decided my part in the meeting was done, and I needed some fresh air. I left Augusta my keys and sneezed my way to the door.

The moon hung above the village and kept me company as I made my way home. I trudged along in the street since no one had plowed the sidewalks since the last storm. It wasn't the first time I'd walked the streets of Winslow Falls alone after dark, but it was the first time that I'd ever felt scared. Even with the friendly moon I kept casting looks back over my shoulder. Each creak of a tree branch dangling above my head or flash of a night prowling cat hurried me along more urgently. I broke into an awkward trot, my legs wobbling from the unfamiliar effort of running.

It isn't that small towns don't have arsonists and burglars and people who mess with kids. It's that we all know who they are and behave accordingly. You know which kids were most likely to be found smoking behind the barn and catching it alight "by accident." So you shoo those kids from your property. You know which woman is hiding bruises and find ways to hire her quietly for odd jobs to help her build a nest egg for flight. You know years ahead of time which girls will be buying back-to-school clothes in the maternity department some September. You send your son to visit relatives out of state if he starts dating one of them one summer. Not knowing who could be acting this way was the scary thing. Faces of the people at the meeting and post office patrons flitted through my mind as I pounded along as well as the image of Beulah's charred body.

Winslow Falls had been good to me and to my boys when Peter died. If it hadn't been for people like Clara, Winston and Dinah, I don't know how we would have held on, which made it all the worse that I was asking myself if one of them could be lighting the village on fire.

And if one of them had set out to kill Beulah.

FIVE

Clive Merrill was the first customer at the post office the next morning. Even for an old guy, he was out early. Usually the geezers spend the early morning with Dinah at the store, getting coffee and filling her ears with nonsense. Once Dinah's patience has worn out they move the whole operation to post office lobby and repeat it for me. I always plan on being able to put up the mail without benefit of their company until around nine-thirty.

Here it was only seven-fifteen, and Clive was giving me a grin that turned his face into a jack-o-lantern — missing teeth, wild, swirling eyebrows and pointy, wrinkled ears. Someone once told me that men with ear wrinkles were destined for heart attacks. If that's true, Clive was in my post office on borrowed time.

"Morning, Gwen. Have you seen the paper this morning?"

"No, Clive. I have to be here bright and early. As much as I'd like the mail to stuff itself into these boxes, it hasn't happened yet. Unlike you gentlemen of leisure, I don't have the opportunity during the week to read the paper over a cup of coffee."

I'm not as patient as Dinah. She's an independent business owner. I'm endowed with the inalienable right as a postal employee to provide whatever level of customer service I see fit.

"That's what we all thought over at Dinah's, so I took it upon myself to bring you a copy of today's issue. I knew you'd want to know how thoroughly the press is covering the trouble with the fires."

Clive slapped a newspaper on the counter and tapped his finger on a large color photo. *Local Postmistress Takes Charge at Fatal Blaze* read the caption. My sushi pajamas and I filled the foreground of the shot. My head was turned sideways with a double chin clearly silhouetted against the fire truck's headlights. I scrutinized the photo. Photographic credit was given to Ray Twombley. I should have known.

"Thank you for bringing this in, Clive. May I keep it?"

"I bought it especially for you." He grinned some more. "You want me to buy up the rest of the copies at the store before anyone else sees them? Winston and I could get some guys together and clear 'em out of all the home delivery boxes, too. I expect that you don't want your lingerie getting so much publicity."

"On the contrary. Not everyone has the opportunity to make the front page." I forced a smile as I tore the photo from the paper. I came around in front of the window and taped the picture at eye level for all the customers to see. That ought to take the sparkle out of his cider. Still smiling, I handed him his mail.

His shoulders sagged, and his feet scuffed as he trudged back out the door.

All morning long patrons filed in with copies of the paper in hand. I smiled until my face ached. By the time lunch hour rolled around, word must have gotten out that I'd seen the photo. The last six people I waited on were empty-handed when they came in. By then I felt I really deserved a juicy cheeseburger from Dinah's. Instead, I had a lunch date with Ethel to pick up those photos.

Ethel glanced at me as I came through the door and hurriedly shoved some sort of book into her desk drawer. Was there something she didn't want me to see? Beulah's death was making me question things I never would have before.

"You're having a real problem with punctuality lately, aren't you?" She marched to the filing cabinet at the other side of the office and yanked open a drawer.

"I closed for lunch two minutes ago. How fast do you think I can walk over here? Do you have the clippings?"

"I said I did, didn't I? Fortunately, the water damage didn't reach this section of the building." She lifted up on her tiptoes and peered into the drawer. Flicking through the contents, she pulled out a folder.

"Is this everything?" I reached for the folder.

"Those are the only copies, unless there are more at Beulah's. So don't spill anything on them or any other nonsense." Ethel slammed the drawer shut and then screwed her magenta lips into a smile at the sound of footsteps from behind. The insurance appraiser had arrived. I escaped while she was greeting him.

On the way out, I met Hugh coming in. The wind slipped under the end of his red beard and flapped it like laundry on a line. I gazed up at the clouds creeping across the sky and inhaled deeply. The air smelled like snow was on the way. I planned to go to visit Harold at the hospital after work, but I hated driving in a storm. That was one more of the things Peter did that I really still missed, even after seven years.

"Anything new?" I asked, hoping the medical examiner finished Beulah's autopsy and we could schedule the memorial service.

"Nothing significant. I was just at the store getting my ears filled up with reasons the DaSilvas are responsible for everything from missing dogs to grand theft auto. Some guy named Chris really hates them."

"He's married to my clerk Trina. He has lots of opinions and thinks people are interested in them." I glanced at my watch to see if there was still time to grab something at Dinah's before I had to reopen the window.

"Got to be somewhere?" Hugh asked.

"Too many places. I have to be at work in twenty minutes. I want to grab a cheeseburger, and I feel guilty that I'm not visiting the fire chief at the hospital," I said.

"I can't help with your work schedule, and I don't have a cheeseburger on me, but I'm planning on going to Riverton this evening to ask Harold some questions. It's supposed to snow, but my truck's got four-wheel drive. Want to carpool?"

"Five-thirty?"

"I'll stop in at the post office." Hugh climbed up the museum stairs two at a time and was out of sight. Despite the looming clouds, my day suddenly felt brighter. Lost in thought, I was back at the post office and open for business before I realized I hadn't stopped for lunch after all.

"Nothing on but those damn soap operas," Harold said. Hugh had dropped me at the front entrance, since the snow was already falling, and I found my way to Harold's room on my own.

"I'm surprised they allow something so exciting in the cardiac unit. Your heart rate might spike dangerously."

"As bad as these actors are," said Harold, "they won't coax a tremor, let alone a spike. Did you bring anything to eat?"

"Don't they feed you in here?"

"I've had fake scrambled eggs, Popsicles and watery tomato juice."

"Sounds sensible," I said, "considering."

"Considering," Harold said, "they're trying to starve me to death. Haven't you got a candy bar or some such a thing in that bag of yours?"

"I could be prosecuted by the chief of surgery for feeding a sick man that crap." Cards, flowers and balloons crowded the top of the television. I added the stuffed Dalmatian I'd brought to the other gifts.

"In my condition every meal could be my last meal," Harold said. "Prisoners on death row get Kentucky Fried Chicken if they want it."

"Fried food's what got you into this mess. When's the surgery?"

"Day after tomorrow." Harold pleated the top sheet on his bed with his gnarled hands. Hard to believe just a couple of days ago he'd been hauling an eighty-pound hose and shouting orders to the crew.

"Where's Bernadette? I was told she was watching over you morning to night."

"I sent her down to the cafeteria. No reason both of us should waste away." I'd never thought of Bernadette being in danger of becoming too thin, but you never knew.

"We missed her at the Historical Society meeting yesterday," I said. "We're putting on a fundraiser to repair the clock tower."

"I hear the state's sent someone to investigate." Harold pleated harder on the bed sheet.

"That's right," I said. "How'd you hear about him?"

"I may be down, but I've still got my sources."

"Unlike you, he's taking the problem seriously," I said.

"I took it plenty serious," said Harold, "as serious as a heart attack."

"That really surprised me," I said. "Were you closer to Beulah than I knew?"

"How could I be?" Harold said. "You know

everything worth knowing in town." The beeping on Harold's heart monitor sped up a bit. It was like watching a lie detector test in front of my eyes.

"What do you think happened in there?"

"I guess a heater used by the construction crew probably caused it. A gust of wind could've come through the opening in the roof and blown it over."

"Chief Seeton?" a deep voice called from the open doorway. Hugh stood there, a potted geranium clutched in his giant grip.

"Come in," Harold said. "Come on in. Everyone's been telling me about the guy from the state." Standing nigh onto seven feet and sporting a smoldering red beard, Hugh would be easy to describe.

"I drove down with Gwen to get your opinion on the fires," Hugh said. "I've heard a lot around town and figured I'd better go straight to the top guy." I rolled my eyes and settled down farther into my chair.

"Gwen means well," Harold said, winking at Hugh, "but the truth is she ain't got the foggiest notion what she's doing. She only joined the fire department to be closer to her boys."

"So," Hugh said, "whatever she thinks should be discounted?"

"I wouldn't like to say that," Harold said. "She's just a little overzealous. Typical hysterical woman."

"I'm not the one who had a heart attack," I said. "Talk about an overreaction."

"But you did lose your supper all over my boot," Hugh reminded me.

Harold looked over and shook his head. "Have you come up with anything?" he asked. "Have they finished the autopsy?"

"I've asked for the lab to hurry," Hugh said, "but it'll take a couple more days."

"What about the cause of the fire?" Harold asked. "Arson is Gwen's pet idea."

"From all appearances it was caused by a construction heater," Hugh said.

"That's what I thought," Harold said. "Those heaters ought to be illegal."

"What about," Hugh asked, "the idea floating around that the DaSilva boys might be setting the fires?"

"It's possible," Harold said. "Kids are responsible for a lot of arsons."

"So you didn't agree with Gwen that the fires are connected and deliberate and that it's someone more purposeful than kids messing with matches?" Hugh leaned back and stretched his legs. They reached halfway across the cramped private room, all the way to the front of my chair. We could have played footsie if we'd wanted.

"Connected? Deliberate? I think we're getting all het up over a bunch of foolishness." Harold stared at the television instead of making eye contact with me.

"It was foolish not to call in the Fire Marshal before someone ended up dead," I said. Harold's heart monitor beeped faster again, and Hugh knocked my foot with one of his big boots. It was like being kicked under the table when you were a kid because you admired your grandma's ability to grow a mustache.

"I think Gwen means the Fire Marshal's office is always happy to assist when arson is suspected. I'm sure you would have taken us up on the offer if it seemed necessary, right Chief?" Hugh kept his hoof within striking distance as I squirmed in my chair.

"Darn right, I would've." Harold tugged his sheet higher and shrank back into his pillows. "I'd never've let it go on if I thought anyone would get hurt." Bernadette bustled in and glared.

"This here's a sick man," she said. "I don't know what you're thinking pestering him with questions."

"Don't fret," Harold said. "I could use the distraction."

"You need rest," Bernadette said. "I want you out this instant." Hugh stood, looking sheepish. I knew enough to hustle out of there. Bernadette's not someone to cross once she's made up her mind. Harold wouldn't be answering any more questions today.

"Good luck with the surgery," I said. "I'll be thinking of you."

"Just give a holler," said Harold, "if you've got more questions." Bernadette herded us out the door and stood in the threshold, blocking any attempts at re-entry.

"Don't even think about it," she said. "The doctor said any more stress could set him off again."

What I wanted to know was, what set him off in the first place?

SIX

Snow had piled up while we were in the hospital. Hugh drove well under the speed limit to keep the truck on the greasy road. Small flakes clustered together tightly and reduced visibility to a few feet. The weather report sounded grim. Six inches on the ground, and they were predicting snow all night.

"How far do you have to go to get home?" I asked, wondering if he would need a place to hole up for the night.

"Just over in Langley, about five miles off the pike. It usually would take me about twenty-five minutes." Hugh kept his eyes on the road and his grip firm. He drove like a native, steady and resigned to taking as long as it needed in order to get there in one piece.

"Are you near the Peppermint Patch?" I'd spent too many hours and far too many dollars wandering through the area's largest garden center. Peter used to complain about the cost until I put in vegetable and herb gardens. Our grocery bill was halved, and he loved eating the produce.

"I'm only a couple of miles from there. That's my favorite nursery. Do you shop there?"

"I'm their best customer. I can't get out of there

with less than a trunk full of plants every time I visit."

"I'd have guessed you garden." Hugh slid his eyes from the road for just a second to glance at me. My stomach fluttered. I told myself I was hungry.

"What gave it away? My stooped back or my blisters?"

"Gardeners are caretakers. From what I've picked up around town, you fit the bill."

"Someone's been filling your ears with enough rot to fill your compost bin. I don't take care of anyone. I live alone. I'm cranky. I don't like dogs. Or cats. Well, except the hairless ones. They're kind of cute."

"So you've got something against hair?" Hugh took one hand off the wheel and stroked his full red beard. "I've been thinking of shaving this off." My stomach flipped and rolled like a load of wash. I wished we'd hurry up and get back to the village so I could get out of the truck. I never was good at flirtatious banter, not even when Peter and I started dating in college, and it wasn't like I'd been practicing in the intervening years.

"From the looks of the weather you'd be better off saving your shearing till spring." I concentrated on the road. The snow was mesmerizing. Hugh put both hands back on the wheel and changed the subject. The state plows hadn't made it this far north yet, and the road had completely vanished beneath the snow. The only guide was a faint track from the last vehicle that had traveled this way.

"Harold's heart monitor didn't sound too happy when we asked about the fires, did it?" Hugh asked.

"You noticed that too? I don't say he's lying, but something is stressing him, and I don't think it's that he isn't running the investigation."

Hugh slowed even more and pulled onto the exit ramp. We were three miles from the village, and the road had worsened. Bill Lambert would be up all night with his crew of five guys plowing and laying down salt and sand as fast as they were able.

Rounding the corner, Hugh slammed on the brakes. Another truck was sliding into a skid. About twenty feet in front of us it fishtailed and then circled completely around before broadsiding Hugh's side of the truck. The force of the impact shoved us off the road and into a snow bank where we were well and truly stuck. I felt my seatbelt tighten up as my body lurched into it with all its weight. My head tried to keep on going. Fortunately it was still attached to my neck.

"Gwen, are you hurt?" Hugh leaned toward me. "Are you all right?"

"Just scared. How about you?" My hands were shaking, but I felt nothing but relief.

"I cracked my head on the door, but it's not damaged."

"What about the other guy?"

"I'll check." Hugh released his seatbelt and tried shoving his door open. It groaned but wedged shut.

"The impact must have jammed it," I said. "Let's try my side. " I pushed open the passenger door and slid off the seat into a snow bank. The cold and wet seeped through my trousers as high as the middle of my thighs. Hugh landed behind me with a decided height advantage. The snow barely reached his knees.

"Why don't you climb back into the truck and try to keep warm? I'll holler if I need help."

"No way. I wouldn't hear you over the wind." Snow scoured my face and dove into my ears. I pulled up the hood of my parka and waddled up the slope with as much dignity as I could muster. Hugh outpaced me, and I soon lost sight of him as the snow swirled between us. I followed his tracks, which filled up almost faster than I could trace them. I heard him yelling down into another ditch on the opposite side of the road.

"Hey, buddy, are you hurt?" I heard him shouting. I squinted and could just make out another figure standing. I waded toward them and got a better look at the other driver. He was a skinny guy, not much taller than my own five feet three inches. I probably outweighed him by forty pounds. Compared to Hugh he looked like a hobbit and a scared one, at that. His brown eyes darted back and forth between us and the road.

"Please, I drive for boss," he said. He was shaking, and I didn't think it was just the cold.

"I'd like to see your driver's license and registration." Hugh tucked his flashlight under his arm, then flashed his badge. The skinny guy took one look and lifted up like he was part of the Rapture. He was gone before either of us could say another word.

"Unbelievable. Absolutely unbelievable." Hugh stood trying to follow the fugitive with his flashlight beam. Bits of snow clung to his beard as the wind tried to tear off pieces of his nose and ears.

"I hope he doesn't die of exposure. That guy didn't look built for this weather." I tugged on the drawstring of my hood to block out more of the storm.

"Some days I hate working with the public. Let's look in his truck for a registration." Hugh pointed his flashlight beam down the hill. I lost my footing and slid down the slope. Hugh tromped down toward the other truck. It was even more damaged than Hugh's. The front end was crumpled, and it was lodged down a much steeper embankment. We slid off the road. This guy slid off a cliff.

"He was lucky to walk away from this." Hugh leaned in and checked for the registration under the visor and in the glove box. Slamming it shut, he pulled something large draped in a granny square afghan across the truck seat. I peered around him and watched him unwrap it. Even in the meager light I recognized the outline of the giant wooden hand that had sat on top of the museum's clock tower, the one everyone had thought had burned along with the rest of the tower.

"What are the chances of two of those hands being in the same village?" I asked.

"About as good as us being able to drive my truck the rest of the way back to your house. Do you know who he was?"

"I can't say that I do."

"You can't or you won't?" Hugh scowled into the dark. From the tone of his voice, I got the feeling his patience was running thin.

"I've never met him. I've never even seen him."

"How many families in Winslow Falls have an accent?" Hugh pointed the beam in my direction, like a low-budget interrogation technique.

"As far as I know, just one."

"That guy looked enough like the DaSilvas to be related, don't you think?"

"I think that's like saying every redhead in Langley must be related to you."

"Every redhead in Langley *is* related to me. There are about three dozen of us. People wear sunglasses to Sunday dinner to cut down on the glare." I couldn't tell if he was joking. How do you fit three dozen redheads built on the same scale as Hugh around a table? Maybe they rented the Odd Fellows Hall.

"Why don't we argue about this more after we've gotten out of the storm? My face is stiffening up." I thought about the scarf I forgot on the bench in my mudroom and gave myself a mental kick in the pants.

"How far is it back to your house?"

"About two miles by road. In the growing season we could shave off half that by cutting cross lots, but with all the snow on the ground it'll be easier to stick to the road, especially carrying that hand."

"No one is going to steal the hand."

"Someone already stole the hand. I'll carry it." I reached in and dragged the thing toward me. It was a lot heavier than I'd imagined it would be, but I'd already opened my big mouth. I reached round it with both arms and started up the hill.

"You're going to give yourself a hernia," Hugh called after me.

"No, I won't. I'm just going to throw out my back. It'll be fine." I heard Hugh laughing as I kept on trudging. It was hard work, but it warmed me up. By the time I reached the top I was sweating. I laid the hand on its afghan, tied two corners in a knot, and started dragging it like a sled.

"This is crazy. I've got my cell phone in the truck. I'm going to call Ray about the accident. Maybe he'll give us a ride."

"Don't count on it. Tell him about the hand while you're at it." I shoved the hand off the road and hunkered down on it to wait. I probably should have worried that someone would come along and run me over, but I was so cold and miserable I was thinking dead would be a nice change of pace. A couple of minutes later Hugh thumped down next to me.

"No signal. We'd better get moving. It isn't going to get easier as it gets later." Hugh stood and swung the hand onto one shoulder then took off breaking trail through the snow drifting into the road. I followed, too grateful for the help to think of anything feminist to say.

Twenty minutes later I felt rumbling underfoot and turned to see a town plow heading toward us.

"Hugh! Let's flag it down!" I yelled, trying to make him hear me over the wind. We were on the wrong side of the road. The plow was bearing down on us, and we weren't going to have time to cross to the other side. A wall of snow plastered me before Bill saw us and slammed on his brakes. He hopped down out of the plow and hurried toward me.

"What the hell are you two doing out here?" Bill pulled his baseball cap off his head and brushed me off the best he could. And I thought I was miserable before. Snow caked my face. Hugh had gotten some of the plow's spray also. Fortunately for him he was tall enough that it didn't quite reach his face.

"We were returning from visiting Harold and were run off the road by another driver. My truck's in the ditch, and my cell phone didn't work."

"What're ya carrying?" Bill pointed to the hand.

"Evidence. Is there room in your truck for all of us?"

Bill nodded, and with a complete disregard for personal space we all squeezed into the truck. There have been many times I've been grateful for plows but never more than that night. Squashed up against Hugh, the hand bumping against my leg, I wondered about the skinny guy and whether someone would find his picked-clean skeleton in the spring.

SEVEN

Bill dropped us at my house. The driveway was impassable, and the snow had drifted so much you couldn't see the porch steps. Once again Hugh broke a trail and I followed. Lights were on in the kitchen, and Augusta had flipped on the porch light, too. Hugh reached the mudroom door and stood there waiting

"Go on in, I never lock it until I go to bed," I said. I followed and almost cried at feeling the warmth of the woodstove drifting down into the mudroom. Hugh stood there dripping all over the flagstone floor.

"Peel off your wet things, and we'll dry them by the stove." I shucked my boots while tugging off my mittens. I wanted to strip to the skin and toast myself like a marshmallow in front of the woodstove, but considering the present company, I decided to slip into my flannel pajamas instead. I gathered soggy clothes and climbed the steps up into the kitchen.

Soup was bubbling away on the stove. I lifted the lid on a kettle and inhaled deeply. Clam chowder, my least favorite food on the planet. I longed for the cheeseburger I hadn't gotten at lunch time.

"I wondered if you were ever going to turn up." Augusta appeared in the doorway wearing an elegant, silky blue robe and matching nightgown. Blonde tendrils of hair had escaped the artful pile on her head, but her makeup was flawless. If I'd felt bad about my appearance before, it was nothing compared to how I felt now. Augusta-the-bombshell made me look like something salvaged from a shipwreck. Any second now, Hugh would lope through the door and see us side by side.

"I was in a car accident. With a mystery man." I contemplated how long it would be before she noticed I was shedding clumps of snow.

"A mystery man? Was he cute?"

"Somehow that didn't seem important at the time. I was trying to tell if he was hurt, but between the howling wind and his accent, it was hard to understand him."

"An accent. Yum. I hope you brought him back with you. I expect he needs warming up." Augusta's last two husbands had deep, rumbling accents.

"He ran off into the storm. You're out of luck."

"Something smells delicious." Hugh emerged from the mudroom, completely distracting my sister. A real man beat a mystery one every time, even one without an accent.

"Maybe I'm still lucky, after all." Augusta fluffed her hair and batted her prosthetic eyelashes at Hugh. "I keep hearing about an investigator down at the store, but no one mentioned you were so handsome."

Hugh stared at her, the corners of his mustache twitching. "I've been called a lot of things, but handsome's never been one of them." I studied Hugh and contemplated that. He wasn't classically handsome, but Augusta made a good point. Even though his height and hair were the most striking things about him, the rest of him was worth looking at. His eyebrows, as expressive as a Schnauzer's, sheltered inky blue eyes. The parts of his lips that peeked out through his facial hair were generous. His chest was about as wide as a barn door.

"Don't be modest. Every man looks good in a uniform." Augusta licked her lips and took a step toward him. It was time to intervene. Another twenty seconds and Augusta would be slurping Hugh up along with the chowder.

"He's not in uniform, and he ought not stay in what he's wearing since he's soaked to the bone. Why don't you dish up some dinner while I find him some clothes?" Augusta winked at Hugh and began pulling soup bowls from the cupboard.

I hurried upstairs to Josh's bedroom. He still kept clothing in the drawers for his visits home from college. Rummaging produced some sweatpants that would be knickers on Hugh but would at least be drier than what he was wearing. I grabbed a tee shirt and an Irish fisherman's sweater I'd knitted one Christmas for Josh that he had been polite enough to wear once. It had taken months to complete and was monstrously oversized. It appeared to be a perfect fit for Hugh. I added a pair of hand-knit socks to the pile and decided it was the best I could do.

"I found you some things," I said.

"Thanks," he said. "Where should I change?" I

pointed toward the bathroom. When he came out, I burst out laughing. Augusta worked hard not to.

"You look like a Revolutionary War re-enactor," I said, pointing to his high-rise pant legs. "The sweater fits, though."

"It's warm, too." Hugh ran his hand over a sleeve. I've made a lot of sweaters, and they never ended up the way I planned. The sleeves would be too long for the intended recipient or the body too short. A couple of years ago I started knitting the sweater I felt like making, then figured out who to give it to once it was done. From the way it fit, I'd been making this one for Hugh.

"Let's make a party of it," Augusta said. She opened the fridge and pulled out a bottle of wine. Hugh followed me to the dining room for wine glasses.

"I don't suppose there's a rental car agency in Winslow Falls?" He gently took the two glasses I handed him and held them like he was sure he was going to snap the stems.

"No, there isn't. Besides, it's not a night for traveling," I said. "The house is plenty big enough, even for you."

"I don't want to put you out."

"Augusta has the actual guest room, so you're the one most likely to be put out. Josh's room is cluttered, but I don't think it smells." Hugh followed me back to the kitchen.

"Thanks," he said. "I appreciate it." Back in the kitchen Augusta ladled out bowls of chowder while I poured the wine.

Three servings later, Hugh pushed his bowl away and groaned.

"I hope you saved room for apple crisp." Augusta stroked her French manicure across Hugh's sleeve.

"I did," I said. "Any ice cream to go with it?"

"It's too cold for ice cream," Augusta said. "I made rum raisin hard sauce." Hugh lolled his eyes around in his head.

"With the way you cook, you ought to be the sister on the fire department."

'Not likely," my sister said. "Gwen's the tomboy in the family."

"She sure is a trooper," Hugh said. "You should have seen her bumping down the hill on her backside to see if the other driver was hurt, not to mention dragging that giant hand along like a sled dog."

I jumped up and moved the dishes to the sink to crust over until morning. The last thing I wanted was for Augusta to tell Hugh about some of the tomboy escapades of my childhood.

"What hand?" Augusta asked. Hugh went to the mudroom and brought in the sculpture. He set it on the kitchen table and peeled back the afghan.

"It doesn't seem too damaged for something supposed to have burned in the museum fire." I ran my hand over the flaking paint. Time and the elements had silvered the exposed wood and roughened the surface, but the carving was clearly the work of a skilled craftsman. The hand was about four feet high and eighteen inches wide. The index finger pointed skyward while the rest of the fingers were closed into a tight fist. Fingernails were etched into the fingertips, and a ring was carved onto the ring finger. In place of a stone set into the ring was a star.

"Is it from the museum?" Augusta asked.

"It sure looks like it," I said, looking over the sculpture for signs of scorching.

"How did it escape being burned?" Hugh asked.

"There was scaffolding set up at the museum for the roof repair," I said. "Maybe someone used it to climb up and take it."

"Okay," Hugh said. "Why would anyone do that?"

"There would have to be a good reason," I said. "The clock tower was too high to shimmy up there for the view."

"Agreed. Could it have been a prank?"

"Like a fraternity thing?" I asked. "The Odd Fellows are the only organized group of guys around here, and they are mostly past it for prime tower climbing."

"It could be kids."

"You mean the DaSilva kids."

"I mean if it was a prank, kids are the first on the list."

"It seems too big for a kid to handle," Augusta said.

"I think the best possibility is the skinny guy. He had the thing in his possession, which is more than we can say for anyone else."

"Why would he want it? Some sort of hand

fetish?"

"Maybe it's valuable," Hugh said. "It has to be pretty old. Does anyone know much about it?"

"If anyone does," I said, "it would be Ethel. Or Gene Ramsey. He's on the museum board of trustees because of his knowledge of antiques."

"Once the storm clears up," Hugh said, "we ought to talk to them.

"I've still got to buy my mother a Christmas gift. I can ask Gene about it while I look around at his shop, The Hodge Podge. If he doesn't know, I'll go ask Ethel."

Augusta moved closer to the sculpture and scrutinized it. "I've seen that before," she said.

"Of course you have," I said. "It was on top of the Museum."

"No," Augusta said, "somewhere else."

"You mean this isn't the only one?" I asked. "It seems pretty unusual."

"I remember, it's a symbol of the Know Nothing Party. They were big in the 1850s."

"Are you sure?"

"Absolutely. I saw something about it on a television antique show. Some lady had a hand sculpture from the steeple of a de-consecrated church. She bought somewhere in Kentucky. The show's expert said it was really valuable. There aren't too many of them left anymore."

"When did you see this program?" I asked.

"I don't know, six months ago."

"And you're sure about the sculpture?"

"I'm sure. You know how it is when the expert on those programs has good news. They dither around twitching and congratulating the owner on their good fortune."

"If you say so. I don't watch them," I said.

"They spent a lot of time on it. I felt sorry for the woman who was up next. Her item turned out to be a Victorian version of a velvet Elvis."

"Did Beulah insure the building taking the sculpture into account?" Hugh asked.

"I'm not sure. I've got all the paperwork for her estate. I can check in the morning," Augusta said.

"I'm too wound up to sleep. I'll see what I can dig up on the internet about the Know Nothings," I said.

"Would you like some company? I'm not sleepy yet either." Hugh said.

"Great idea. Gwen could use the company of an able-bodied man late into the night. You kids be good, and don't do anything I wouldn't do. Not that I can think what that would be." Augusta winked elaborately in Hugh's direction and floated up the stairs.

Augusta had always held herself in high esteem in the sexual adventure department. Me, I'm more of a prude, and I've come to accept that. As far as I can tell there are no wild oats in my Quaker box. Even if I was in the market for a date, I couldn't get one with my sister around. She oozes pheromones like a pantry pest trap. If chemists could bottle essence of Augusta into a perfume, there would be no more lonely women in America.

"You and your sister aren't much alike, are you?" Hugh watched her go.

"No one believes we have the same parents. The computer's in here." I tried to stop blushing as I led the way into the den and pulled a second chair up to the oak table Peter had set up as a computer desk.

"She doesn't leave a guy much room to enjoy the chase does she?"

"Augusta likes to live fast. Subtlety slows her down." I'd always admired Augusta's direct approach. I hadn't considered that it might backfire sometimes.

"I like subtle." Hugh settled in the second chair and eyed the room. "This is a comfortable room. Are you a travel buff?" I followed his gaze as it landed on the framed antique maps hanging around the room.

"They were my husband's. This was his office." It felt strange to be sitting in Peter's chair, explaining his space to another man.

"Divorce?" Hugh sounded genuinely interested.

"Car accident. Sort of."

"Sort of?"

"Peter was a surveyor. One afternoon the driver of a car didn't slow down for the Men Working sign and struck him. Peter died before the ambulance could even get to him."

"That's pretty grim. How long has it been?" Hugh leaned forward a little and studied my face. It felt like he was listening with his whole self, not just a little corner of his brain like most people do.

"Seven years."

"Have you been on your own that whole time?"

"No. I had my sons to finish raising. Owen was sixteen and Josh was twelve when it happened. Now the boys are grown, and I'm on my own."

"Do you get lonely rattling around in this big house?" Hugh brushed his arm against mine as he reached for a pad of paper and a pen on the table.

"Sometimes." Blushing again, I bent my head over the keyboard, flicked the power switch and started searching for the Know Nothing Party. I typed the name into a search engine and waded through a bunch of entries with nothing to do with history. Eventually I picked up a line on them and started following it.

They were an ultra-secret society, like the Steadfast Order of the Loon only more paranoid. They blew onto the national political scene in the 1850s and caught on like a paper fire. Apparently, they had an arson problem, too. As radical anti-immigrant, anti-Catholic conspirators, they set fire to churches, making it impossible for any Catholic churches in the Northeast to procure property insurance. The tide of anger against an influx of Irish and German immigrants fueled support for their activities.

"Listen to this," I said. "The Know Nothing Party, also named The Order of the Star Spangled Banner, rose from obscurity to prominence in the 1850s. At the height of their power, ninety U.S. Congressmen were affiliated with the movement. In 1856 the party unsuccessfully supported the candidacy of Millard Fillmore for President. Little is known concerning the party as each time an individual was asked if he belonged to the group, he reportedly answered, "I know nothing," thus giving rise to their name. Their power base covered Maryland, Kentucky, Pennsylvania and New England where immigrants competed with native-born peoples for manufacturing jobs. Anti-Catholic sentiment already running high was fueled by the sensational book entitled *The Awful Disclosures of Maria Monk*."

"That's quite the title," he said.

"There's more. 'Their influence was mostly over by 1860 but laws remained on the books in New Hampshire until 1877 banning Catholics from holding public office.'"

"You're kidding," Hugh said.

"I wish I were."

"Sounds familiar doesn't it?" Hugh said.

"What does?"

"All the anti-immigration stuff. It's like we've been treading water for a hundred and fifty years and nobody even realized it."

"We may not have realized it, but I bet the DaSilvas sure did," I said.

EIGHT

The next morning I woke late. The excitement of the last few days had worn me out, and the plows had interrupted my sleep. Fortunately, Trina works on Fridays for me so at least I wasn't late for work. Augusta's snores rumbled toward me as I staggered to the kitchen to start some coffee. I wasn't looking forward to clearing the driveway with my ornery snow blower, but it had to be done.

Someone had filled the woodstove and stoked the fire. A piece of paper lay on the table. I unfolded it and ran my eyes for the first time over Hugh's handwriting. He had caught a ride with a plow driver back to his truck. He mentioned that he'd call me later. I read the note over several times, then asked myself why I would do such a thing. Just as I was resolving to get dressed and tackle the driveway I spotted Diego DaSilva scooping snow at the end of my driveway.

I raced down the mudroom stairs. "What are you doing?" I called out from the open doorway, wishing once again that I wasn't showing the village my pajamas. It was getting epidemic.

"Shoveling. I was passing and the fireman asked me if I wanted to earn money. Is okay for you?"

"It's great. I'm delighted." He turned and went back to the end nearest the road. I admired the way he began with the hardest part first. Every time the plow passed in the night it had built the bank at the end of the drive up by a few more inches. There must have been two feet of it packed in hard. I closed the door on the sound of his shovel scratching and poured myself some coffee.

The giant hand was still sitting in the middle of the kitchen table. I wrapped the afghan back around it and lugged it into the room I called the library. The name was a little pretentious, but it was crammed full of books. Peter and I were both avid readers. One of the first projects we had tackled after buying the house was to build floor-to-ceiling bookcases around the room.

I carefully sat the hand on one of the wingbacks flanking the fireplace and left. Returning to the kitchen, I opened the folder of clippings from Ethel to look over while I breakfasted on leftover apple crisp. I fanned out the yellowed bits of newspaper across the table. The photos were interesting, and many of the buildings seemed altered by changes in the landscaping.

In a photo from a 1904 Fourth of July issue of the *Courier* the museum showed clearly as a backdrop for a parade. Behind a beautiful hat worn by an ugly woman, a plaque was attached to the wall of the building. Squinting, I could read nothing more than the word Mill before my eyes grew blurry.

By the time I finished a third cup of coffee, the

drag of the shovel was getting closer to the house. When I looked out the window above the sink, I saw Diego bent over, hacking at some ice that had adhered to the pavement. Pretty thorough for a kid with little experience with snow. The driveway was cleared generously. He hadn't tried the usual trick of making the opening just barely wide enough.

People who put in a poor investment early with their driveway clearing invariably paid for it later. Winter caves in on the lazy. You have to push back the first few snowfalls much farther than necessary to leave room for what's to come, sort of like wearing stretch pants to Thanksgiving dinner. Make sure you've got room, or things are going to get uncomfortable. The shovel went silent, and I heard a knock on the mudroom door.

"Do you have salt to put on the walkway? Someone will fall."

"It's in the barn in a five-gallon bucket near the door. Come on in as soon as you're done." I watched him push open the barn door, and for a second I could have sworn it was one of my own boys. Same dark scruffy hair, same slouchy posture bundled up in a parka two sizes too big.

Nostalgia this early in the day didn't bode well. My days off were always the hardest days without the boys. When Owen and Josh were small those days were full of church services, family dinners and drives to visit elderly aunts. When Peter was gone, they were the best way to keep some stability in our lives. The Sunday dinners that had been cooked by Peter turned into ice cream sundaes and popcorn enjoyed over board games. Eventually Owen got tired of the junk food and learned to cook. Just thinking about his lasagna made my mouth water.

I ran my eyes over the photos again and wondered whether the sign was still on the Museum. I decided if I worked up the courage to get dressed, I'd check.

Diego let himself back in and stood dripping all over the floor. His ratty gray sneakers were soaked through, and his hands were red and raw.

"Kick off your shoes and leave your coat on a peg. I bet you'd be willing to eat a snack and drink something hot."

"I am hungry. I didn't have breakfast."

"You're a hard worker for a guy with an empty stomach. I wonder how you'd do if you ate before you got going?"

"I don't know." He surveyed the kitchen carefully. Part of me wondered if he was casing the place to break in later with his little brothers in tow.

"Do you like apple crisp?"

"I don't know."

"Do you like apples?"

"I don't know."

"Let's give it a try. Do you want some hot chocolate?"

"Do you have coffee?"

"Are you old enough to drink coffee?"

"My brother drink coffee. He is two." I peered into his dark eyes and remembered an awful lot of coffee comes from Brazil. Probably Brazilian children are weaned on it.

"What do you take in it?"

"If it is hot I will drink anything." I filled a mug and handed it to him with the sugar bowl and the cream pitcher.

"Fix it however you'd like." I dug around in the cupboard and found some chocolate syrup. "You want to stir some of this into it?" He nodded. While he dressed his coffee I microwaved a heaping plate of crisp. Watching him, I noticed his wrist bone poking out as he stirred his coffee. I scooped a big blob of vanilla ice cream onto the hot crisp before placing the plate in front of him. He poked at it with a fork then dove in. He shoveled food as efficiently as he shoveled the driveway. Watching him eat was inspirational. With his alternating shoveling and sipping he could teach hot dog eating contestants a thing or two.

"It is good."

"Want some more?" I asked as he picked up the last flakes of oatmeal with the back of his fork.

"Please." I refilled his plate and poured him more coffee. He leaned over the newspaper clippings while he waited for seconds.

"Is this Winslow Falls?"

"Yes. I'm doing some research for the historical society. Ethel Smalley asked me to volunteer for a presentation about the building at a fundraiser to repair the clock tower." He scowled at me when I mentioned Ethel's name.

"I guess you share most people's opinion of Mrs. Smalley," I said.

"I hate her. My family, we hate her."

"That's pretty sad, don't you think, that so many people don't like her?"

"Whose fault is it that no one like her?"

"I'd have to say it was hers."

"Then she get what she wanted. Why is that sad?"

"Good point. Do you always look for shoveling jobs when it snows?"

"Yes."

"Why haven't I ever seen you on my street before?"

"Usually I find jobs near to my house. This morning no one wanted to hire me so I keep trying until I got here."

"Do people usually hire you more easily than that?"

"Yes, but they think my family is making the fires, so they don't want me near their houses." He took another tug at the coffee.

"Are you?"

"Would I tell you if we were?"

"Probably not, but I thought it was worth a try. One of my sons went through a pyromania phase. It wouldn't surprise me if most men on the fire department are volunteering to make up for something they lit on fire as a kid. But I don't think any of you were involved with what happened to the clock tower or with Beulah, and to prove it, how'd you like a shoveling contract?"

"What do you mean?"

"I'd like to contract you to shovel the post office

parking lot as long as it doesn't interfere with your school work. Do you want it?"

"What will you pay?"

"You tell me what your time is worth. I'll tell you if I agree." Diego glanced up and down at my flannel-clad figure like a car salesman who sees you pulling into his lot with smoke billowing from under your car's hood. "Fifty dollars. Cash."

"Done. But you have to present me with a written bill like any other contractor. I work for Uncle Sam, and he doesn't like me to spend his money without accounting for it in writing."

"Does your Uncle Sam own the post office?"

"Yes. He does. Your spoken English is very good. How's the written English coming? Can you make out a bill?"

"I think so. Is spelling important?"

"Yes. You must look professional. Think up a name for your company, and then ask Miss Gloretta if you can use one of the computers at the library to make up an invoice to give to me. If you don't know what that means, use one of the dictionaries at the library to look up the word invoice. Do we have a deal?" He looked startled. Maybe the library wasn't one of his usual hangouts. Gloretta might not be too happy with me before the winter was through.

"Yes. It is a deal."

"Can you start today?"

"I can do it."

"Good. I'll be by later to check on it."

"I will go." Diego pushed back his chair and

headed for the door.

"Wait a minute. You ought to wear something on your hands if you're going to be out in the cold." I rooted around in a basket I keep in the mudroom for a pair of wool mittens that didn't look too girly. Near the bottom, I found a heathered charcoal gray pair. They looked like the right size.

He slid them on and checked the fit. "Thanks. These are warm."

"They'll stay warm even when they get wet," I said. "That's the beauty of wool." I watched as he hurried down the street balancing his shovel across his shoulders like a milkmaid with her buckets and yoke. I wondered what I'd gotten myself into.

NINE

Tramping along Clement Street through salty puddles, I squinted at the sun sparkling off the snow as it draped the bare branches of the trees. Passing the Thimbleberry Inn on the corner, I admired the wreaths and sleigh bells festooning the wraparound porch and the tall windows. All around, neighbors were digging out from the storm. The sound of snow blowers and the smell of exhaust filled the air.

Stopping in front of the Museum I searched for the plaque. At first glance it wasn't visible. Beside the steps was a yew that wasn't in the 1904 photograph. It covered the windowsill and blocked light to the building's interior. Wedging my body between the shrub and the building, I pressed the branches away from the building and saw a plaque screwed onto the wall. It was brass and caked with decomposing yew needles. Using my mitten as a scrub brush, I cleared it off enough to read it.

Millard Fillmore Slept Here read the inscription. Not what I was expecting. I thought the Mill I'd seen in the photo referred to one of the many mills in Winslow Falls' history. I didn't remember hearing about a presidential visit. In New Hampshire we're used to attention from would-be presidents. With our first-in-the-nation primary, we're a tourist information booth on the road to the White House. They never seem to look back, though, once we've given them a boost or buried their dreams. With just under two million residents, we're a presidential leap year, existing only once every four years.

I stepped back and took a longer view of the Museum. The roof of the clock tower had been burned completely at the peak. An average-size adult standing in the tower room would find her head sticking up into the outside with an unobstructed view of at least half the village as well as the river. The side of the tower opposite the street was burned down more than the rest of the tiny room. It had mostly crumbled under the pressure of the fire hoses while we were trying to save the rest of the building.

I stopped by the post office on my way home to check Diego's work. The lot was as clean as a carving board after the dog's licked it. Diego was worth every penny.

I had to pass Dinah's on my way home from the post office, so I thought I'd stop and see if she'd fried any blueberry doughnuts that morning. Dinah's blueberry doughnuts make you forget it's winter.

"I was about to head to your house to interrogate you about the accident," Ray called out, churning blueberries and doughnut around like his mouth was a cement mixer. Videos of Ray chewing could be sold as appetite suppressants. Clive perched on his favorite stool with the paper spread in front of him.

"You should talk to Hugh. He was the one driving," I said, picking up some sugar-free gum instead of a doughnut. Ray wiped his mouth on the back of his hairy hand and pulled out a notebook that looked exactly like Hugh's.

"I don't put much stock in what he has to say. I heard from Bill he couldn't even hang onto a skinny fugitive." Ray scratched one of his teeth with a grubby forefinger.

"Is that right?" Clive joined in. "Couldn't hold him, huh? I thought he was some kind of police officer along with being a fireman."

"He's supposed to be," Ray said. "Says he's a state trooper, if you can believe that. The cream of the crop."

"I've never heard tell of a Statie letting someone flee on two feet before, have you?" Clive rattled his paper for effect.

"Can't say that I have. I guess every group's got its bad eggs." Ray consulted the notebook again. "So, Gwen, tell the truth, was Hugh drunk or just speeding?"

"I'm not even going to answer that," I said.

"So both." Ray stuck out his tongue and slowly wrote something in his notebook.

"You should be more careful with your accusations. Besides, I think you should be more worried about the other driver. Hugh and I were unharmed, but I'm not sure about him. He could have died of exposure by now."

"Good enough. It would save me the trouble of

arresting him for trespassing." Ray grinned, a bit of blueberry skin sticking to the front tooth he hadn't scratched.

"Trespassing? How do you figure that?" Clive swiveled away from his paper and gave Ray his full attention.

"If you're illegally in a country, anywhere you go is trespassing. The entire state is off limits. Keep out!" Ray waved his arms in front of his body.

"That's not the intention of trespassing laws, and who says he was illegal?" I said.

"Fleeing an accident scene is illegal. That's good enough for me," Ray said.

"Probably stole the truck too," Clive added. "Did you recognize it?"

"It was dark, and my eyelashes were freezing together. I was up to my waist in a snow bank, recovering the museum's hand. So no, I didn't notice whose truck it was."

"Some investigator you are." Ray snorted and bit into another doughnut.

"There wasn't a registration in it," I said. "The back plate was missing. The front end was wedged in a snow bank."

"You didn't recognize it?" Clive gawked at me. In a town of about six hundred and fifty people, everyone's vehicle is recognizable. Not only do you know who's in it, you can usually guess where they're going based on the day of the week or the time.

"No, I didn't," I said. The door bells jangled, and Trina rushed in, shivering. She and Chris moved here from California, and even after a couple of years she isn't used to the cold. I glanced at my watch and realized it was time for her lunch break. She nodded to us and sat next to Clive.

"Bill was in the post office this morning telling about your accident and how miserable you looked when he picked you up," Trina said. "He said you'd been dragging the hand from the museum at least a mile by the time he rescued you."

"Bill embroiders the truth. Hugh carried the hand most of the way, and I'm sure I didn't look that bad."

"Probably no worse than you usually do," Clive said staring at my puffy parka and muddy boots. Trina and Ray both nodded.

"Why was the hand in the truck in the first place?" I asked. "Why didn't it burn up with the rest of the tower?"

"I know why it didn't burn," Trina said. "Chris said he had one of the crew take it down before they started the roof job. He didn't want it getting knocked off while they were stripping shingles. I guess he was worried about it dropping on someone's head."

"That explains it," Ray said.

"It doesn't explain how it got into an unidentified truck," I said. "Trina, did Chris say where he stored it?"

"No. He just said it was no picnic getting it off the roof." Trina pulled a pink nail file out of her purse and started sawing away.

"I wonder how they got it up there in the first place," Clive said.

"Why was it put up there?" I asked. "Why a giant hand? It seems weird when you think about it."

"God," Clive said. "They built the museum before airplanes and such. Back then there was just God."

"Have any of you heard it was valuable?" They all shook their heads.

Augusta had gotten up and dressed by the time I reached home. She consented to go shopping for a Christmas gift for our mother. We decided to try our luck locally since Mum loved antiques of all sorts.

"How about this?" Augusta held up a teapot shaped like an old man smoking a pipe.

"It doesn't say Merry Christmas to me somehow." Everything in The Hodge Podge was packed in tightly enough to make me nervous just standing still. Crystal knife rests, silver hairbrushes, baby carriages full of doilies and framed artwork, and documents filled the large store. The building was constructed as a hotel when the mills were still bustling and the railroad stopped at least once a day in town. Now the building attracted a different sort of visitor. People on the way to the White Mountains would often stop in to buy a souvenir of their trip to New Hampshire.

Gene, the owner, smiled at Augusta as he wrapped up a Depression glass lemonade set for another woman. He escorted her to the door and then made his way to my sister's side.

"Anything special you're looking for today?" he asked.

"A Christmas gift for our mother. Any suggestions?"

"I suggest you have dinner with me this evening." Gene reached for her hand and cradled it between his own. Augusta fiddled with the top button on her red silk blouse. This needed cooling off. I didn't want Augusta to get any ideas about extending her visit because of a new romantic interest.

"Gene, why would the museum have a plaque on the front saying *Millard Fillmore Slept Here*?" Gene dropped Augusta's hand and gave me his full attention. As a teenager I'd always imagined how it would be to distract a man from Augusta. Millard Fillmore had never factored into the fantasy.

"When did you see that?"

"This morning. I saw a photo of the plaque in an old newspaper clipping Ethel gave me for the fundraiser research. It's right behind that big yew to the right of the stairs."

"I suppose," Gene tapped a long finger against his thin lips, "it could have been because Daniel Webster served as the Secretary of State under Fillmore." Daniel Webster is arguably New Hampshire's most famous son."

"That might explain him being in New Hampshire, but it still doesn't explain why he'd be in Winslow Falls."

"Maybe he had friends here." Augusta worked her way back into the conversation. "Maybe he was visiting the White Mountains on holiday and stopped at Dinah's for a doughnut."

"Speaking of food, make my day and consent to dine with me," Gene said. I spotted the stairs to the second floor and escaped. Gene always struck me as a man that oozed. I'd no desire to watch him grease his way across Augusta.

One of the rooms upstairs had been set up like a nursery. A second was an adult bedroom furnished with a matching bedroom set complete with a vanity table and a freestanding wardrobe. The doors to the wardrobe were open, and long dresses and men's coats hung from the rod. I pushed open a closed door at the end of the hall and peered down a narrow hallway. There wasn't a sign saying the space was closed to the public, so I went on through.

Leaning up along the walls were dark oil paintings and framed letters written on yellowed paper. One of them, a letter signed by Franklin Pierce, had a price tag of nine hundred dollars. It didn't seem like the paper was in good shape, but it looked impressive enough mounted in a dark wooden frame. A roll-top desk with cubbyholes pressed against one wall. An inkwell and quill pen rested on top. A silver letter rack and letter opener set caught my eye. My mother loved to write newsy letters to family members about the latest scandals at her active seniors community in Florida. With a box of stationery and some stamps, it would be a perfect gift. I picked up the set and returned to the counter to check out.

"Where do you manage to find so many beautiful things?" Augusta was in full in flirt mode, her hand resting on Gene's forearm.

"Sometimes they just walk right in my door," Gene winked and leered.

"I hate to break up whatever's going on here, but I think I found the perfect thing," I said. I placed the rack on the counter.

"This item is not for sale," Gene tugged at his collar.

"Why not?" I asked.

"It hasn't been priced yet. You helped yourself to it out of the storage room."

"Sorry. Besides, time is money right? By turning this over quickly you'll make a better profit. Augusta, isn't this perfect for Mum?"

"She'll love it. Please, Gene."

"I suppose I can make an exception," Gene said, "but only if you'll agree to have dinner with me tonight."

"We don't have any plans, do we, Gwen?" Augusta didn't even look in my direction. "I'll be ready at seven."

TEN

"What a pack rat." Augusta held up a ratty dishrag.

"Granny Binks was just as bad," I said. "I think Mum moved to Florida just to avoid clearing out Granny's house when she died." We were in Beulah's attic, rummaging through her boxes and looking for anything useful for the fundraiser. So far, it was looking grim. Boxes, bags, trunks and crates were crammed into every nook. From the way Beulah had kept house downstairs, no one would suspect she was living under this mess. At least once a year Beulah mentioned she needed to clear out up here, but I hadn't realized it was this bad.

"Have you checked behind those boxes shoved up against the chimney?" I asked.

"Not yet. I'll give them a go now." She tugged at the cardboard flaps on one of them.

"Papers." Augusta dragged the carton to a tiny cleared space in the center of the attic. We settled in front of the box and began to lift out envelopes and pamphlets. Yellowed newspaper clippings made up the top layer. "Look at these." Augusta held up three pamphlet-type books entitled *Maria Monk's Awful Disclosures*. "Who needs multiple copies of this?"

"Sounds racy," I said. "Set it aside, and we'll read it later." I began spreading out the newspaper clippings in an arc around me on the floor. They were from newspapers from different states. The only thing they seemed to have in common was election results and advertisements selling miracle cures for consumption. The local obituary page was included for several of them. Others had listings of local meetings.

"Look at that dressmaker's dummy. Can you believe anyone ever had a waist that small?" Augusta asked. The slender dress form wore a red and white vest beaded with white stars.

"Depressing, isn't it?" I pulled out two wooden spoons and a porcelain hatpin holder from the box. "Do you think Beulah even knew what was up here?"

"Probably not. I'm guessing most of it wasn't even hers to start with."

"Considering she was born in this house, a lot of this must have belonged to her parents and even grandparents."

"This is interesting." Augusta moved aside a crispy bundle of letters and held up a scrapbook. One of its brass hinges hung limply, and the blue velvet cover was tattered.

"I remember that. You liked to make fun of all the big mustaches," I said. Augusta scooted closer and gingerly opened the cover.

"Eighteen fifty-five," Augusta read. "Property of Eustace Freemont Hartwell." She turned the page and there, drawn in carefully, was a family tree. A tightly controlled hand had written in the names and birth dates of generations of family members. Vreeland Price Hartwell was there and so was the Judge, Ambrose Hartwell Purington. All the pages were decorated with colored stars.

"Was this guy a patriot, or what?" Augusta said. "There's more red, white, and blue here than a car dealership having a Fourth of July sale."

"Maybe he was born on the Fourth," I said, "or married that day."

"Not according to this," Augusta said, flipping back to the first page. "I'd guess he was kind of a nut."

"Maybe he was a veteran," I said. "Was he old enough for the War of 1812?"

"Nope. He was born in 1830."

"Anything in here that could help with the fundraiser?"

"Maybe. Here's another picture of the Museum. It doesn't have the hand on the clock tower, though."

"That's weird," I said. "I thought the building was designed with it."

"I bet Ethel knows something about it." Augusta kept turning pages. Newspaper clippings and programs from local events were pasted onto the pages. A postcard of the dam and the former woolen mill still clung to the final page.

"One of us should ask her, and I've got to work tomorrow." I squinted at my sister in the fading light, searching her face for signs of weakness.

"Perfect. You can ask her when she comes in for the mail." Augusta and I always fought about chores when we were kids. She usually won then, too. "If she says none of this stuff is valuable, I think we should just call a junker."

"That's heartless. Don't you remember playing here when we were kids?" I asked. "When Mum and Dad played bridge with Beulah and Granny?"

"Sort of." Augusta leaned against a stuffed chair with broken springs. "I think we were here a few times." She stashed the album back in the box.

"I can't believe how bad your memory is. We played in this attic every Thursday night for years. It's like you never lived here at all."

"I can't help it if my memory's like a wad of cheesecloth. Besides, you can't move forward if you're always looking back."

"We played dress-up and damsel in distress. You always wore one of those fox stoles and played the princess. You made me be the prince who rescued you." I stood up and scouted around for the trunk that held the dress up clothes.

"That sounds right," Augusta said. "You were a tomboy and never wanted rescuing." She had a point. The idea of waiting for someone else to fix what ailed me never held any charm.

"Help me look for the dress-up trunk," I said. "We'll see if the clothing jogs your memory." Just as Augusta stood up to join the search, I thought I heard a thumping noise at the base of the stairs. I froze and strained my ears. The arsonist spooked me more than I wanted to admit.

"Gwen, you've got to see this," Augusta called

from the far end of the attic. I kept glancing back over my shoulder as I followed the sound of her voice. A low wattage bulb hanging in the center of the room was the only source of light besides the grimy windows tucked into each gable. Augusta stood silhouetted against the fading sunlight and pointed into a long narrow box.

"What is it?" I would have sworn the floorboards behind me creaked.

"I believe it's meant to bring you face-to-face with your own mortality. I bet it belonged to a secret men's society." Augusta moved sideways, and more light shafted onto the box. Inside the satin-lined box lay a skeleton, its bones held together by metal pins. Out of the corner of my eye, I caught sight of a shadow moving steadily across the floor. I screeched and hurled myself to the far side of my sister. Knocking against the underside of the roof, I gouged my scalp on a protruding nail.

"You can't be frightened of this old thing." Augusta reached into the box and patted the skeleton so high up his thigh that his ghost was probably blushing.

"It's not him. Something's moving around up here," I whispered.

"You're imagining things. No one's with us except this guy, and we can handle him."

"Shh," I whispered, squinting under the dusky eaves.

"Oh," squealed Augusta, spotting Beulah's cat Pinkerton. Like all men, he made a beeline for

Augusta and displayed interest in her legs. "We forgot all about you. You must be half starved." Puffs of fur drifted off Pinkerton's oversized body as she squeezed him to her chest. She picked her way across the cluttered floor to the narrow stairs. I followed as closely as I dared, sneezing and blinking my watering eyes.

"He must have a kitty carrier around here somewhere." Augusta tugged on her coat.

"Where are you planning on taking him, Gusty?" I gave a little cough, hoping she'd remember my allergy.

"Home, of course. He can't stay here." Augusta buried her face in his neck and made a smooching sound.

"I'm allergic to cats. He can't stay at my house."

"I'm starved," Augusta said over the wails coming from the cat carrier.

"Let's pick up something at Dinah's on the way home." I brushed at dust and grime clinging to the legs of my sweatpants.

"We're not going anywhere with you looking like that." Augusta pointed a manicured finger at me and looked to the cat for support.

"Like what? I wear this outfit all the time." I glanced down at my flannel shirt hanging unbuttoned over a fundraiser tee shirt from when Josh was in elementary school.

"That makes it worse. Besides, remember my date

with Gene?"

"I'd forgotten." Actually I hadn't, but I hoped she had. I didn't want to spend the evening alone while Augusta went out. It was easier not to date if no one else was doing it either.

"Maybe Gene has a friend. We could double." She nudged me in the ribs.

"I don't need anyone to fix me up." She looked at me like I was a dog with three legs trying to run, spunky but pitiful.

"We'll see."

"I'm not in the market."

"Everyone's in the market. Even married people are in the market. It's biological." Augusta locked the door behind us. It was probably the first time the door had been locked since Beulah had visited our mother in Florida four years earlier.

"The batteries in my biological clock have corroded." I jerked open the car door and shoved the keys in the ignition.

"Then you just need new batteries." Augusta slid in beside me and pulled my keys out. "I think you need a change."

"I'm fine. Everything is great." Augusta stared at me, and I did my best to stare back. "I'm used to being me, and everyone else is, too."

"Who cares about everyone else? For once stop thinking about everyone else and start looking in the mirror. Try it right now." Augusta dug in her purse, which could double as a moving van in most of the world and dragged out a compact. Flipping it open and clicking on the map light, she shoved it in my hand. "Does this look like a woman who should be worrying about everyone else?"

I took stock of myself. My face looked like my sweatpants, grimy and worn out, covered in wrinkles and bits of fuzz. Even my eyes, which I thought of as my best feature didn't hold any sparkle. Actually, they were red and felt gritty.

"It just isn't important to me, Gusty. Raising the boys and working are my priorities." I closed the compact and handed it to her.

"The boys are grown. You have time for yourself now."

"I'm busy with village commitments. I'm a museum trustee, a historical society member. I'm on the planning board."

"Don't forget the fire department."

"See? I don't have time."

"Why do you choose not to have time?"

"I don't choose it. People ask for help, and I can't say no."

"Everyone else says no. What makes you so special?"

"Being the postmistress is kind of a default public official. People expect it of me."

"Well, they ought to stop expecting it. I'm not just talking about your wardrobe, Gwen. I'm worried about your happiness and health. When I say you don't look good, it isn't just your hair or clothes I'm talking about. You look run down and discouraged. And lonely. If you don't do something about it soon,

I'm telling Mum." She leaned over and stuck the keys back in the ignition then fastened her seatbelt. I backed down the driveway wondering which was worse, reinventing myself enough to satisfy my sister or having my mother decide to come take care of me.

It had happened once before. Once Owen was born, my mother decided the baby and I needed round-the-clock care, so she moved in with us for two weeks. Unfortunately, her version of care involved sitting in the rocker holding the baby and telling me stories about the women she knew whose babies died of mystery illnesses.

"You do that, and I'll be sure to mention how you brought a cat into my house. You know she worries about my allergies."

"They're all in your head."

ELEVEN

Fuzzy nuzzling woke me the next morning. At first I thought it was Peter's armpit hair tickling my nose. I stretched and draped my arm over what I thought was his chest. Picking a hair off my tongue, I remembered Peter was still dead. Pinkerton had taken his place next to me. That summed up my life at present, nothing in my bed but a writhing mass of allergens shedding all over me.

I threw back the covers and dug my feet into my slippers. Maybe it was my imagination, but it felt like my face was on fire. I clomped to the bathroom and peered into the mirror. Raised welts covered my face, leaving just enough space for my eyes to squint out.

Beulah's funeral was going to be the most-attended in town since Elmer Burrows' twelve years ago, necessitated by an icicle dislodging from his roof and driving through his skull. Staying home sick was not an option. I needed to be there, but I didn't want my face to be bigger news than Beulah's death. Besides, I wanted to look professional if Hugh showed up to compare notes. This called for groveling.

I knocked on Augusta's door. No answer. I pushed it open and saw my sister sprawled on her back, a red satin eye mask on her face. Her blond hair fanned across the pillow as if she'd been posed by a fashion photographer or a serial killer making a statement. It was going to be painful to grovel before the queen of beauty.

"Help." I hoped I sounded sad enough to evoke sisterly pity.

"Help," I tried again in a louder voice. Nothing.

"Help!" I shouted, shaking the foot of the bed like a caged gorilla. Augusta surfaced from slumber like a rescued drowning victim. Lurching upright, gasping and clawing at her eye mask, she took one look at my face and burst into hysterical laughter. She stumbled out of the bed and staggered down the hall. The bathroom door slammed, but laughter still echoed down the hall. I slunk back into my room to get dressed. It was 5:45 a.m. according to my digital alarm clock.

I dressed more carefully than usual. Nothing was going to offset the face entirely, but perhaps the artful use of accessories might help. In my jewelry box I found a pair of large, gold hoop earrings I never wore. Yanking a multicolored scarf from a box at the bottom of my closet, I tied it around my neck as a distraction from my face. Twisting it to the left, then the right, I wondered how foreign women on TV always looked chic in scarves. They throw them on any old way and look glamorous while I couldn't manage one that wasn't made of worsted wool and designed to ward off frostbite when you fed the chickens. I pulled it off and tried it on my head.

"Are you a gypsy or a pirate?" Augusta asked from the doorway.

"Neither. I can't go to work looking like this," I said, pointing at my blistering face.

"Well, you can't go looking like that either." She snatched the scarf off my head and placed an antihistamine and a glass of water into my hands.

"Take that, and we'll get you started drinking about a gallon of water. We need to flush whatever is bothering you out of your system."

"I told you not to bring that cat here."

"He would have died if we'd left him."

"I could have died from anaphylaxis."

"Because you've been having a hard week, I won't mention you're overreacting."

"Thanks," I said. "What am I going to do about my face? I can't go to work or the funeral like this." She left the room, and I stood there alone, twisting the scarf around and around in my hands and wondering how I was going to live through a day full of Winston, Clive and Ray laughing at me.

Augusta breezed back into the room with a pitcher of water and a mini steamer trunk. She heaved it onto the bed and shoved Pinkerton onto the floor.

"Scoot," she commanded the cat, and like most men, he obeyed. She popped the latches on the trunk and selected some brushes and jars. She turned to the closet and flicked through the clothes. "Don't you own anything that doesn't look like you washed the car with it?" She frowned at fleece vests, ratty cardigans and baggy pleated wool skirts.

Augusta shuddered as she crossed the room to the dresser. Opening the top drawer she rooted around and held up a pair of white cotton granny panties and a sports bra with holes for inspection. She slammed the drawer closed and tried the next. Augusta tossed faded turtlenecks and University of New Hampshire sweatshirts in a heap on the floor in the corner.

"And I thought your face was in bad shape." She shook her head at me and left the room again. Returning with things from her suitcase, she held dozens of garments up to me before settling on an outfit.

"Drink another glass of water and put those on." She pointed to the pile.

"We aren't the same size."

"How can you be drinking water and talking at the same time?" she asked. I drank some water and picked up a black turtleneck sweater. It was soft and looked three sizes too small. A lacy bra topped the pile. It was reinforced in ways that were probably regulated by a government oversight board.

"I'm not desperate enough to borrow your bra."

"Yes, you are. You just haven't realized it yet. You have to learn to harness the power of your bust for good instead of evil. Your sports bra presses your breasts under your armpits and turns them into back fat." Thinking about my photo in the paper, I conceded that she might have a point. Swallowing my pride along with some more water, I took the bra.

"What is that?" I poked at an under garment that looked like it belonged to the Victorian era.

"A foundation garment. It sucks in all the jiggly bits."

"It looks like something Granny Binks would have worn."

"Where do you think I get my fashion sense? You'll love it."

"I'll try it."

"Good. You get dressed while I start some coffee. I'm not up to giving you a makeover without caffeine."

Thrashing and squirming, I wedged myself into the underwear and then moved on to a pair of gray trousers. The pants slid over my hips and even zipped. I was attempting to hook together the bra when Augusta returned.

"Not like that. It will work miracles but not without cooperation from you."

"I've been wearing a bra since I was thirteen. I know how to put one on."

"Obviously, you don't. You have to lean forward and scoop everything available into the cups. That's where the harness part comes in. Flab can be your friend. You just have to know how to use it." With that Augusta bent forward and demonstrated. Her technique explained the discrepancy between my saggy bust line and her perky chin rest. I bent forward to give it a try for myself. My bust was naturally younger than hers by two years. The results would have to be at least as good. I stood up and inspected my work in the mirror.

"I think you need to work on symmetry." Augusta

squinted at my handiwork. I agreed. About two more pounds of fat had gotten piled into the right cup than the left. It would be a more convincing look if both of my cups would runneth over instead of just one. After a few more tries I had no more difference between the sides than a mother whose infant was full after nursing on only one breast. It was a look I'd been comfortable with twenty years before. Not exactly how Augusta had planned on making me look younger, but it was all we had time for that morning.

I slid the turtleneck on and checked the mirror again. I turned to get a rear view and sure enough, no back fat. I stared at Augusta with new respect.

"Now sit over here, and we'll fix your face," she commanded. I perched gingerly at the edge of the bed. Cat hairs were scattered about the quilt like allergy land mines.

Augusta dabbed light beige foundation around my face. The cream felt cool on my flaming skin, and I was less itchy than I'd been before.

"Hold still. I'm moving on to your eyes." She zeroed in on my eyebrows with a pair of tweezers and began sighing loudly. I couldn't remember plucking them since Peter died. Humiliatingly enough, she plucked some things off my chin too.

"Are you going to be much longer?" I asked.

"Beauty takes time, Gwen, especially when there's been so much neglect." Augusta rolled up a tube of her favorite lipstick.

"I'm not wearing that. I'll look like a hussy."

"Are you saying I look like a hussy?" Augusta

asked, eyes wide and innocent looking.

"No, but you don't look like you are from around here."

"I'll take that as a compliment. The only belles around here are the ones in the church steeple." She had a point. Traditionally, New England women have been too practical to be more decorative than useful. From the time the Pilgrims landed, we've needed all hands on deck to survive. A lot of New Hampshire has no more than a hundred frost-free days per year. Between snow, rain and mud season, the most practical footwear you can own is a pair of insulated boots. Predictably, the region's leading fashion designer is L.L. Bean.

"Your hairdresser should have her license revoked." Augusta lifted my curls off the back of my neck.

"What hairdresser?"

"Figures." She grabbed a round, prickly brush and a pot of goo that she worked through my hair like she was kneading bread dough. I sat there waiting for my scalp to rise until doubled. I was sure the only thing left was for Augusta to bake me until golden brown and hollow sounding when tapped. "Okay. Take a look."

Augusta steered me toward the mirror. If someone had shown me a photo of the woman looking back at me, I would have suspected I'd seen her somewhere but couldn't quite place her. A cousin perhaps, but not me.

I turned sideways. No pouch popped out where

my abs were supposed to be. Turning frontward, my saddlebags were missing. My bust stood front and center, proud of itself for the first time in forever. My thighs no longer looked like two sand bags left by the army corps of engineers once the river stopped threatening to jump its banks. But my face was the biggest miracle of all.

Augusta had managed to hide or flush out all the redness from my face. I actually had eyelashes. My lips were pouty and voluptuous. Where there had been only one brown eyebrow sprinkled with graying hairs, there were now two—with no gray hairs in sight and no hairs of any kind sprouting from my chin.

"I don't mean to hurry you, since you're obviously enjoying yourself, but it's getting late. Isn't that yummy fire investigator supposed to be there this morning?" I glanced at the clock and sprinted toward the stairs. Before I got to the base she called out to me.

"Shoes make or break the outfit. Catch!" Augusta tossed down her black high-heeled boots and waved.

TWELVE

I surveyed the post office's cleanly shoveled parking lot. I was grateful for a well-sanded walkway as I crunched across unsteadily in the borrowed boots. Diego was a man to be trusted. That reminded me to drop by his house later to pay him.

I hung up my coat, started a pot of coffee, and checked the computer for email updates. I deleted most of the incoming messages and left the rest to be dealt with later. I heard the scrunch of snow under tires as Ernie, the rural deliveryman, pulled up to the back door to drop off the day's mail. I unlocked the door again and held it open for him as he lugged in three large drawstring sacks.

"What happened to you?" asked Ernie.

"I had an allergic reaction to a cat," I replied.

"Allergy attacks suit you," Ernie said, a gap-toothed grin parting his gray-stubbled chin from his sorry excuse for a mustache.

"Thanks, I think," I said. As soon as Ernie left I opened the service window and unlocked the front door. Before long customers were rattling the locks on their P.O. boxes and stomping snow off their feet.

Yellow slips announcing the arrival of packages

too large to fit into the boxes get sorted and stowed first, followed by first class mail. Third class and bulk mailings are low on the priority list. At this time of year there is a lot of bulk mailing of seed catalogues and catalogues selling home improvement gadgets. I was busy with the yellow slips when Clive appeared at the window.

"What happened to you?" he asked.

"A health problem," I said. "Is there any postal business that I can assist you with, because I have a lot to do back here besides discussing my appearance?"

"Don't be so darned touchy. I just meant that you are more dressed up than I ever remember seeing you. You aren't jealous of your sister, are you?"

"Go away, Clive," I turned my back to the window. I continued stuffing the boxes as people streamed in. Saturday morning is always busy, but today was even busier since people wanted to talk about Beulah. I decided to take advantage of all the traffic and try to find a new home for her cat.

"Does anyone want to adopt Pinkerton? Augusta brought him home from Beulah's, but I can't keep him. Worst of all, he's taken over my bed," I said.

"You should be grateful that any male creature would get into your bed, considering your taste in pajamas," said Winston.

"I bet it was because he thought that the sushi was real. You know how cats love fish," added Clive.

"Aren't you allergic to cats?" asked Gloretta, the village librarian.

"That's just the problem."

"The only kind of cat I like is one that has been to the taxidermist," Winston said.

"No way. Brandy hates cats," said Clive.

"Brandy hates everyone except you," I said. "Maybe he could live at the museum once it's repaired."

"You could give him to the DaSilvas," Clive suggested. "They'll probably eat him for Sunday dinner."

I rolled my eyes and changed the subject. "What do you know about Millard Fillmore?" I asked Gloretta as I slid her mail over the counter.

"He was the thirteenth president, taking office after the unexpected death of Zachary Taylor."

"Did you ever notice the plaque on the wall beside the front steps of the museum?"

"I can't say that I have."

"I hadn't either until I spotted it in an old photo. It's behind the giant yew. It says *Millard Fillmore Slept Here.* What was Millard Fillmore doing in Winslow Falls?"

"I don't know. You should ask Ethel."

"Is there anything special about the sculpture that was on the clock tower?"

"Besides that it was kind of strange?"

"Yeah, besides that it was a giant wooden fist with the index finger pointing skyward."

"We're lucky it was the index finger. No, I guess I never really thought about it. When you've lived with something all your life, you don't really notice it do you?"

"I suppose you don't. Do you think anyone might know if it was valuable? I'm wondering about a special insurance rider."

"I'd ask Ethel about that, too. I would have thought that she would be bragging about it though." Gloretta waved and went back out to face the cold.

By the time I closed the post office that afternoon, clouds had barreled into the village, and the weather channel posted a storm warning for the evening. Eighteen to thirty-six inches were predicted by a cheerful weatherman somewhere in sunny Florida. I sipped coffee as I sorted through the week's mail. I hate to admit it, but I'm always in arrears with my own mail. I don't even pick it up each day.

Augusta swept into the kitchen just as I'd opened my fourth credit card offer. She was dressed for the funeral, if a black knit dress that hugged each of her curves and cherry red lipstick can be considered mourning. To be honest, most people attending the funeral would be there more for the social aspects of the event than because they were grieving. Most people would miss Beulah, but death at age ninety-one doesn't shock many people.

"We need to leave here a little early since I said I'd help set up the church hall for after the funeral."

"You go on ahead. I'm going to ride over with Gene. He offered to help sort stuff at Beulah's. We'll go straight over after the service."

"Don't be late."

"I won't. Save us seats."

I nodded and hurried off. With my heavy coat and a scarf tucked up under my chin, the brisk air was refreshing. On Mill Street I passed Tilly McElroy's house and noticed chickadees and blue jays jockeying for position at her bird feeder. As eager as they were for food at this time of day, a big storm must be on the way.

The walk took only five minutes, and the service wasn't due to start for at least half an hour, but cars already lined both sides of Church Street. I entered the Hartwell Church through the back entrance to the church kitchen and fellowship room. The peculiar church smell of old wood, burned coffee and apple juice filled my nostrils.

Women bustled around peeling foil off platters and Pyrex dishes. Children in Sunday best played tag around the tables. Old men chatted about the cost of heating oil. A satin banner emblazoned with the words *Let Us Worship the Prince of Peace* hung on the wall above Trina's kids, Kyle and Krystal, who were pulling each other's hair.

Ethel stepped in and took things in hand. Just the sight of her froze the tag players in their tracks. The men made themselves useful by untangling folding chairs and setting them into place. Even Trina's children ran for the shelter of their mother's arms. I was the only woman caught without a job.

"Nice that you could join us Gwen. I was expecting you earlier."

"I am early. I can't help it if everyone else is even

earlier," I replied.

"At your age you should have learned to be more responsible. Which reminds me, have you finished the research for the fundraiser?"

"You do realize," I said, "that it's only three days until Christmas?"

"Which means the fundraiser is just over a week away. I can count on you, can't I?"

"Between Christmas rush and the fire invest-igation," I said, "I'm swamped."

"Not too busy to get yourself tarted up, I notice. I'll expect the research tomorrow." Ethel turned her back and slapped Kyle's hand as it reached toward a cookie plate. I escaped upstairs along with anyone else with any wits about them.

The church is mostly used for weddings, funerals and special services throughout the year. The Baptist church down the street holds services every week, and most of the religious activity in town revolves around that building. Like most tiny New England towns, there were more churches built than the community could support in a thriving fashion. Ten years ago the congregations combined and hammered out a custody arrangement that offered visitation to each building.

I saw Hugh had taken a seat as close to the back as possible. I've heard in some parts of the country seats in the front of any sort of public forum are the first to fill up. This cannot be said in New England. It doesn't do to put one's self forward, especially in church. Besides, it makes things that much more painful to persons arriving late to have to slink past the entire group on their way to the front than to slip quietly into a seat at the rear. In this way, the offenders have been taught a lesson by those more virtuous than themselves. Very few families are late two weeks in a row.

Hugh waved me over and patted the pew next to him. He looked even more oversized than usual. I felt eyes following me from every corner of the sanctuary.

"I wasn't expecting you to be here," I said, surprising myself by noticing how well his navy suit set off his blue eyes.

"I always attend funerals of victims when I work a case." Hugh clanked his knees against the seat in front of him as he stood to help me remove my coat. My face flushed as Pastor Norling stared over the top of his bulletin.

"Quite a turnout." Hugh seated himself close enough for me to feel the warmth radiating from his body.

"I told you Beulah was well liked." I noticed the DaSilvas sitting by themselves at the front of the church. Luisa was holding the littlest one in her lap, and the others were sitting quietly, hair plastered to their heads, neatly pressed shirts on their backs. Before the pastor even started to speak, I saw Luisa wiping away tears. By the time he started to pray, she had a steady stream flowing down her face.

Just as the pastor was winding his way toward an amen, I felt the pew bow beneath me, and Augusta and Gene slid in.

"Where have you been?" I whispered as we all

turned to hymn number one thirty-five.

"We got distracted," Augusta answered as Gene winked at her.

"Just remember that my house is not a rent-by-the-hour motel," I said a little louder than I'd intended. Ethel shot me a look.

"We were checking the weather report."

"Uh huh," I said, staring at a lipstick smear on Gene's cheek.

Exactly twenty minutes after the service began, Pastor Norling gave the benediction, and Viola Labrie sent us on our way toward the refreshment table with a recessional hymn. Over Styrofoam cups of scorched coffee people discussed everything from the citizens most likely to run for office in March to the programs they had watched on television the night before. Some people were talking about Beulah but mostly in terms of how she died or whether the Museum was likely to reopen.

Winston and Clive headed toward Augusta and me. Clive balanced a mound of rice pudding and three finger sandwiches on a flimsy paper plate. Winston sipped coffee and sported a tomato sauce stain on his dress shirt.

"I thought for sure you'd be wearing black pajamas to this event," joked Winston.

"I don't even own any black pajamas." I excused myself as Luisa entered the room.

"Your boys were very well behaved," I said, hoping to make up for the unpleasantness at her house earlier in the week.

"Thank you." Luisa's eyes were red and puffy.

"Are you okay?" I dug around in my purse for a tissue but gave up and handed her a napkin from the refreshment table.

"Beulah was good lady. She helped me much." Luisa honked her nose lightly.

"We're all going to miss her. Did you work for her at her house as well as at the museum?"

"Sometimes I clean her house, but not for money. She helped me so much. I not take money. She give me baby things. She was helping me speaking English."

"I'm sure you took as much from her as you could get your grubby hands on." Ethel spoke loudly enough for her voice to carry across the room. I felt the whole room staring. Luisa took a step backward. Diego clenched his hand into a fist.

"I'm sure Beulah wanted to help. She loved babies. And big kids, too," I added, remembering the older boys were listening. "She mentioned several times the lovely job you did at the Museum. She would be touched that you thought so much of her." Luisa spoke to the boys in Portuguese, and they hurried toward the exit.

"Disgusting. Can you believe they have the nerve to show up here after what they've done?" Ethel shook her fat little hand at the door. "That's it. I'm calling Immigration." Diego glared at Ethel before slamming the door behind them.

THIRTEEN

I was embarrassed. Embarrassed for Luisa and her boys and embarrassed for Winslow Falls, that we had someone so ignorant living amongst us. I wish I felt like Ethel was the only one, but in all honesty, I didn't notice anyone leaping to Luisa's defense.

I took stock of the room. The outburst seemed to bother some people, but I wasn't sure if it was because no one liked witnessing a scene or because they, too, felt Luisa had been mistreated. Winston and Clara were gathering up their coats and avoiding looking at anyone. Clive had gone back to the refreshment table for seconds. Hugh came up behind me and placed a giant hand on the small of my back.

"You forgot your coat upstairs. I thought you might be ready to get out of here." He held my coat open, stooped a little to help me slip it on, then took my arm and steered me out the door.

"Can you see now why I said Ethel might have been the intended victim in the fire?" I asked, feeling a few flakes of snow spatter my cheeks as I craned my neck to look him in the face.

"She makes a strong impression."

"Like a skunk makes a strong impression. Did you

see Diego's face?"

"I did. Angry isn't in his best interest."

"What do you mean? Of course he was angry."

"Some people already believe the DaSilvas are responsible for Beulah's death. Giving Ethel a killer look only strengthened that impression."

I turned down Hugh's offer of a ride home. Unreasonable as it was, I was irritated at him for pointing out what everyone was thinking. I felt uncomfortable with my hometown's dirty laundry flapping in front of a stranger, especially one who was so perceptive. I wanted to check on the DaSilvas, and I didn't want an audience. I decided to hand-deliver payment for Diego's shoveling work and take the kids a bag of mittens, hats and scarves I'd knitted. I tucked a couple of adult-sized things in the bag for Luisa as well.

Luisa opened the trailer door, and once again I was struck by how out of season she was dressed in tight jeans, open-toed shoes, and a silky, fluttery top. I know I never looked like that with a toddler balanced on my hip.

"What are you wanting now? We do nothing wrong." She clutched her toddler tighter, her eyes snapping at me.

"I wanted to pay Diego for his work at the post office. He did a great job, and he shouldn't have to wait for his money. And I brought these for you and the kids." I stretched my arm toward her and handed her the bag. "It's stuff for the cold, hats, mittens. I like to make them, but I don't always have someone to wear them since my kids have both grown up." Luisa took the bag and peeked inside. She looked at me and stepped back to let me come in.

I followed her to the kitchen where she spread the contents of the bag out on the counter. I'd found a knitted giraffe that I stuck in among the clothing. Luisa handed it to her child and put him on the floor to play.

"Will you drink coffee?" she asked.

"I'd love some. It's freezing out there."

"I'm not believing I can be so cold. Every day I am missing Brazil."

"You might want to start wearing heavy socks and sweaters." I peeked down at her shoes.

"I like to be cold more than to wear those things." Luisa pulled a boiling teakettle off the stove and slowly poured water from it into a filter that looked like a jelly bag. Dark coffee strained through into a glass carafe.

"I guess if you want to be beautiful you have to suffer."

"Is true. The boys don't like to be cold. Thank you for the things."

"It's my pleasure. How old is the baby?" I watched him twisting the neck of the giraffe.

"Two." Luisa handed me a cup of coffee and slid over a sugar bowl. She passed me a Thermos bottle filled with steaming milk. I stirred some into my coffee and wondered how to ask politely about her motivation for coming to Winslow Falls.

"Does he have grandparents nearby who get to see

him, or are you here on your own?" Luisa eyed me
over the rim of her coffee cup, taking her time with
her answer.

"My family is in Brazil. I come to New Hampshire
with sons only."

"New Hampshire seems like a strange choice. I
know there are a lot of Portuguese-speaking people in
Massachusetts, but I don't know of others here."

"That is reason I coming here. No Brazilians. No
Portuguese."

"I thought immigrants usually liked to live near to
each other to help each other in a new country."

"Yes, in a group I find help, but my sons get no
English, only Portuguese. They not mix in America,
just stay Brazilians in a small Brazil in America."

"I'd never thought of that."

"Is true. Help at school, Brazilian food at store.
People talking Portuguese. Even on television is
Portuguese. Diego, Ronaldo and Tulio have more
English two months here than two years in
Massachusetts. I want to be Americans with Brazilian
family, not Brazilian family in America."

"I noticed that Diego speaks English surprisingly
well."

"He is intelligent. He is much help."

"Do you get any help from their father? Is he
Brazilian too?" I wondered if I'd overstepped my
bounds, but she didn't seem offended.

"He is Brazilian. He not help. He has other
woman, and he wants to be with her and talk
Portuguese and have Brazilian friends. I say we

should go to a place with no Latinos."

"Winslow Falls was a good choice then. No Latinos here. We all still think tacos are exotic."

"We don't eat tacos. Or tortillas. Or chili." Luisa sighed deeply.

"Isn't Brazil in South America?"

"One day you come for dinner. I show you. We are not Spanish peoples. In the south, where is my family, we not eat spicy foods."

"I'd like that. I don't cook, but I love to eat." I drained my coffee cup and carried it to the sink. The counters, stove and sink gleamed. With four kids and full-time work, it was a remarkable level of cleanliness.

"One day we do this." She walked me to the door and held it open.

"Luisa, if you need help with something, please let me know. Everything is hard if the language isn't easy."

"Why you are helping us? You are not knowing us."

"My husband Peter was killed in an accident when my two sons were twelve and sixteen. I know what it's like to raise kids on your own. If people in town hadn't helped me, I don't know how we would have made it through."

"Beulah helped us, and look what Ethel say today. We are better with no help." Luisa snuffed her nose like she was about to cry again. "I knew when she say me not work more at museum she not like me, but I not know she go to say bad things in front of many people and my sons."

"Ethel fired you from your job at the museum?"

"She say she not need me there. My work was no good."

"But Beulah hired you. Did you tell her that Ethel fired you?" Luisa shook her head, sending her black hair swirling around her face.

"No. I say nothing to Beulah. I want no trouble with anyone." She shivered and hunched her shoulders as cold air blasted through the open door. I wasn't shivering. My growing fury was toasting me nicely from the inside out. It kept me warm all the way to Ethel's house.

FOURTEEN

I meant to confront Ethel before I cooled down, but as I approached her house it was dark, and I needed to use the bathroom. I shouldn't have gone home. By the time I'd attended to the call of nature, I'd lost my nerve. The house was warm and smelled of freshly baked bread. Augusta was there fixing dinner.

"I thought you'd still be out with Gene." I opened the oven door and peeked at a roasting chicken and scalloped potatoes.

"Always leave them wanting more. That's my policy." Augusta wiped her hands on an apron I'd forgotten I owned.

"You have a policy for romance?" I slumped in a rocker as she bustled about the room washing greens for salad, slicing a loaf of bread.

"Everyone has a policy whether they acknowledge it or not. Even you." Augusta pointed at me with the bread knife.

"My life is devoid of romance."

"That's because that's your policy: no romance."

"It's not a policy. It's a lack of opportunity."

"You've got a seven-foot-tall redheaded opportunity knocking on your door pretty frequently lately. I'd say he's interested." My cheeks flamed, and I gnawed my thumbnail. I haven't bitten my nails since the second grade when my father promised me a whale-watching trip if I quit.

"What makes you think he's interested?"

"Because despite my best efforts, which are considerable, he kept his attention on you the night he stayed over after the accident. And what about at the funeral this afternoon? Who was holding your hymnal for you and fetching your coat?"

"He has good manners. That has more to do with a proper upbringing than any particular interest in me."

"Why is it so hard for you to believe someone might find you attractive?" Augusta thumped the bowl of salad on the kitchen table. I drew a deep breath and let it out slowly, feeling my shoulders slump forward. Augusta pulled out a chair and dragged it close to me. "What is going on here?"

"Peter was cheating on me. He was involved with another woman when he was killed." My eyes smarted.

"Peter?" Augusta squeezed my hand. "Are you sure?"

"Ethel told me." A tear skidded off my cheek and plopped into my lap.

"How would she know?"

"The woman was a bank teller over in Langley. Ethel was making a deposit one day and saw Peter leaving the bank with her. Being the hateful busybody she is, she followed them. They drove to the woman's house during the lunch hour. Ethel found it interesting enough to keep tabs on him for a couple of weeks."

"She told you this?" Augusta's eyes widened.

"One morning about a month after Peter's funeral she dropped in at the post office and told me how lucky I was to be a widow instead of a humiliated divorcee. She suggested I check Peter's credit card statement for dinners at the Italian restaurant in Hoyt's Mills."

"Good Lord. Did you check?" Augusta's nose twitched like she smelled something rotted.

"I did. Purchases I didn't know anything about at restaurants and jewelers and florists showed up for over a year."

"What a bastard, and you couldn't even confront him about it."

"I wanted so badly to ask him why he did it, what was wrong with our marriage. What was he finding with that woman that he wasn't finding with me?"

"I don't know, Gwennie. I just don't know."

"You know what the worst thing was? Being so angry I could hardly breathe and having to pretend to be a grieving widow. Every day people would stream into the post office with condolences, and I'd have to fake it when what I really wanted to do was to grab them by the shoulders and shake the pity off their kind faces."

"The boys don't know, do they?"

"Certainly not. I've never told anyone. As far as I know Ethel hasn't told anyone except me either. I've never heard about it if she has."

"And we both know you would have heard." Augusta jumped up and rummaged through the fridge. Pulling out a bottle of champagne, she set it on the table and went to the dining room. Returning with the flutes Peter and I had used at our wedding reception, she ripped off the foil and deftly untwisted the wire cage.

"I don't feel like celebrating," I said.

"I've been divorced four times. Believe me, I know exactly what it takes to get over a marriage. Come on, on your feet." Augusta grabbed the bottle and led me into Peter's office.

"Shrines are no good. I made that mistake with Walter." Augusta had met Walter in college. Probably they'd still be married if he hadn't arrived home from work one evening with a nineteen-year-old girl in tow and announced that God had called him to become a polygamist.

"You felt keeping Walter's money constituted building a shrine?" I looked around at all of Peter's things I hadn't had the heart to get rid of.

"Absolutely." Augusta popped the cork on the champagne and poured us each a glass. "That's why I spent it all. No shrines. And this," Augusta swept her hand around the room sloshing champagne as she pointed, "is definitely a shrine."

"The boys needed a place to remember their dad." I focused on the bubbles rising to the top of my flute instead of looking at Augusta.

"The boys don't live here anymore. Neither does Peter."

"I like this room the way it is."

"You like the taxidermy fish and the collection of miniature tractors? You like the annoying plastic clock that makes a different bird sound every hour on the hour?"

"Maybe it's a little outdated. I really do hate that clock." I took a sip of my champagne, then drained the glass. Augusta promptly refilled it.

"You start taking down the maps from the walls, and I'll get some boxes from the barn. And another bottle of champagne."

By two in the morning we had dragged everything I no longer wanted or needed into the barn or into the hall. The room looked like possibilities instead of memories. The change felt good.

"What are you going to do with it?" Augusta asked, sitting on the floor and leaning against a wall.

"I still need an office, but it needs some new wallpaper and fresh paint."

"We'll go out to a home improvement place in the morning and maybe back to Gene's for a few pieces of furniture that are more your taste." Augusta yawned.

"I haven't budgeted for buying furniture at Christmas time, at least not at Gene's prices."

"Don't worry. I'm sure I can get you a great deal."

"I don't want you to do me that sort of a favor."

"Don't fuss. It'll be my pleasure." Augusta wrapped me in a perfumed hug. "Tomorrow's going to be a busy day, and we both could use some beauty sleep." Augusta led the way up the stairs and fluttered her hand at me as she reached the guest room door.

I slipped into my pajamas in the dark and crawled between the chilly sheets. I wished someone was there to help warm the bed, but my mind didn't wander to thoughts of Peter and the past. It was lingering on the present when I realized I wasn't alone after all. Switching on the bedside light I spotted Pinkerton snuggled down at the foot of the bed. Holding him at arm's length I stomped down the hall to the guest room and tossed him in to join Augusta. Returning to my own room, I yanked the quilt off the bed and dumped it in the hall until I decided what to do with it. I didn't want the cat hair in my own washer, but there was no way I could avoid cleaning it.

I wiggled my feet down to the spot Pinkerton had warmed and drifted off to sleep, wondering again what it would be like once more to have someone to cuddle with. Someone tall. Maybe someone with red hair.

Opening my bedroom door the next morning, I spotted Pinkerton curled up once again on the quilt. I shooed him away, carried the blanket downstairs and then set off for Suds Yer Duds. The Laundromat was just the place to leave Pinkerton's fur. I had to pass Dinah's on my way and noticed Winston coming out dressed for church. He rattled a white paper bag at me with one gnarled hand and held a half-eaten doughnut in the other.

"Eggnog doughnuts this morning. Get 'em while you can." He ambled down the sidewalk, dribbling crumbs on the icy pavement behind him. Five minutes later, clutching a doughnut sack of my own, I stood in front of Suds Yer Duds, a single-story building clad in fake brick siding. The rusty metal roof dripped melting snow down my back as I struggled with the door.

I stuffed the furry quilt into a machine and settled in a ripped vinyl chair to flip through an old *Reader's Digest* and munch a doughnut when Ray burst in carrying a stack of laundry baskets.

"What're you doin' here?" Ray eyed my doughnut bag as he thumped his baskets down on a washer.

"Laundry." Not sharing doughnuts with Ray was helping him to avoid becoming a stereotype. At least that's what I told myself as I slid the bag under the *Reader's Digest* in my lap.

"I thought it was probably something like that. What's in the bag?"

"Feminine hygiene products." Ray threw a hand up to shield his eyes like I'd turned a laser pointer full in his face. He hummed loudly and busied himself with his dirty uniforms and crusty socks. I pulled the doughnuts out from under the magazine and parked them in the open. It didn't look like they were in any danger from Ray.

"So where's your boyfriend?" he shouted over the slap of the washer once he had run out of tunes to hum.

"What're you talking about?"

"Same thing as everyone else, your love life." Ray plopped himself in the rickety chair next to me. Absentmindedly, he picked at a rip in the upholstery with a hairy forefinger.

"Not that it's any of your business, but I have no love life."

"That's what I told Winston, but he said to keep an eye on you. What do we know about this guy anyway?" Crazy as it was, I felt a little touched by Winston's concern.

"What guy?"

"You know, Mr. Big Shot Investigator."

"He's not my boyfriend. What other rumors are gallivanting around behind my back?"

"I heard Augusta killed Beulah to get a hold of her estate."

"She wasn't even in Winslow Falls when Beulah died. Who said that?"

"I don't know who started it. I just know Clive repeated that he had heard it somewhere else." I wondered what Clive had to gain from saying such a thing. Had he had anything to do with Beulah's death himself and wanted to throw the attention elsewhere?

"You know Augusta better than that and so does Clive. Besides, there were other people who might have had a reason to kill Beulah."

"Like who?"

"You're the Police Chief. What's your opinion?" I didn't want the village churning itself up against Augusta, but I wasn't going to toss anyone else into the fray as a distraction.

"We all know who did it. The only mystery around here is why your boyfriend is holding off on arresting them."

"He's not my boyfriend. Just humor me for a

minute and pretend someone else could have set the museum on fire. Who else could it be?"

"Well, if it wasn't those kids, I'd have to say Pauline could be a good possibility. She was pretty steamed up about Beulah not giving her the job as curator."

"Ethel said the same thing at the meeting the other night."

"I suppose even Ethel could have done it. She got the job at the museum, but maybe she didn't like answering to Beulah. She was a good lady, but she could be hard to take when it came to the museum."

"That wouldn't explain why she'd set fire to the museum. She couldn't have control over a building that burned to the ground."

"Maybe she had a lot of faith in the fire department. Maybe she thought you guys would do a better job." Ray's radio blared from his belt. "That was Farley. Phil Lawrence just hit a deer out on County Road."

"Is anyone hurt?"

"Nobody but the deer. Phil wants me to help him toss it into his truck. No sense good venison going to waste. I'm gonna be gone a while. Don't leave my wash in the dryer too long. It doesn't look professional if my uniform's wrinkled." Ray slammed the door on his way out, sending a chunk of ice crashing down off the roof. As far as I was concerned, no amount of laundry care was going to help Ray look professional. When my quilt was clean, I took it home to air dry.

FIFTEEN

Augusta was up by the time I got home, and we spent most of the morning sitting at the wallpaper counter in a home improvement place down in Riverton. We eventually settled on wallpaper and paint and celebrated our decisions over a late lunch at The Lobster Pot. Augusta dropped me off at the house to start painting and continued on to The Hodge Podge to look for a desk and a lamp.

Peter and Ethel both filled my thoughts throughout the afternoon. The more I dabbed and swiped, the more I felt my anger at Ethel returning. She had humiliated me when I was the most vulnerable. I had an overwhelming desire to give her a piece of my mind. Augusta still hadn't returned by the time I washed out the paint brush. Before I could lose my nerve again, I stuffed my feet into my boots, grabbed a Mag-Lite and dashed out the door.

Ethel's house stood dark in the dusk of the evening. The street lamp outside was the only light shining nearby. I barreled up the steps to her front door and knocked, but there was no reply. Ethel's blue town car hunkered in the driveway, and I'd never thought of her as much of a walker.

I stomped through the snow around the side of the

house to try to peek inside. Curtains along the side of the building were still drawn shut. At the back of the house I raised on tiptoe to peek through the flapping plastic covering the kitchen window. A puff of wind lifted the corner of the plastic and revealed the kitchen. Light glowed from the digital clock on the coffee pot, and I could barely make out a jigsaw puzzle covering one end of the table.

I poked my flashlight through the gap and flicked it on. As I swept it around the room, the beam landed on the ceramic tile. Ethel lay sprawled on the floor in front of the wood stove. Even from this distance she didn't look too lively. Her eyes were closed, but the angle of her body looked too uncomfortable for natural sleep. Jasper was walking across her back and kneading her with his claws. I could hear the flannel ripping from where I stood. I tried the handle of the back door, but it was locked.

I waded back through the snow and pounded down the street as quickly as my out-of-shape legs would take me. Bursting through the door at Dinah's, I was glad for the first time in my life to see Ray.

"It's about time you decided to get some exercise." Ray pointed at me with a half-eaten hotdog. "That photo in the paper wasn't exactly flattering."

"Gwen doesn't exercise," Clive said from the stool where he always ate his supper.

"Something's wrong with Ethel," I said. "She's laid out cold on her kitchen floor with the cat climbing all over her." Ray stuffed the rest of the hotdog into his mouth with one shove, and Clive sprang for the door. The three of us climbed into the town's only police car. Ray was so excited to flip on the siren he forgot to close the car door before pulling away from the curb.

Squealing to a stop in front of Ethel's house, Ray threw the cruiser into park and dashed up the front steps. Over and over he slammed his shoulder into the heavy door, getting absolutely nowhere. I stood wondering how we were going to get in when I realized Clive had disappeared. Retracing my steps through the snow, I rounded the corner of the house and saw Clive using a key to open the back door and step inside. Jasper streaked past me into the dark as I entered the kitchen. I bent down and felt Ethel's wrist for a pulse. I couldn't feel anything, but the truth is, I never got the hang of pulse-taking, even during the eighties when everyone was into aerobics and target heart rates. Still, from the bloody paw prints tracked away from her head, I'd say Ethel's heart rate was definitely at the resting stage.

Clive must have let Ray in because there he was, hot and eager. He'd pulled out an exact copy of the notebook Hugh was always scribbling in.

"We'd better call the ambulance," I said. I searched for the phone and found it, cleverly disguised as a plastic napping cat. As it rang, I noticed a kerosene heater tipped over on its side, just like the one at the museum. I gestured for Clive to take the phone and checked out the heater.

It was less than four feet from Ethel's body. A little fuel had leaked onto the ceramic tile floor and trickled toward her corpse, but as I joggled the heater I couldn't hear sloshing in the fuel reservoir. I surveyed the room and couldn't see why the heater tipped over. The base was wide and the floor even. Jasper wasn't heavy enough to have knocked it over by rubbing against it. I couldn't see him getting dangerously close to a working heater anyway.

Clive hung up the phone. "The ambulance is on its way." He hung back from Ethel's body instead of flapping over it like he had with Beulah's. "Do you think she had a heart attack or something and then hit her head when she fell?"

"It looks like a lot of blood for bumping her head on the floor," I said, "even if it is ceramic tile." A blotch of rusty red spread from the crown of her head.

"Don't touch anything." Ray hooked his thumbs into his belt and rocked back on his heels. "You don't have any official standing here."

"You deputized me at the post office the other day." As much as I disliked Ethel, I didn't feel right about leaving Ray in charge. After all, he has to read the directions on microwave popcorn every time he makes a bag.

"Nice try. You turned me down flat. The fire may have been your jurisdiction, but this is mine. You wait in the other room until I can take your statement." The ambulance came to a stop in front of the house and cut off my opportunity to respond. Lucky Ray. Winston came through the front door. Right behind him was Hugh. He motioned me over, notebook in hand.

"I was on my way back into town and noticed the

ambulance so I decided to follow it in case I could help out." Hugh was talking to me but he was focusing on the activity surrounding Ethel's body.

"I'm glad you stopped. Ray knows even less about what he's doing than I do."

Hugh caught sight of the overturned heater. "Was that tipped over when you came in?"

"Yes, it was. I wondered about it, too." Hugh crossed the room and bent to inspect the heater. He glanced back up at me and shook his head. Ray noticed us and made a beeline for Hugh.

"There's no fire this time. I'm the guy in charge here."

"I think it may be more complicated than that." Hugh pointed to the heater, and Ray started chewing his bottom lip.

"It's just a heater. What I've got here is a dead woman and no fire. That means no cooperating with you."

"What we've got here is a probable arson attempt and a dead woman. Have you gotten a good look at her body yet? Any superficial indication as to the cause of death?" Hugh stood and loomed over Ray.

"I hadn't gotten around to that yet when you burst in." Ray stuck his hands on his hips like a mother in a fifties sitcom.

"What you mean to say was that you couldn't bring yourself to do it," Winston said. I knew where Ray was coming from. From the brief look I had gotten at Ethel's head wound, it wasn't anything to be too eager to see.

"Allow me." Winston handed Hugh some latex gloves, and we all watched while Hugh knelt over Ethel's body. "From the looks of things, I'd say this had nothing to do with a fall. There's a deep, trough-shaped wound on the back of the head. She was hit with something dense to cause that much damage to her skull." Clive let out a little squeak. I noticed he looked as green as I felt.

"Do you think she was struck and then someone tipped the heater over to try and hide the real cause of her death?" I asked.

"It could be. There doesn't seem to be a reasonable explanation for why this heater tipped over on a level floor. I'm treating this as part of the museum investigation."

"But it's my case." Ray's arms drooped at his sides, his notebook forgotten in his hand.

"'Fraid not. If that's a problem, take it up with the Fire Marshal. I'm sure he'd love to hear from you." Even though he'd never admit it, I'd say Ray looked relieved.

"Gwen, you found the body, right?" Hugh asked. I nodded. "Then let's get your statement." He gave some more directions about measurements and photographing the body to Ray and Winston, then met me in the living room.

"At the museum fire you mentioned the idea of Ethel being the intended victim." Hugh paged back through his notebook. "It looks like you were onto something I didn't take seriously."

"I doubt it would have made any difference in the

end. I told you it wouldn't surprise me if Ethel had made someone angry enough to try to kill her. I still couldn't have told you who did it."

"The strongest lead we have connecting the two victims at this point is kerosene heaters in both places. Any ideas?" Hugh's eyes wandered the room as he was talking. I wondered if he was evaluating the decorating or assessing the flammability of all the clutter.

"We could ask at Dinah's about kerosene purchases. She sells it at a pump outside the store."

"Do you think anyone would be foolish enough to buy it in the same place he was intending to use it?" We both eyed the group in the kitchen. Winston and Clive stood watching as Ray tried to unstick the zipper on a plastic evidence bag.

"I think it's possible."

"Well, maybe. Anyone have an argument with her recently besides the DaSilvas?" Hugh asked.

I lowered my voice so the crew couldn't hear me. "I think we should talk to Pauline Lambert. She applied for the curator job and was bitter about Ethel getting it instead. Ethel rubbed it in her face at the meeting the other evening."

"You think it was enough for her to kill Ethel over?" Hugh's forehead pleated right between his red eyebrows.

"Pauline hasn't spoken to her own sister in fifteen years because they both wanted to name their sons after their father. Patty got pregnant with a boy first and used the name."

"What was the name?"

"Horace."

"And I thought my ex-wife held a grudge," Hugh said.

"Most ex-wives are angry," I said. "It can't be that bad."

"She tried to burn down our house," Hugh said, "while I was asleep inside it. She said she was sick of me getting called out to fires every time she made a nice dinner."

"Were you a fire investigator when she married you?"

"I was investigating a possible arson in her apartment building," said Hugh. "After the divorce I wondered if she had anything to do with that fire, too. She had a lot of complaints about the landlord."

"It sounds like you've had the right kind of experience to handle Pauline," I said.

"Does that mean you're not coming with me?"

"Oh, I'm coming," I said. "You want to head over as soon as you've wrapped things up here?" Hugh nodded and got back to work. I thought about who could have killed Ethel. Pauline had sounded angry enough to kill her, but there wasn't any shortage of people who might have liked to do it, including the guys processing the crime scene.

SIXTEEN

Pauline's Ford Escort sat in the driveway looking as new as it did back in 1987 when Bill picked it up for her at a liquidation sale. Pauline, in ratty sweats and fuzzy slippers, answered the door. Seeing Hugh, she put a hand up to her hair and scowled at me.

"Is your telephone broken?" she asked. "Most people call before stopping by." She had a point. Pauline isn't someone you drop in on. She has some admirable qualities, but spontaneity isn't one of them.

"Ma'am," Hugh said, "this visit's official." Pauline sighed and allowed us to squeeze into the tiny hall. The smell of cigarette smoke mixed with a scented candle so cloyingly sweet it made my teeth ache. She motioned for us to follow her into the tidy living room.

The couch and two easy chairs were draped with colorful acrylic afghans. Pauline plunked herself in a chair and tucked her feet under her. Waving toward the sofa, she thumped a cigarette from a crumpled pack and lit it. She muted the television but didn't turn it off. Twirling ballroom dancers flitted across the giant screen. "If you wanted to speak with Bill," she said, "he's not available. He hasn't gotten a good night's sleep in days on account of all the snow."

"Actually," Hugh said, "I wanted to talk to you. About Ethel Smalley."

"Ethel? God almighty! You're interrupting my evening to ask me about that bitch?" Pauline drew deeply on her cigarette.

"So the two of you weren't friends?" Hugh asked.

"It's no secret. I expect Gwen filled you in." Pauline flicked her hand in my direction, spilling ash down the front of her gray sweatshirt.

"I prefer to let people speak for themselves," Hugh said. "Where were you today, starting right after Beulah's funeral?"

"What's this about?" Pauline's eyes squinted a little.

"Gwen found Ethel with a nasty dent in her head about an hour ago. We wondered if you know anything about how that could have happened." Hugh pulled out his notebook and clicked open a pen.

"Bill!" she called loudly over her shoulder. Bill appeared in the doorway, a paperback in his hand.

"I didn't know you had company." He glanced down at the book.

"Of course you did." Pauline stubbed out her cigarette. "You just weren't feeling sociable. Ethel's dead."

"Dead? A heart attack like Harold?" he asked. I shook my head slowly. "Why are you talking to my wife?"

"We're talking to anyone with a reason to want her dead," Hugh said. "I understand Pauline was disappointed about the curator job." Pauline shot me a look that made me grateful we weren't in a dark alley littered with broken bottles.

"I wasn't the only one who hated her. The entire Historical Society referred to her as Satan's Bunion whenever she wasn't around. Why aren't you talking to Clara? Or Bernadette?" Pauline picked up another cigarette and rolled it between her fingers.

"We will, but you were the one displaying hostilities at a meeting this week so we decided to talk to you first. Where were you after Beulah's funeral?"

"I was here finishing some Christmas baking," Pauline said, "and before you ask, no one was with me. Ashley was out babysitting, and Bill was at work."

"That's right. With the forecast predicting more snow I had some equipment to check out at the town barn," Bill said.

"That brings me to another concern." Hugh cleared his throat. "I understand Ethel was making some ugly accusations about marital problems."

"I don't like where this is headed. I want you to leave," Pauline said.

"A woman you admit to hating has been killed, and someone tried to light her house on fire to cover up the crime," Hugh said. "It would be best if you were co-operative."

Bill loped over and took up a position behind Pauline's chair. He dropped a ragged hand on top of her shoulder and gave it a squeeze. "Pauline and I didn't give that woman credit for having enough sense to ask her what she thought of the weather." He gave her another squeeze. "We sure didn't worry ourselves about her opinions on other matters."

"Was that the sort of thing she said about you often?" Hugh made a note.

"I wasn't carrying on." Bill rifled the book pages with his thumb and gazed down on Pauline's honey colored hair. "I already told you Ethel was just trying to stir things up."

"That had better be all it was, or you'll be in line for a head wound of your own." Pauline shrugged Bill's hand off her shoulder and reached for a cigarette lighter.

"No one else has been saying that sort of thing," I said, hoping to drop Pauline's defenses. "People bring more rumors to the post office than mail. Ethel bringing it up at the meeting the other night was the first I'd heard of it."

"See, Darlin'." Bill put his book on the side table next to Pauline's recliner and draped his arms back over the chair to massage her shoulders. "I told you that old cat was just stomping on ya. If Gwen hasn't heard about it, it isn't happening."

"But why would Ethel have had it out for you in the first place?" Hugh asked. "Ethel had the job as curator, not Pauline. If there was going to be animosity, it should have been the other way around." It was a good question. I still hadn't thought of a way to bring up the bank account I knew Beulah had shared with Bill. I had to wonder if Ethel harping on Bill and Pauline was somehow related and if so, why.

"If my husband hasn't been stepping out on me, I have no idea what was the matter with her other than general spitefulness. You know what she was like." Pauline turned to me for agreement. I nodded.

"There's every possibility Ethel was just enjoying seeing them squirm," I said to Hugh. "She'd do that sort of thing every chance she'd get. She's done it to me, too."

"Having that foreign family murdering people is worth it if they managed to take Ethel down," Bill said. "Why aren't you giving them the third degree?"

"Before we go, there is something I have heard about." I felt cheap bringing it up, but someone had killed two people. "Some people are saying the two of you had too much control over Beulah's finances."

"What are you saying?" Bill stepped from behind Pauline's chair. "Are you saying we had something to do with what happened to Beulah?"

"Did you?" Hugh asked, standing and knocking his head against the ceiling fan.

"We're done here. Next time you're walking down the street in a storm, don't expect a ride from this plow driver." Bill jabbed a beefy finger toward the door.

SEVENTEEN

"You've been holding out on me." Hugh backed down the long, twisting driveway with ease despite the dark and the trees crowding both sides. I turned over my answer in my mind. On the one hand, as a law-abiding postal employee, it was not my way to discuss anything I saw coming through the mail. On the other hand, the situation in town had escalated with Ethel's death.

"I'm not a gossip." I fiddled with an emerald ring on my right hand. Peter had given it to me when I was pregnant with Owen and my wedding band wouldn't fit. Even though I'd stopped wearing my wedding band a couple of years ago, I kept wearing the emerald. Green was my favorite color.

"I never said you were. When it comes to tattling on your neighbors, you have a case of lockjaw. I'd see a doctor about a tetanus booster if I were you." Hugh took one hand off the wheel and tapped my knee. "I've been working this investigation as though we were partners. Have you?"

"I was being discreet. Look at how much misery Ethel caused flapping her jowls. Besides, I have a conflict of interest." My knee tingled where Hugh had tapped it. Maybe it was time to stop wearing the emerald.

"Is it a professional conflict or a personal one?" Hugh asked as he pulled onto the main road.

"I take my professional life very personally. I'm not sure I can distinguish between the two anymore."

"Nothing you tell me will go any further than this vehicle if it doesn't impact the case. If it does, I'll be as tactful as possible."

"All right. Beulah was getting more and more feeble. After her hip surgery she couldn't ignore it any longer. Bill had been plowing her out and fixing things up around the house that needed repair for years. Pauline even drove Beulah to the grocer when she did her own shopping every week."

"Sounds neighborly." Hugh stopped at the corner of Main Street and Elm where the village Christmas tree lit up the darkness with its twinkling lights. "What's the problem?"

"People started saying Bill and Pauline were just helping Beulah out to get remembered in her will or worse, to get control over her money. She was a wealthy woman."

"Anything to substantiate the rumors?"

"Several months ago I noticed Bill's name as the second name listed on a bank statement addressed to Beulah. I couldn't very well ask her about it, but she must have mentioned it to someone, because the rumbling started."

"How does it have any bearing on the fires or the deaths?" Hugh pulled to a stop in front of my house.

The porch light was off, and the house was dark. For just a second I wished I was Augusta and was the kind of woman who knew how to invite a man in for a nightcap casually. I think of myself as self-sufficient, but after what happened to Ethel, I was spooked. My dark house didn't look inviting. I imagined myself sneaking from room to room checking behind doors for lurkers and yanking open the shower curtain to make sure no one was there. I hoped Augusta hadn't made plans to stay out all night.

"No one liked Ethel, not even Beulah. In order for Beulah to give the curator job to Ethel instead of Pauline, she had to be pretty unhappy with Pauline and Bill."

"Unhappy how?"

"Beulah was as generous as they come, but she wanted to be asked. She'd give you every pumpkin in her patch if you told her you admired them, but if she caught you taking one without asking, she'd have Ray arrest you and then call everyone she knew to tell them about it."

"You think Bill and Pauline were helping themselves to her pumpkins?"

"It's just a feeling. I can't even tell you an instance when they might have done it."

"Either of them ever been violent?"

"Not if you don't count the scuffles that break out at town meetings." Winslow Falls views politics as a contact sport. Deep in the bowels of winter there's no better way to warm up than by attending a budget committee meeting. Bill had gone off in the cruiser a couple of times to cool down. Pauline had managed to avoid arrest but only because Ray liked it when she flirted with him.

"Sounds like we should keep them in mind. After what happened tonight I don't like you heading into a dark house alone, especially since I expect everyone knows you don't lock your doors." Relief flooded through me as Hugh walked me to the mudroom door and followed as I flipped on lights.

"This isn't the first time I've come home to a dark empty house."

"But I bet it's the first time you've returned home after suggesting someone might be a killer. I'd feel better about leaving you here after I look around." The fire in the wood stove had gone out, and the room felt cold. Hugh pulled the poker from the stand next to the stove. In no time he had stirred up the coals, gotten the kindling crackling, and perched a fat log on top waiting to blaze up.

"Not bad for a guy who's supposed to be an expert at putting out fires." I filled the teakettle in the soapstone sink.

"Two sides of the same coin. Do you want to stay here while I check around, or are you coming with me?" I set the kettle on the stove and started to wipe my hands on my trousers until I remembered they belonged to Augusta. I grabbed a dishtowel from the refrigerator door handle instead.

"Let's call it a house tour. That way you can roust any intruders, and I can keep my sense of independence." We made our way from the kitchen to the dining room. Hugh glanced around quickly and moved on. There was nothing but china and crystal hidden there.

We moved toward the living room. I watched him poke the drapes and peek behind the door. We entered the library, and I looked around the room. The books were still wedged onto shelves haphazardly. The wood box next to the fireplace was undisturbed. All the picture frames hung straight.

"You must be a devoted reader." Hugh crossed the room in two long strides and stopped in front of a bookcase heaving with gardening books. Running his long index finger over the spines he pulled one entitled *Sensual Gardens* from the shelf. "Is this any good?" Hugh locked his eyes on mine.

"I think the answer depends what you are hoping for in terms of subject matter. You're welcome to borrow it." I'm forever pressing my favorite books on anyone who expresses the slightest interest. If they don't return them, it makes more room on my shelves for new purchases. Hugh tucked the book under his bent arm and nodded approvingly as he scanned the room.

"It doesn't look like anyone is in here either," Hugh said. I glanced around, ready to agree, when I noticed something.

"The hand is gone." I stared at the spot next to the wingback chair where I'd placed the sculpture for safekeeping. There on the floor, looking as if it had slid off the arm of the chair, was an afghan.

"Are you sure?"

"That isn't mine. It was wrapped around the hand." I pointed to the afghan and noticed my hand trembling. I felt robbed. Someone, probably someone I knew, someone I smiled good morning to at Dinah's, had used my sense of community against me. The same easy flow of information that put me in a position to help Hugh with the investigation had allowed someone else to know that I had the hand here and never lock my doors.

"You don't think Augusta could have moved it?" Hugh asked.

"She's never lifted anything heavier than her own purse."

"Let's check the rest of the house just to be sure." Hugh left the library and took the front stairs two at a time. He popped his head into the sewing room, which had been Owen's bedroom until he had graduated from college and I realized for certain that he had grown up. No giant hand. Hugh stopped at the guest room.

"It would be easy to lose the hand in here," he said, viewing Augusta's entire travel wardrobe spread over every available surface. The search was slower as Hugh tried to find places to land his enormous feet other than on top of discarded panties and stockings, but the result was the same. The bathroom held nothing unusual except for Augusta's army of grooming products crowding the sink, toilet tank and window sill.

"How long is your sister staying?" Hugh asked, unplugging a curling iron Augusta had left, hot and dangerous in the sink.

"She hasn't said." I backed out of the bathroom and threw open the door to Josh's room. I'd vacuumed and dusted in anticipation of his trip home over Christmas break so this room, at least, was easy to check. Still no hand. Lastly we entered my own bedroom. Everything was neat as always. The quilt on the bed was smoothed across tidily, the pillows were fluffed. My sushi pajamas lay neatly folded on the blanket chest at the foot of the bed. Pinkerton reclined on top of them. Seeing Hugh, he jumped down and waddled toward him, his belly dragging along the floor as he twined Hugh's legs.

"I think your cat could use a diet."

"It isn't mine. It was Beulah's. I'm hoping it eats itself to death."

"Not a cat fan, I take it?"

"I'm allergic."

"Want me to take him home with me? You could tell your sister that whoever stole the hand took the cat too."

"Thanks, but you can't even imagine the drama involved if Augusta is given the ghost of a chance. She'd have Ray wasting taxpayer money day and night until Pinkerton was found and the guilty party was hanging from the village Christmas tree."

"It would give Ray something to do besides trying to help in the fire investigation." Hugh bent down and scratched Pinkerton between the ears.

"It still wouldn't be worth it, but thank you." I grabbed my pajamas and took them to the laundry room. The door of the linen closet hung open. On the floor in front of it lay a pile of abandoned pillowcases and sheets.

"Even Augusta wouldn't do this. What was the intruder looking for?" I asked.

"Anything missing?"

"I'm not sure yet." I started folding the linen. All the pillow cases had their matching sheets except one set. "A top sheet."

"A plain sheet would make a less conspicuous wrapper for the hand than that gaudy blanket," Hugh said.

"I was feeling a little frightened. Now I'm just angry. Who has the gall to sneak in here and steal my sheets?"

"I'm guessing it wasn't a ghost. Who had the opportunity to break in here?" Hugh had his notebook out again.

"I was gone all morning. I went to the Laundromat and the home improvement center. I was home long enough to do some painting before leaving for Ethel's. I haven't been home since."

"You didn't notice the hand was gone when you came home this afternoon?"

"I didn't go into the library or upstairs."

"I don't like the idea of you staying alone. Do you know where Augusta is?"

"She went to the Hodge Podge to look for some furniture for the office. She and Gene have been seeing a lot of each other lately, so I expect they went to dinner or something after he closed the shop."

"Can you call her? Will she come home?" Hugh stuck his notebook back in his pocket and steered me down the stairs.

"I wouldn't want to mess up her plans. I'll be fine." Meeting up with Ethel's killer would be safer than interrupting one of Augusta's dates.

"I'll call, then. What's the number?" Hugh strode into the kitchen and picked up the phone. A draft blew in from the mudroom, and I heard the door slam shut. Augusta appeared looking as radiant and put together as ever.

"I hope I'm not interrupting anything." Augusta winked at Hugh and flashed me an eager smile.

"Someone broke in here sometime during the day and stole the hand sculpture," I said. Augusta's smile turned into a perfect O of surprise.

"I told you to lock your doors. Someone could make off with Granny Bink's china. How would we explain that to Mum?"

"It's more complicated than lost valuables. Gwen found Ethel dead in her home this evening," Hugh said.

"You don't know our mother," Augusta said then turned to me again. "So, did you kill her?" My jaw tightened, and I could feel my stomach acid being churned like butter. A second murder, a break-in and now an accusation of murder by my own sister. It was too much.

"Thanks, Hugh, for checking out the house for me. I'm going to bed." All night long I startled myself awake with nightmares of Ethel being crushed to death by a giant wooden hand. More than ever, I wished my bed weren't so lonely.

EIGHTEEN

"Damned shame about Ethel." Winston stood at the counter Monday morning looking like it was anything but. He had a rosy glow that he only dragged out for Dinah's two-for-one dessert specials.

"It was a surprise." I slid him his mail over the counter. Technically I'm not supposed to do that, but a lot of my older customers fumble with the combinations on their boxes. Sometimes adhering to the letter of the law constitutes unnecessary cruelty.

"I can't see how it was a surprise." Winston scratched his chin stubble with an envelope. "Those people are on a rampage."

"Which people?"

"You know darn well which people." The door creaked open, and Ray stomped in dropping snow all over the tile floor.

"What do you think, Ray? Do we need to look further for who's responsible for the fires? Or Ethel's death?"

"Case closed, in my opinion." Ray stepped up to the window.

"Real policemen are tightlipped about ongoing investigations," I said.

"We're in the middle of a crime spree perpetrated by illegal aliens," Ray said.

"There's one of them now," Winston said. Diego stood next to the bulletin board, holding a box and looking at the posters of deadbeat dads.

"Diego, do you need to mail a package?" I asked.

"Hey, kid, do you know a skinny guy who ran Gwen off the road and then murdered Ethel Smalley? Heard he had an accent," Ray asked.

"Cut it out, Ray. You can't assume two people know each other because they both have an accent. I don't assume you and Hugh are both able to solve crimes because you each have a badge."

"What about it, kid?" Ray stepped closer to Diego and rested his hand on his gun holster. "Guy looks a lot like you. Sneaky, illegal, inclined to steal?"

Diego stiffened, and I motioned for him to come up to the window.

"Well, I can't stand around here jawing all morning. Some of us have work to do." Ray strutted toward the door. "I'm watching your family. Tell that to the skinny guy when you see him."

Pauline Lambert stuck her head in the doorway as Ray was leaving. "Winston, I've got a week's worth of trash stinking up the back of my station wagon. Are you gonna open the dump, or should I leave it on your front porch?" Winston broke into a trot getting out the door.

"So where's this package going? Brazil?" I don't get to send many international packages, and I always enjoy them.

"I am not sending. It is for you." Diego handed me the box. I'm ashamed to say that for a second I caught myself wondering if it contained a bomb. Or anthrax. Suspicious packages in the post office get a lot of press these days. Maybe I'm no better than Ray or Winston.

"For me? Should I open it?" Diego nodded, and I lifted the flap. No respiratory distress.

"My mother make these for you. She says thank you for mittens and hats." I peeked inside and saw some little brown balls rolled in sprinkles.

"She didn't need to do that. It was my pleasure. What are these?" I leaned closer and smelled chocolate.

"*Brigadeiros*. They are Christmas sweets. Taste, please." He pointed at the box.

"Only if you have one too. I hate to eat alone." Diego plucked one out of the box. His fingernails were chewed down so far it made my own fingers ache just looking at them. I bit into one of the sweets.

"You like?" Diego asked, his full mouth making his accent all the more challenging.

"Delicious. Will you tell your mother I said so?" Diego nodded and turned to go.

"You'd better take a couple more for the road." I pointed to the box and was pleased to see him flash a chocolate-toothed smile as he took two more.

"Diego, if you do know the man Ray was talking about, I want you to give him a message, too." Diego stared at the floor instead of at me. "Tell him if he wants to talk about what happened, he should come to me or the man who came with me to your house asking questions. Tell him to stay away from Ray." Diego nodded and bolted out the door, nearly colliding with Augusta.

"I have some good news and some bad news." Augusta handed me a package addressed to our mother. "Mum's gift is all set."

"Is that the bad news, that her Christmas gift will be late?" I asked.

"That's not the bad news."

"I've got no more room for bad news," I said. "Ethel's death filled the last space."

"Josh called." Augusta got right to the point. "He's snowed in."

"Snowed in?" I asked. "As in not coming home for Christmas?"

"Yeah. It happens a lot when you are trying to get from Buffalo to Boston in the winter." Brilliant. Owen had just started a new job out of state and didn't have any vacation time. Now Josh wouldn't be here. Even Mum had decided to stay in Florida. No one would be home for Christmas except Augusta. And a cat.

"It could be worse. You could be spending Christmas waiting for your husband to be operated on. To cheer you up, I'll drive you down to visit Harold and Bernadette after you get out of work." Without waiting for an answer, Augusta swished out the door.

Augusta dropped me at the front door of the hospital and went to look for a parking spot. I took the elevator to the cardiac floor and peeked through the open door of Harold's room. His faced the window and spoke quietly into the phone. His free hand bunched the bed sheet, and his jiggling foot rattled the bed. His voice rose, and I could make out his end of the conversation.

"Are you sure there won't be any more? I'm supposed to be avoiding stress," Harold paused. "It better be the last time." Harold banged down the phone, and I heard his heart monitor beep faster. I was deciding whether or not to call a nurse when a round little duck of a woman pattered toward his room. I backed away from the door and heard her scolding Harold from several doors down. Around the corner Bernadette sagged in a plastic chair darting a crochet hook in and out of an acrylic afghan.

"Gwen, I hardly recognize you. What are you wearing?"

"A couple of days ago Augusta gave me a makeover. How're you holding up?" I asked.

"I've had better Christmases." Her beefy shoulders drooped, and she was wearing the same trousers and sweatshirt she'd had on when Hugh and I visited her three days earlier.

"I guess you've heard about Ethel." Bernadette might look rumpled, but she'd have to be in the morgue instead of the waiting room to have been pruned from the village grapevine. Unless I missed my guess, Clara told her first thing in the morning, if not earlier.

"It was like hearing that flu season has left your area of the country," Bernadette said. "You couldn't find anyone who wasn't happy to see her go."

"You really think no one will miss her?"

"No one I know of." Bernadette jabbed her hook in and out of her work like it was Ethel laying there instead of an afghan. "Everywhere she went that woman stirred up trouble. I called Dinah's yesterday to ask how Beulah's funeral had gone, and the shouting in the store was so bad Dinah couldn't hear me. She called me back later when the fuss had died down."

"Do you know what they were yelling about?" I asked.

"Dinah stays in business," Bernadette said, "because she knows what to pass along and what to leave out. She said it was Ethel and Bill Lambert, and it was nothing exciting, just the usual."

"Knowing those two," I said, "they were probably arm wrestling for the last bag of barbecue potato chips." I got to my feet and laid a hand on Bernadette's fleshy arm. "Let me know if you need anything." Bernadette nodded and started adding another row to her blanket. I punched the lobby button in the elevator and thought about what Bernadette had said. It looked like I needed to ask Bill some more questions.

"How's the patient?" Augusta stood near the exit looking at some lobby artwork.

"Harold's holding his own." I said.

"I was talking about you," Augusta said. "You look like death warmed over."

"It's been a long week."

"You need a pick-me-up."

"The last time you said that to me I spent a weekend in a Tennessee bog looking at timeshare property.'

"It'll be better this time. I'll get the car."

Augusta dragged me to the mall. Christmas spirit was so thick in the air there should have been a health advisory for asthmatics and the elderly. We joined the fray and picked up a few things for the DaSilva kids and Luisa. I used love to shop for Christmas, but since the boys have grown up, their Christmas lists are as much fun as unsalted oatmeal.

My Christmas cheer returned as we gathered up board games, wooden puzzles, stuffed animals, building sets and a sled. And a red, angora sweater for Luisa. She could keep warm and still look glamorous.

Once the shopping was complete Augusta muscled her way through the crowds toward a beauty salon.

"I've done all I can with her," she said to the bubble gum-popping child behind the counter. "The hair is best left to professionals." She gestured toward my head as she consulted with the child.

"Enjoy your hair appointment while I find you a new wardrobe," she said.

"Shouldn't I go with you to pick out what I like?"

Augusta looked me over from head to toe. "Good God, no. I'll be back in a couple of hours."

I should have known the direction things would take when they had me sign a waiver before they started. I should have spoken up when my scalp began smarting from the chemicals, but Augusta's words about beauty hurting rang in my ears, and I kept my mouth shut. When the girl spun me toward the mirror, I prayed the fluorescent lighting was unflattering. From the way the salon staff refused to make eye contact, I suspected it was more serious than the lights. I paid quickly, then slunk off.

"Do you want me to slip a hat in your stocking Christmas Eve?" the mall Santa yelled out to me. His elves snickered and elbowed each other. Thankfully, I saw Augusta hustling in my direction, her arms weighed down by shopping bags. She marched straight past. Clearly, I was so altered, not even my own sister recognized me.

"Hey, over here!" Augusta stopped, flicked her eyes across the crowd and eventually landed on me. Digging in her purse, she pulled out a pair of dark sunglasses. She grabbed a complimentary wheelchair and shoved me into it. She dumped the bags in my lap and whipped off her wool coat. Throwing it over my head, she broke into a trot.

"Ma'am, do you need some help?" someone asked. I couldn't see anything but I guessed it was mall security.

"No. I'm just in a hurry to get Granny back to the rest home. She gets unruly if I don't have her back in time for tapioca pudding night."

We didn't speak during the drive home, not unless you count the hiccupping gasps coming from Augusta every time she glanced in my direction. Pulling into the driveway forty-five minutes later, I broke the silence.

"We can hope the orange will come out with a good shampooing."

"What we can hope is that it all falls out and Santa brings you a wig for Christmas."

"He already offered me a hat."

"You must be on the naughty list, because if you'd been nice he'd be bringing a wig." I lowered the visor and peeked in the mirror. I looked like I was related to Hugh. It was a good thing I'd spent so many years knitting hats. I was going to need them all if I was going to hide this mess.

"Can't we just dye it again? We could just pick up one of those kits at the drug store."

"Do you want your hair follicles to commit suicide? Any more chemicals, and it will fall out."

"Are you saying there's nothing we can do?" That explained the gasping.

"I may be able to track down a specialist, but don't get your hopes up. I can't believe you did this."

"What are you talking about? This was your idea." *Damn, damn, damn.*

Augusta shuddered. "This was not what I had in mind."

NINETEEN

Augusta had another date with Gene so I decided to console myself with fast food from Dinah's. One great thing about winter is no one notices if you pull a hat down tightly on your head. Nobody could see any hair at all. They could barely see my eyes.

Dinah was sliding out a pizza when I arrived. Despite the low temperature outside, Dinah's cheeks were flushed, and sweat ran down the gully of her cleavage. She was always generous with her cleavage display. She used it to pacify the geezers at the lunch counter. It was harder for them to give her lip when their tongues were lolling out.

"I'm just pulling your order out now. Give me a minute to box it up."

"No hurry." I grabbed some soda and chips and placed them near the cash register. "I stopped in to see Harold today and heard something from Bernadette that I hoped you could clear up."

"What's that?" Dinah neatly sliced the pizza into eight wedges.

"An argument between Bill Lambert and Ethel the day she was killed. Bernadette said it was loud enough that you couldn't hear her on the phone."

Both Dinah and I are in a position to spread a lot of rumors and cause a lot of grief. Neither one of us does. I would have understood if she declined to answer.

"Ethel accused Bill of using the town plow to make money plowing private customers. She said Beulah told her he did it for the Museum as well as some other people."

"Why would she care?"

"She said it was an abuse of power and she wasn't going to stand for corrupt town officials."

"How did she think she was going stop him?"

"She said she'd convinced someone else to run against him for road commissioner. The last thing Bill needed just before the election was accusations about using the plow for private purposes."

"Who'd she have in mind for the job?"

"Clive," Dinah said grinning. "He was having a thing with her."

"A thing? With Ethel?" I was astonished. "Are you sure?"

"Yeah, I'm sure. I caught them coming out of the bathroom together." Dinah's bathroom is a one-holer that makes airplane bathrooms look spacious.

"Maybe there was a plumbing problem," I suggested.

"Ethel's blouse was untucked and buttoned wrong, and her magenta lipstick was smeared onto her chin. And from the goofy look on Clive's face there wasn't anything wrong with his plumbing." Dinah slapped the pizza box shut and handed to me.

*   *   *

Wind flapped up the lid of the pizza box. Within sight of the house my fingers froze into the gripping position around the shopping bag. My hat had crept so far down my forehead it was nearly impossible to see. Wobbling up the steps while balancing the bag of junk food and the pizza, I squinted through pinpricks in the hat to see where I was going.

Turns out I was going down. A patch of ice had formed on the third step. My feet slipped, and my ankle crumpled beneath me as I skidded to a stop at the base of the stairs. The pizza shot out of its box and landed in my lap. I pushed up my hat and looked around.

Headlights swept into the driveway, and Hugh pulled in next to Peter's old red truck. "Was that your dinner?" He studied the mess covering me.

"Help me up." I stuck out my hands and waited for Hugh to show what a state fire fighter was made of.

"What kind was it?" I had to admire his priorities.

"Loaded, extra cheese." I stepped forward and felt my ankle give out from under me.

"Hold up there." Hugh put an arm around my waist. "Let's get you inside and see if you fared worse than the dinner."

"Watch out, the third step is glare ice."

"You ought to put down some salt."

"I can't seem to remember. Peter always took care

of those sorts of things." I surveyed the mess and thought that it was more likely I'd remember in the future.

Hugh helped me into the kitchen and parked me in the rocker next to the wood stove. I unzipped my coat and yanked off the dangerous hat.

"Wow, I thought my hair was red." Hugh patted my head experimentally, like he was evaluating a carpet he might purchase.

"I left my sense of humor out under the pizza."

"Enough said, Raggedy Ann. Which ankle is it?" he dragged over a chair from the table and lifted my legs onto it.

"The left one." I held my breath as he worked my boot off. He raised an eyebrow as he peeled off my sock and pushed up my trouser leg.

"Not a complete makeover, I see," he said staring at my hairy calf.

"Is your bedside manner always so tactful?" I asked.

"I can give you a list of references." Hugh grinned as he flexed my foot and rotated my ankle.

"Careful!"

"It's pretty banged up, but I don't think it's broken." He walked to the fridge and dug round in the freezer. "Have you got an ice pack?"

"Probably not. The boys always poked holes in the blue kind. I switched to bags of frozen peas years ago and never went back after they moved out."

"I don't see any peas either. Were you saving these cranberries for anything important?"

"I was hoping that someone would appear and turn them into muffins."

"So your dream guy is the muffin man, I assume."

"Just give me the bag." Hugh wrapped the bag in the dishtowel and dropped it in my lap.

"Not much chance of frost bite with the pelt you're sporting, but it never hurts to be careful." He strode back out onto the porch and disappeared from view. I contemplated my ankle and the whereabouts of Augusta. She hadn't mentioned being gone at dinner time. I scanned the room as best I could from my rocker. No note propped against the toaster. No light blinked on the answering machine. And no smells emanated from the oven. I was thinking about licking the pizza sauce off my jacket when Hugh returned. A plastic bag releasing the unmistakable smells of Chinese takeout hung from his hand. He deposited the bag on the table and started pulling plates and wine glasses from the cupboard. Rooting around in a drawer, he scrounged up a couple of forks and serving spoons.

"And you thought dinner was a total loss."

"How did you know I love Chinese food?"

"I tapped your phones and tallied up the number of times you called Lo Mein's for takeout in the last month."

"Well, then, you must know exactly what I always order."

"Crab rangoons, vegetable lo mein, Schezuan chicken and egg rolls. The beef and broccoli and the moo goo gai pan are for me, no sharing allowed."

"I'm impressed. Maybe you're a real detective after all. How'd you really do it?"

"Your pajamas gave it away. Can you get to the table on your own, or should I carry you?"

"I think I can manage."

He found a corkscrew in the cutlery drawer. With the skill of a trained hunting dog, he zeroed in on a bottle of Pinot Grigio I'd been saving in the back of the fridge. Expertly pulling the cork, he poured out a glass for each of us as I lurched toward the table.

"Wow. It really hurts when I put pressure on it."

"I'll take another look at it after dinner. Shoot! I left the report on Ethel's death in the car. Seeing you splattered all over the driveway aroused my knight in shining armor side, and I forgot why I was here in the first place."

"I should try that more often if it will make takeout magically appear on my table."

"I'm not sure how many of those kinds of falls you should attempt without a stunt double." Hugh headed out the door again.

I settled myself at the table and propped my foot up once again with the bag of cranberries in place. Reaching across the table I opened the takeout boxes and tucked spoons into each. While he was gone I snitched a piece of broccoli out of his beef and broccoli. My cheeks bulged with crunch and MSG when Hugh returned with a file folder.

"I thought I said no sharing."

"How do you know I was eating your food?"

"I'm a detective, remember?" He tossed the folder

on the table between us and handed me a wine glass. "Wash down the pieces of broccoli stuck between your teeth with a swallow of this." I gulped the wine and opened the folder. I skimmed the jargon and gave my attention to the medical examiner's report. While I was reading he snagged an egg roll from a carton, bit off the end and dunked it knuckle deep in the duck sauce.

"That constitutes double dipping."

"That's to get back at you for helping yourself to my broccoli."

"So it was a head injury," I said. Her head had been a mess. The thought of it was enough to make me lose my appetite. Well, almost enough. I reached for an egg roll of my own.

"Something hit her prior to her death."

"The diagram in the report shows an injury to the back of her head. Could she have fallen against something as she was losing consciousness?"

"The wound is on the back of the head, and she was found on her stomach. If she had hit the stove and fallen, the wound would have been on the front of her head, or we would have found her on her back."

"What do you think happened, then?"

"Either someone decided to kill her and blame it on the fire bug, or someone killed her and someone else felt like starting a fire. It seems to me unlikely that it would be two separate perpetrators, but I guess we can't rule it out quite yet."

"If anyone was going to be the target of two different hostile neighbors, it would be Ethel."

"Either way, it's a homicide."

"How does that affect Ray's involvement?" I asked

"It's complicated. I think the best thing to do is to wait and see how involved Ray wants to be and in which way we can each contribute to the case." Hugh gestured toward my leg.

"How's the ankle?"

I shifted the bag of cranberries to get a better look. "I think it's swollen to twice its normal size." Hugh reached over and poured me another half glass of wine.

"Where do you keep the pain relievers?"

"In the downstairs medicine cabinet."

He plunked the bottle of ibuprofen on the table in front of me. I twisted off the cap and downed two pills with a gulp of wine.

"Still no real idea who's been starting the fires?" I asked.

"You've heard something?"

"People at the post office keep mentioning the DaSilva kids as the likeliest possibility. Harold said something like seventy percent of fires are set by juveniles."

"Unfortunately, that's correct."

"I don't want it to be them," I said.

"Anyone you'd rather it was?"

"No one except Ray," I said, "or maybe Clive. I really hate his dog."

"I don't think the statistics show dog owners are more likely to start fires."

"Speaking of Clive, I heard something interesting

from Dinah while I was getting the pizza," I said. "She says Clive Merrill was romantically involved with Ethel."

"Had you heard about this before?"

"It was a total surprise."

"Then I guess we'd better go talk to him. Are you up for it with the ankle?"

"Miss out on hearing from the one guy who liked Ethel? No way."

TWENTY

The weathermen had been right. In the time it had taken to finish dinner and round up a pair of crutches left in the barn from the winter Josh broke his ankle skiing, the flakes had piled up at least three inches. I was grateful for the four-wheel drive on Hugh's truck when we turned onto the road that led to Clive's camp. Most of the lake residents cleared out by Labor Day, but Clive lived here year round. The road was private so the town didn't plow it. A rutted track had been ground down by Clive's jeep. No street lights lit the way, and it wasn't salted or sanded. It looked as bad as my porch steps.

He had bought the property on the cheap from a couple getting a divorce. The house crouched below the level of the road, and the driveway hadn't been plowed. Hobbling down with crutches and a bum leg was not going to be a pleasure. Hugh put the truck in park and peered down the hill.

"Do you want me to go in alone," he asked, "or should I give you a piggy back ride?"

"I'm not about to just sit here," I said, "and I'm too big to be carried." I pushed open the truck door and swung my legs out. I was hip deep in a drift before I remembered my crutches were in the back of the truck. Stepping out on my good leg, I made a grab for the truck bed and failed.

Hugh called down from above me, "Most people lie on their backs to make snow angels." He watched me struggling to turn over.

"Are you staying in the truck," he asked again," or am I carrying you?"

"I'm not within ideal parameters on the height and weight charts," I said. "You'll never be able to carry me." Hugh crossed his seven-foot wingspan across his chest and grinned down through his red mustache.

"They don't even list my parameters on the charts," he said. "Besides, I'm a fireman, remember? I have to be able to carry helpless women out of burning buildings no matter what size they are." He reached down, hoisted me out of the hole I'd created, and slung me over his shoulder. "Stop swinging your leg like a caged elephant," he said," or we'll both go down this hill like Jack and Jill."

"I may be a little plumper than I ought to be," I said, "but I think calling me an elephant is going too far."

"I didn't say I thought you were an elephant," Hugh said. "You worry too much."

"You'd worry, too," I said, "if you had to explain things like this to my customers."

"No one will know." Hugh raised his free hand to knock on Clive's door. Before he landed the first blow the door popped open. Hugh slid me off his shoulder, and I grabbed his arm for support since we forgot my crutches in the truck.

"Mr. Merrill?" said Hugh. "I think we met at the fire the other night?"

"You're the one whose boots got the tail end of Gwen's lunch," Clive said.

"That's right," Hugh said. "We'd like to ask you some questions about Ethel Smalley."

"I just can't believe she's gone." Clive still looked a little shook up. His shirttail was untucked on one side, his shoelaces were flapping, and he wasn't wearing his fishing hat. Clive doesn't even take off his hat in church. He wore it at Beulah's funeral.

"Could we come in, sir?" Hugh asked. Clive stepped back and pulled the door open wide. A large fish mounted on a wooden plaque hung on the wall. It looked like Clive had stolen it from one of the neighborhood grill-type chain restaurants steadily invading the lower third of the state. A coat rack constructed of deer antlers from salvaged road kill loomed near the door.

At the ready next to him was his dog Brandy. She had a long reddish coat and loved to bite anything that wandered by. Kids in town called her Brandy Snap and ran in the other direction whenever they saw her. I felt like running too. The last time we met, I was out for a walk, and Brandy had nipped at me and growled until I managed to flag down a passing car for a ride. Hugh squatted and started stroking her fur. She promptly dropped down and exposed her belly for a full massage.

"I've never seen her do that with a stranger

before," said Clive. "Do you have a dog?"

"No," Hugh said, "not anymore." Hugh dug in with both hands and finished off the scratch. Brandy lolled, nearly comatose with joy. As I limped past her she barely managed a gurgle down low in her throat where the growl should have been. Hugh had obviously missed his calling. He could have been the Pied Piper of dogcatchers.

At the end of the short hall I saw a large brick hearth with a working wood stove settled on it. I hobbled toward it and flopped onto a disreputable easy chair. Russet dog hairs made up the dominant color scheme in the room. Hugh sat opposite me on a drooping plaid sofa. He grimaced at me when a snapping sound erupted from the sofa's underpinnings as Brandy jumped up to lay her head in his lap. Clive took the rocker and turned on the television.

"'Fishing with Walter and Earl' is just starting." Clive said looking at the television. He didn't need to worry. Between the sofa that was threatening to bust out under him and the journey back up the hill lugging me on his shoulder, Hugh probably wanted to get a move on.

"I'm sure you've heard that Ethel's death has been determined to be a homicide." Hugh stopped stroking Brandy's head to tug his notebook out of his shirt pocket.

"Ray was talking about it down to Dinah's." Clive tore his eyes from Walter reeling a thrashing fish up out of a lake and picked up a packet of Juicy Fruit gum from the side table. He deliberately pulled out a stick and carefully unwrapped it. "Why are you asking me about it?" He stuffed the gum into his mouth and began folding the wrapper into smaller and smaller squares.

"I understand that you got along with Ethel better than most of her neighbors," Hugh said. "We wanted to get a complete picture of her, and so far opinion seems to be going only one way." Clive reached for another stick of gum and added it to the first.

"She had a talent for irritating folks," Clive said, "but she got things done. No one seemed to appreciate all the hard work she put in around the village. Committees and such."

"Did she ever say that anyone in particular didn't appreciate her?" Hugh asked. "Did she ever mention feeling threatened?"

"Ethel wouldn't have felt threatened by a charging bull if she was standing three feet in front of him wearing a red bathrobe," Clive said. "That woman was fearless."

"Maybe her fearlessness got her killed," I said. "At one time or another she managed to tick off just about everyone in town."

"Including you," Clive said. "If she was murdered, I don't know that it's such a hot idea having you on the case." Brandy lifted her head off Hugh's lap and remembered how to growl.

"Don't worry," I said. "Hugh will make sure that everything is on the up and up." I gauged the distance to the door in case Brandy decided to attack.

"What was the nature of your relationship with Ethel?" Hugh asked." Were you just friends?"

"We were keeping company," Clive picked up the gum packet again. "We had an understanding."

"So," Hugh said, "you were a couple, then?"

"I guess that's a way of putting it." Clive dropped the gum back on the table, pulled out a dingy handkerchief and daintily honked his nose.

"I'm sorry for your loss, sir." Brandy twisted her head to check on Clive, and Hugh stroked her back into submission. "How long had you known her?"

"She moved to Winslow Falls about eight years ago, but it wasn't until about two months ago at a ham and bean supper at the Grange that we seemed to hit it off. She brought a lemon meringue pie that tasted just like the ones my mother made. When I complimented her on it, she invited me to supper a few days later. That was that. One dinner at Ethel's, and I was hooked." Clive dabbed at his nose with the handkerchief again.

"You both were awfully quiet about the whole thing," I said. "I'm surprised I hadn't heard about the two of you before."

"Ethel wanted to keep it under her hat," Clive said. "She said the secrecy spiced things up." It was official. Ethel's love life was more interesting than mine, and she was dead. Maybe Augusta was right. Maybe I did need to get back in the dating game.

"You didn't mind," I said, "not letting everyone in on your secret?" Brandy growled at me again.

"'Tweren't nobody's business but ours," Clive

said. "We'd no one to answer to. I don't see you giving out the details of your love life." Hugh stopped scribbling in his notebook and peered at me beneath arched eyebrows.

"If there was anything to report, Clive," I said, "I'm sure you would have heard it at Dinah's, just like all the other news. Speaking of which, did Ethel tell you why she was fighting with Bill Lambert the day she died?"

"She mentioned a tussle with Bill," Clive said, "but she didn't tell me about it. If I had to guess, it would be about the plowing."

"You remember Bill," I said to Hugh.

"Plow driver?" Hugh asked. "Married to the chain smoker?" Clive strained his wrinkled ears through conversation for bits of gossip the way mothers use a colander to get bugs out of a kiddy pool. He wasn't going to get any dead insects from me. I gave Hugh my best post mistress glare.

"Did Ethel say something about plowing, or were you assuming?" I asked.

"She said she was going to stop him from using the town plow for personal use," Clive said. "When she got all het up the best thing to do was to let her sputter."

"Anything else she had been sputtering about lately?" Hugh asked.

"She was royally ticked off by that foreign family," Clive said. "She said the mother did a terrible job cleaning the Museum, and those boys pestered her cat and broke her window."

"Did you have problems with them? See them hanging around fire scenes?" I asked.

"Nope, I didn't." Clive snuck a peek at the television. "I just know she said they were responsible for the fires every chance she got."

"Did you think about marrying her?" I asked.

"A man needs his freedom," Clive said. "Besides, she kept dropping hints that maybe she would be getting back together with another fella."

"She had another guy?" I asked. "Who?"

"She never said, but she was really disappointed that it didn't work out."

"She never even gave a hint?" I asked.

"I got the impression that he was pretty well off," Clive said, "like she had been planning on a six-star Caribbean cruise, and then it was back to clipping coupons for early bird specials at Bonanza." Brandy must have grown tired of Hugh paying more attention to his notebook than to her. She jumped off the sofa and parked herself in front of me, growling and raising her hackles.

"That's it for now, sir," Hugh said. "If you think of anything else, you can reach me at the number on my card." I tried to stand, but Brandy leaned closer and growled more throatily.

"Cut it out, Dog," Clive said. "Let her go, and I'll fix you a can of beans." The dog hurtled toward the kitchen, and Hugh and I made a dash for the exit. It would explain a lot about Brandy's disposition if her digestive tract was frequently subjected to baked beans.

*   *   *

"Are you going to be difficult or gracious?" Hugh asked, pointing up the snow-covered hill toward his truck.

"Why is it gracious," I asked, "to get someone I hardly know to carry my bulk up a steep hill through a snow drift?"

"If we get to know each other better," Hugh said, "will you be more cooperative?" He scooped me up with an unflattering grunt and slung me onto his shoulder.

"I doubt it." The going wasn't easy on the way back up the hill. By the time he set me down next to the truck, he was panting like an overweight German shepherd.

Neither of us spoke most of the way back into town, I on account of humiliation, Hugh because he was trying to catch his breath. In the short time we'd spent at Clive's, the storm had worsened. The roads were slick with sleet, and visibility was reduced to almost nothing.

"Sounds like there were hidden depths to the victim," Hugh said once he regained his breath. "Clive made her seem like a hot ticket."

"You have no idea," I said thinking of the acrobatics involved in a tryst in Dinah's bathroom. "You should try to get home before the storm gets worse."

"Are you trying to get rid of me?"

"I don't want you getting stuck again."

"Don't worry about me. When I was a Boy Scout my troop camped in the woods every winter. I got a merit badge in snow shelter building."

"Are you an Eagle Scout?"

"Yes, I am. Anything else you'd like to know about me?" Hugh slid to a stop in my driveway.

"That about does it," I lied.

TWENTY-ONE

Beulah's house was cold when I stopped in after work Tuesday evening for more cat food for Pinkerton, cold enough to make me worry about bursting pipes. I checked the bathroom and under the kitchen sink and decided to inspect the basement just to be sure.

I pulled the string for the twenty-five watt bulb at the top of the cellar way and eased down the wooden steps on my crutches. Even in the driest part of the winter the basement air felt clammy.

Overhead, copper pipes crisscrossed the ceiling. I picked my way across the cement floor, focusing my eyes upward to check for leaks. Beulah had gone to the trouble of having a separate laundry room carved out of a back corner of the cellar. I headed for it and pushed open the door.

Carefully draping a wooden drying rack with Beulah's panties and support stockings was a skinny little man. Instinctively, I raised a crutch and whacked him with it. The rack collapsed under the weight of him as he fell. He started to move, and I raised my crutch to whack him again.

"Please, no hitting." I pinned him down with one crutch, leaning on him with all my weight. With the other crutch I gave him a good poke. He turned his face toward me.

"What are you doing here?" It was the mystery man.

"I hurt no one." He stared up at me with enormous brown eyes. His Adam's apple bobbed wildly in his throat.

"What are you doing here pawing through Beulah's underthings? She'd die of shame if she wasn't dead already. Are you a serial killer taking a trophy?" I was starting to get scared. He didn't look like much, and I outweighed him, but you hear about the supernatural strength of the criminally insane. And I did have a bum leg.

"I hurt no one. Luisa say me to stay here."

"Luisa told you to hide here?" His Adam's apple bobbed again as he nodded. "How do you know Luisa?" I poked him again.

"She my sister. She say me to stay here when I break car."

"Why would you stay here?"

"I say to Luisa I break car, and she say police will look for me at her house. She say I go here for hide."

"Someone killed another woman after you ran off, and a lot of people blame you."

"I hurt no one. I am hiding all times, even when someone comes in the house I am hiding."

"Someone was here? Someone besides me?" He nodded. No one besides Augusta and I ought to be in Beulah's house.

"Yes, today. In morning. Is walking over my

head."

"Did you see who it was?"

"No. I hide here. There is loud walking, then I hear door, and then is no walking." I studied him carefully, considering what he had said. He didn't look like a killer, not that I was sure that should look like.

"What were you doing with those clothes?"

"I want make my pants dry. I am cold. I see these clothes wet, and I fix. " He gazed at me with his sunken brown eyes, and I felt more sorry for him than frightened.

"I'm going to let you up. I want to look around and figure out who might have been here. You won't give me any problems, will you?"

"I no am problem." I eased my weight off the crutch and let him up.

"Oh, you're a problem all right. I'm just betting you're not a killer. You go up first." I gestured toward the stairs with my crutch. Just like that, he bolted up the stairs and was gone. I heard the storm door bang shut behind him. There was no way I could have stopped him. Honestly, I wouldn't have tried. I felt more comfortable with him gone.

I hobbled around the first floor of the little cape for a second time, looking for signs of disturbance. Standing in Beulah's living room, I couldn't see anything missing, just signs of dirt tracked around the room. There was dried mud on the floor in front of the desk. I peeked inside. The cubbyholes were stuffed with papers, rubber bands, a roll of stamps. Nothing looked organized, but it didn't look rifled either.

I checked the rest of the room, but everything seemed accounted for, even some small silver items and Beulah's collection of souvenir spoons. Maybe the intruder was looking for modern electronics and didn't realize the value of Beulah's collections.

Upstairs, I poked my head into Beulah's room and the spare room she used for sewing. The tracks were fainter than the ones on the first floor, and they stopped in front of furniture with any storage space.

I limped to the attic door and popped it open. Reaching the top of the stairs, I scanned for any changes. It wasn't a mess, exactly, but it wasn't how we left it either.

Boxes were shifted out of place. The dressmaker's dummy was moved, and the vest was missing. I lifted the flaps on a few boxes, trying to remember what had been there. The grubby dishcloth was still there along with the dried flowers, but the scrapbook was nowhere to be seen. The box with the books about Maria Monk and the paper cutouts was missing, too.

My ankle throbbed, my fingers were numb, and I worried the DaSilvas looked even guiltier than ever. What I wanted was a hot bath and a glass of wine. Unfortunately, what I had to do was stop in at the police station and report the robbery at Beulah's. I hobbled back down the stairs and into the cold.

Ray was up to his ears in gift wrap when I arrived at the police station. Every Christmas the police department does a toy drive to benefit local kids who don't have much. I may not like Ray, but I have to give him credit. He organizes the whole thing from advertising to wrapping and even delivery. As I walked in he was trying to pull a thick index finger from the knot in a tied ribbon.

"Give me a hand, would you?" he said. "My fingers are just too clumsy for this, but I think it looks only half done without a bow." I loosened his finger and tied a quick knot, then curled the ends with the edge of a pair of scissors.

"You're actually useful," Ray said.

"Thanks," I said. "I'm here to talk to you about Beulah's house. Some things are missing."

"Like what?"

"A scrapbook and some pamphlets and a gaudy old beaded vest. I can't think what anyone would want with it."

"Are you sure all that stuff's gone? It's hard to see with a hat pulled down over your eyes."

"I can see fine. The vest was on a dressmaking dummy when Augusta and I were there a few days ago. Now it isn't."

"Maybe Augusta threw the junk out. She was saying at Dinah's that going through everything was no picnic."

"She wouldn't have done that. She's taken the executrix job very seriously."

"All I'm saying is that it would take a pretty strange duck to break into a house to steal a scrapbook and some old clothing." Ray yanked the backing off a green bow and jabbed it onto the top of another package.

"I agree it seems nuts."

"Of course, you never know with foreigners," Ray said. "If you're not smart enough to speak English, you're probably too stupid to know what's worth stealing." Ray ran his finger around the inside of his ear and then inspected under his nail for waxy build-up.

"Ray, you disgust me," I said, "and not just because of your hygiene." I slammed the door to the police station behind me and decided to give the same information to Hugh. He might believe Luisa's brother was involved in the thefts, but I doubted it was because he hated immigrants.

It's not easy to work up a good stomp using crutches, but I was doing my best when a car slowed down beside me.

"You look like you could use a lift," Hugh said. "Hop in."

"Where'd you get the car?" I asked, staring at a classic Chevy.

"It's my personal vehicle," Hugh said. "I felt like taking it out for a spin. Hop in." I yanked the back door open and tossed my crutches in, then joined Hugh in front.

"You look worn out," Hugh said. "Where're you headed?"

"I wish I knew," I said, sinking down and closing my eyes. "In the last few days everything has gone completely haywire." I tried to hold it in but a fat tear slid down my cheek and landed on the pale yellow leather seat.

"I know what you need," Hugh said. He pulled back onto the road and turned up the radio. An oldies station played "Lollipop" as we headed out of town. The sound of slushy pavement mixed with the music as I slouched back and let the tears stream down my face.

By the time we stopped, I'd blown my nose on every mangled tissue I'd found in my coat pockets. I still didn't feel better. I scowled out the window at a rundown shopping plaza. Bob's Dry Cleaning, Center Langley House of Pizza and Rhinestone's Bowling Palace all clustered together in a depressed huddle. Hugh came around to my side of the car and held open the door.

"Whenever I feel things aren't making much sense, I come here and toss around a few balls," Hugh said. From the way the beefy shoe rental woman greeted Hugh I guessed things didn't make sense on a regular basis. She arched her eyebrows at Hugh and asked my size. Hugh led me to the farthest lane and untied his shoes. His toes poked out of his socks. Padding in stocking feet to the ball return, he scrutinized the choices.

"I'm warning you," he hoisted a ball, "pink's my lucky color." With a dramatic heave, he launched it toward the pins. Two pins teetered, then toppled. Hugh spun back around with a giant grin on his face. "What did I tell you? Lucky ball."

"Looks like you're ready for the pro leagues," I said. "Is it also lucky not to wear shoes?"

"They don't have my size for rent," Hugh waggled a naked toe at me, "and I can't justify buying a pair, considering how badly I play."

"I don't think it matters how well you bowl." I watched him toss a black ball straight into the gutter. "It only matters how much you enjoy it."

"I'll think on that advice." Hugh knocked down another pin. "You're up." I lurched toward the balls on my crutches and steadied myself on one leg before aiming down the lane. Imitating Hugh, I lobbed the ball with all my strength. Four pins fell with a clatter.

"You're a natural, even with a bad ankle," Hugh wrote out my score. "I knew this would be good for you." I glanced around. The place looked like a set from "Happy Days" with the jukebox in the corner and the abundance of chrome. Even the staff had frilled aprons and beehives. Oldies poured from loudspeakers above our heads.

"I was thinking about calling you when I got home," I said, feeling the joy of heaving another ball with abandon. "I found the guy that ran us off the road camped out at Beulah's. He said he heard someone in the house. When I checked the attic some things were missing."

"Where is he now?" Hugh gave me his full attention.

"I don't know. He ran off, but I found out he's Luisa's brother."

"Did he hurt you?" Hugh stepped toward me, his eyes crinkled with concern.

"No. I think I scared him a lot worse than he

scared me."

"You were leaving the police station when I found you. What does Ray say about it?"

"He thinks anyone who isn't a native English speaker is automatically a criminal. I told him some things were missing, but I didn't tell him about Luisa's brother. They have enough problems without encouraging Ray."

"I expect you're right."

"It's Christmas. Why can't arsonists, murderers and bigots take a break at the holidays?" Another tear slid down the side of my nose.

"I'll be right back," Hugh slapped his tennis racket-sized feet as he went. He returned with a plastic cafeteria tray covered with fries smothered in cheese, two extra tall root beer floats, and a box of tissues.

"Nothing like fat and sugar to fix what ails you."

"Unless what ails you is a heart condition or diabetes." I reached for a tissue.

"Clinical research indicates comfort food is the best cure for an aching heart." Hugh dug into the fries. "So have at it."

"Have you been talking to my sister?" I concentrated on dunking a fry deep into a puddle of cheese to avoid eye contact.

"It just shows." Hugh reached across the table and covered my greasy hand with his own.

"I thought I'd been better at covering it up than that." I peeked up at him as he squeezed my hand.

"You are. If you hadn't been, some guy would

have had a go at roping you in. And I wouldn't have been able to try my luck because you would have already been spoken for." My throat dried up, and a mist of sweat sprang up across my forehead. I thought about Augusta's comments about the biological nature of things, and that made me sweat more. In college, I barely passed biology.

"Spoken for. That's a phrase I haven't heard in years."

"I'm an old fashioned guy."

I looked around the bowling alley. "I'd noticed. Do you carry a handkerchief you spread over puddles for ladies to walk on?"

Hugh pulled a white fabric square from his trouser pocket. "It's usually for cleaning my reading glasses, but given the right lady, I'd sacrifice it to a puddle." He leaned toward me and I felt my face flush. Actually, the flush must have spread in all directions because the nape of my neck tingled, my stomach fluttered, and my arm hairs stood on end.

"I usually wear galoshes." I tried not to notice Hugh's lips as a he smiled.

"Are you telling me you're definitely not interested?"

"I'm not interested in needing anyone. I've worked too hard at being on my own to give up any ground on that score."

"Going to dinner or out snowshoeing shouldn't mean giving anything up. This isn't a high pressure situation. At least I don't intend it to be." Hugh gave my hand a greasy squeeze.

"I'm in no fit condition to snowshoe."

"When your ankle heals. I've got a whole tangle of trails through the woods on my property. After, I'll make you dinner."

"I thought you only did take-out."

"Take-out is for business dinners. Haven't you heard that firefighters are great cooks?" Hugh's cell phone chirped. "You're not off the hook. I'm going to keep asking you until I get a no. Even then, I may ask a couple of times more just to be sure."

Hugh let go of my hand and reached for his phone. He spoke briefly into it and hung up.

"That was Ray. He's identified the owner of the truck that skinny guy was driving."

"Anyone I'd know?"

"Ethel Smalley."

We bowled another string, but my mind wasn't on the game. I kept thinking about Ethel and the truck I didn't know she owned. I was sure I'd never seen Ethel driving anything but that blue sedan with the yard sale bumper sticker. If it was Ethel's, then she must have registered it at the town office. That meant Clara, the town clerk, knew about it.

TWENTY-TWO

The town office is marginally bigger than the post office. If you're in line waiting to buy a dog license, there is no way to avoid hearing the business of the person in front of you. This morning was no exception. I stood rereading the posted minutes of various town boards to block out Vernon Betts detailing his wife's foot surgery. Ten minutes later he shuffled off, and I got my chance with Clara.

"If only that man would develop a disease of his own so he'd stop coming in here every day to talk to me." Clara rolled her eyes.

"I'm just glad his mail is delivered by the rural carrier. I've got all I can handle every morning with Clive coming in to the post office."

"So what can I do for you?" Clara offered me a mint from a tin.

"You heard about the accident I was in during the storm?" Clara sucked on her mint and nodded. "The truck that hit us was registered to Ethel."

"I heard the guy who killed Ethel was driving the truck that hit you." Clara leaned in, eyes wide.

"No one knows if he killed her. Did you know about Ethel owning a truck?"

"Well, now you mention it, I guess I did. She said something about not wanting to stink up her car with trash going to the dump. I can't say I ever saw her driving it though."

"Did you ever ask Winston if she brought it to the dump?" I asked.

"Ethel wasn't my favorite person, you know that. I didn't talk about her any more than absolutely necessary. If I brought it up, I don't remember his answer."

Hugh pulled up in front of the town office just as I was limping out the door.

"Looks like you beat me to the punch this morning." Hugh got out and walked around to the passenger side and opened the door for me. "Hop in and tell me what you found out." I settled myself and soaked up the heat blasting from the vent. I filled Hugh in, and we agreed to head to the dump.

If you want to win a local election, you campaign at the dump. On a Saturday morning almost everyone in town ends up there at some point. If Ethel had ever brought trash to the dump in the truck that ran us off the road, then Winston would know about it.

"I think you should let me handle this," I said.

"Is Winston likely to be close-mouthed about Ethel's truck?" Hugh looked surprised.

"It's not that. I don't think you'll fit in the dump office. At least, not if Winston's in there, too." We glanced at the tiny outbuilding sided in cast-off galvanized sheet metal and discarded license plates.

"I'll be here when you're done." Hugh came round the side of the car and opened it for me.

"It's my ankle that's out of commission, not my arm, you know," I said.

"I told you I was an old fashioned guy. Now stop complaining, and go dig up some gossip." I tried my best to strut away like Augusta does, all nonchalant with a bit of a hip wiggle. Even with two good legs I can't really manage it. From the stifled chortles leaking out of Winston's helpers I only managed to look like a staggering drunk on crutches. When it comes down to being decorative or useful, I come up useful every time.

Winston was sitting behind his desk made from a hollow core door stretched across a short metal file cabinet on one side and a sawhorse on the other. He reached for a grimy paper cup and spat a gob of chew into it.

Crammed in around him were things people brought to the dump that he couldn't see any reason to throw away. Coils of Romex were draped over nails pounded into the walls. Coffee cans of screws and nails were stacked in the corners. Stuffed animals were piled up to the side of the door. I squeezed in next to a life-sized purple gorilla and just barely managed to shut the door.

"Something I can do for you this mornin'?" he asked, closing a copy of *Transfer Station Monthly*.

"I was wondering if Ethel ever came to the dump in a navy blue truck? Mid-sized, with a cap." Winston opened a three-ring binder on his desk. He flicked through several pages, running his stubby finger down the columns with care.

"Just wanted to double-check before shooting my mouth off." He snapped the binder shut. "Ethel had a dump permit for two different vehicles. One was her sedan, and the other was a truck like you described. She only brought the truck in the one time to get a permit."

"So you never saw it again?" I was disappointed. Why would Ethel have a truck she didn't need? She was too cheap to pay the registration and insurance even if it was a junker that she wasn't making payments on.

"I didn't say that. It came to the dump a lot, just not with her. Chris Davis brought it in every couple of weeks for probably the last six months."

"Chris? Are you sure?"

"I'm sure. I hadn't written out a dump permit for him for that particular truck, so I made a point to look it up when he was here with it the first time. It was Ethel's. The first time I wondered if he was renovating her house or some such a thing. He kept coming in with it, though, and I never heard that Ethel reported it stolen."

"Did you ever ask him about why he was using it?"

"It wasn't any of my business so long as the vehicle had a valid dump sticker." I couldn't think of anything else to ask so I thanked Winston for his time and left him with his magazine.

Hugh was standing outside his car fending off seagulls.

"Who's Chris Davis?" Hugh asked.

"He's married to my clerk Trina. They've been in town about two years." I wondered how to ask Chris questions about secretly using a murder victim's truck without causing Trina to quit at the busiest season of the year.

I really didn't want to spend another Christmas season begging for extra help from the surrounding offices. I've had twenty-three clerks in the past ten years. Donald Petrie at the Langley office simply hangs up now when he hears my voice on the phone.

I gave Hugh directions to the Davis house and slumped back, chewing a fingernail and thinking about how much time I had left until retirement with full benefits. No matter how many vacation days I'd banked, it still wouldn't get me out before the end of this holiday season.

A twelve-foot inflatable Santa waggled in the wind in front of Chris and Tina's house. Another Santa and the reindeer parked on the roof. In fact, every square inch of the front lawn lit up, moved or blared music. The only thing missing was a path shoveled to the door.

"I think you should wait for me," Hugh said.

"I'm fine. I've gotten used to these things by now." I confidently swung my crutches across the crusty snow. I squeezed between a hard plastic camel and an oversized elf. "See?" As I bore my weight down on the crutches, they punched through the crust on the snow. The top of my body lurched forward as my feet slipped out behind me. I whacked the elf with a crutch. He toppled onto Mrs. Claus in a manner that was sure to get him fired. She in turn knocked over Frosty, who leveled the Grinch. Before I could stop myself, I upended the manger and sent Baby Jesus skittering into the street just in time to be crushed under the tire of Ray's police car.

Ray flipped on his lights and got out to inspect the scene. The commotion brought Trina to the front door. Her two kids, Krystal and Kyle, peeked out around her. Krystal started to wail. Ray poked at the crushed Christ Child replica with his boot. It was doubtful this doll could be resurrected.

"Would you like to file a complaint?" he called to Trina. "Looks like assault and battery to me. It might even be a hate crime."

"What am I going to tell Chris?" Trina asked. "He spent all last weekend setting this stuff up."

"Is he here now, ma'am?" Hugh called up to her, from the safety of the driveway.

"No. He's at an architectural salvage place in Portland." Trina said. "He said he'd be home early on account of the holiday." I scooted on my backside until I reached the driveway. Hugh heaved me to my feet and then retrieved my crutch from the middle of the street.

"About those charges, Trina?" Ray asked again. "Want to file them?"

"I guess not," Trina said. "It wouldn't really be in

the Christmas spirit. Besides, if she's in jail I'll have to work her shifts." Trina tugged Krystal back into the house and slammed the door.

"That didn't go the way I was expecting," I said.

"You know, the Fire Marshal doesn't condone torture," Hugh said. "We both stared at the carnage. Somehow the inflatable Santa was punctured in the fray and had lost enough girth to be a celebrity spokesman for a prescription weight loss program.

"Please take me home," I said. Ray, busily snapping photos of the debris, didn't notice us leaving. Staring in the side mirror I saw him stringing up crime scene tape. When we arrived home, Hugh walked me to the door.

"I'll call you if I locate Chris." He pushed open the unlocked door.

"Call any time. I don't have holiday plans since the boys aren't coming home, and Augusta may have plans with Gene. "

"I'll be in touch." He rested a giant paw on my arm before leaving me alone in my empty house. I flicked on the light over the kitchen sink and found a note from Augusta letting me know she'd gone to the grocer for eggnog.

It was still light out, and I had presents for the DaSilvas. I thought the younger kids still might believe in Santa, so I trudged to the barn and dug through the old costume box the boys had loved when they were little. Near the bottom I found a rumpled Santa suit and a long white beard. Not only was it festive, it covered up my tangerine hair.

Augusta had returned with the car by the time I'd wiggled into the suit and brushed out the beard.

"I thought you were more interested in removing facial hair than adding it." Augusta plopped two grocery bags on the table.

"I'm delivering gifts to the DaSilvas. Would you drive me over?"

"Sure. Let me just stick the perishables in the fridge." Ten minutes later we pulled up next to the DaSilvas' driveway, and Augusta helped me to the door before going back to the car to stay out of sight. I adjusted my beard and thumped on the trailer's warped door. Even without a bum ankle there was no way I was squeezing through a chimney, even if the trailer had happened to have one.

"Ho, ho, ho," I bellowed as Luisa pulled open the door. She took a startled step backward, and I took that as an invitation to go on in. Diego and his brothers sat at a coffee table eating plates of beans and rice. The younger ones gasped, and even Diego looked excited.

"Have these boys been good this year?" I asked. Tulio and Ronaldo glanced uncertainly at their mother. Diego nodded, and the toddler cried. "Anyone working hard learning English?" I reached into the sack as Ronaldo and Tulio joined Diego nodding. Luisa closed the door and scooped up her youngest.

I'd handed out all the packages in my bag, and the toddler had stopped crying and started grabbing my beard, when I heard scuffling on the stoop. Luisa said something in Portuguese that I assumed meant not to open the presents until she said so and then opened the door again. A blast of cold shot through the room as a second Santa shoved the skinny guy from Beulah's basement into the trailer in front of him. Alessandro began to cry again.

Luisa ran toward the man, and the only word she said that I understood was "Ernesto."

"I was coming to deliver presents when I saw this guy slinking up the stairs." Even with the Santa suit there was no mistaking Ray's voice. "Look what he had with him." Ray plunked down a kerosene heater that looked just like the ones found at the Museum and at Ethel's.

"He is no doing wrong. Please go." Luisa said shaking a finger in Ray's face.

"Oh, I'm going all right, and this slippery customer is coming with me." Ray dug into the depths of his red suit and pulled out handcuffs. I wondered if he was wearing his entire uniform under there.

"Where is Santa taking Tio?" Tulio asked, putting down a package.

"I'm taking him to the police station for questioning. He stole a truck, fled an accident scene, and killed a couple of old ladies." Ernesto shook his head. Luisa started crying along with Alessandro. Diego was the only one who looked angry instead of scared. He lunged at Ray and pulled off his beard.

"You are thinking it is my uncle doing bad things because we are foreigners. My English is not so good, but I watch television. I know you cannot be here with no search warrant. My mother say to you to get out."

"So this guy is your uncle, huh? Have you got a green card you could show me?" Ernesto tried to pull away, but Ray grabbed him and snapped on the handcuffs. "I didn't think so." Ray shoved Ernesto toward the door. "You folks have a nice holiday."

TWENTY-THREE

The trailer door flapped shut. I hobbled toward it as fast as I could and hollered after them.

"Ernesto! Don't talk to him. Wait for the man with the red hair." I turned to Luisa, who was crying harder. "Luisa, where can we talk privately?" She led me down the hall and opened a door at the end. Folded neatly on the floor near the heat vent sat a pile of blankets and a pillow. A milk crate pushed against the other wall held clothes. There was nothing else in the room.

I pulled off the Santa hat and beard. Alessandro watched me remove what seemed like a piece of my face and howled even louder—or maybe he was as upset about the color of my hair as I was.

"Gwen. I thought was you. I need help my brother. I go with the police." Luisa squeezed her son tighter to her chest.

"Why would you go? He's the one who ran away from the police. He's the one who was hiding at Beulah's."

"He not hurt Beulah." Luisa bounced Alessandro on her hip.

"I'm sure you believe your brother. I want to

believe him, too, but proving he wasn't involved may be difficult. He's acting like a guilty man."

"I can prove. What if I say he is with childrens when fire is happening? Diego will say he is home."

"Luisa, I saw Diego out the window after the fire. I don't think that will help Ernesto. If you know something, you'd better tell me now."

Luisa took a deep breath. "I was with Beulah at Museum."

"When?"

"The night she die."

"What were you doing there?"

"When I clean Museum, I see some things are not the same. Some things are not there. Some things are changed with things that look much like them. I say to Beulah this is happen, and she is not happy."

"I'm sure she wasn't. Were you there when she died?"

"No. I was at Museum for clean, and Ethel say to me to not work there more. I say this to you before." I nodded, remembering our conversation the day before I found Ethel's body. "When she is saying this I think I tell Beulah about missing things before I am forgetting what things look like in Museum."

"So you went to Beulah's house?"

"I walk there from the Museum. I say to Beulah what I think, and she not happy. She say she needs see what things I am talking but she wants no one know she is looking. She say is secret."

"Did you go with her to the Museum?"

"We waited for to be later so Ethel not there. I

drived Beulah in her car. She no can walk to Museum." So that explained how she got there.

"Did you drop her off or go inside?"

"I went in for show her what was gone or changed. She was very not happy. I am to clean at store of Gene Ramsey also, and I say to her we need go, but she say no. She say to me to go to other job and say me to come back later for to get her."

"So you walked to The Hodge Podge and cleaned there and left her alone in the Museum?"

"She say I use her car to go to work. She not want it near the Museum for someone see she is there and is faster for me to come back for her if I drive."

"Did you come back?"

"Yes. I listen fire trucks at Gene's, but I was not thinking Beulah was hurt. I finish clean. When I try to go Museum was fire, and I could not go in."

"Why didn't you tell us she was trapped inside?" I was shocked. We might have been able to save her.

"She say to me was secret she was there. I think she was at her house, so I take her car to her house and put in garage. I look for her in house, but she not there."

"But you still didn't go back to the Museum and tell us that she was there?"

"I scared. I think someone say I hurt her because I no have job at Museum. I say to Diego go to look. I felt bad I say to her about the missing things."

"So you went home and sent Diego to the fire scene?" I asked.

"Yes. I stayed with little boys, and he go look."

"Where was Ernesto when you got home?"

"I not know. I ask him, and he say is better I not always knowing what he is doing." Luisa started to cry again.

"Is he illegal?"

"He come here legal but now he is not legal. Visa for three months only. Now is over one year he is with us." This was not going to be good. Ray would be delighted. I had to track down Hugh as soon as possible.

"Do you think he had anything to do with the fires or what happened to Beulah and Ethel?" Luisa bit her lip.

"I think no. He no hurt people. He does work for boss and worries what it is, but he is good man helping us and getting money."

"Okay. I'll go to the police station and see what I can do for Ernesto. I can't promise anything if Ray gets hold of Immigration, but I can tell you the investigation into the fires and deaths isn't Ray's job. It's mine and Hugh's. Ernesto will get a fair chance with us." I put the beard and hat back on. Passing back through the living room, I waved at the kids and limped out the door. Augusta still had the car running.

"I saw Ray stuffing a skinny guy in the back of the cruiser. Was that the guy that ran you off the road?"

"Yup. He's Luisa's illegal alien brother. I need to call Hugh. I hate to bother him on Christmas Eve, but it's urgent." Augusta handed me her cell phone, and I caught Hugh closer by than I was expecting. He had returned to Chris's house and parked out front to wait for his return.

"He says he'll meet me at the station. I'm sorry this isn't turning out to be a very festive night."

"Don't worry about it, but if you don't mind, I'm going to drop you off and leave you. I don't want to meet the village mystery man looking less than my best." Augusta braked hard in front of the police station and waited for me to get out. The police station had been a store like Dinah's at some point in the past. It was a wood-framed building with huge, street-side windows. Ray had the place lit up for Christmas. Looking in, I could see Santa handcuffing Ernesto to the rail running along the deli case. The case had been too heavy to bother to remove when the police station was brought in, so Ray made the best of things by unplugging it and storing his town reports and speeding ticket booklets on the shelves where the meat and cheese used to go.

I'd just pushed open the door when Hugh squealed up in his Chevy.

"I feel so underdressed." Hugh flicked his eyes from me to Ray. I pulled off my beard but left on the rest of the suit.

"Thanks to you, Gwen, Ernesto here isn't saying anything." Ray dragged a chair next to the deli case and jacked one foot onto it. I wonder how long he'd been practicing that maneuver.

"I believe he isn't required to tell you anything. Besides, this is a fire investigation, not a police matter." I reached into the front of my Santa coat and pulled out the pillow I'd used to enhance my belly. The feathers had been poking me in the tummy for hours and I'd had enough.

"What about the car accident? You could've been killed. Not to mention he stole Ethel's truck. As soon as I get done questioning this sicko about what he did to those two women and why, I'm calling immigration."

"Not so hasty, Ray. The owner of the truck is dead and can't report it stolen. If Gwen, Ernesto and I don't remember being in any accident, you haven't an investigation to pursue. All you've got is a dead woman's truck at the bottom of a ditch." Hugh squinted at Ray and waited for his words to sink in.

"You're not serious. There'll be fingerprint evidence." Ray whipped his leg off the chair and kicked it across the room.

"It was pretty cold out in the middle of that storm. I expect a guy from a tropical country would have been wearing some gloves." Hugh strode over and picked up the overturned chair. "Now let's all sit down and talk about this professionally. Gwen, why don't you get off that ankle and ask this guy a few friendly questions? You know his family right?" I nodded and sat down across from Ernesto.

If anything, he looked even more shrunken than when I'd him pinned to Beulah's laundry room floor. His dark, sunken eyes darted toward my crutches. Hugh took a seat beside me, and Ray remained standing.

"I don't have anything to do with immigration. I

only need to know about the fires. Where did you get the truck?"

"I drive for Boss." Ernesto's eyes darted back and forth between Hugh's face and my own.

"What's your boss's name?" I asked.

"He say I call him Boss. No names."

"So your boss is a man?"

"Is a man. Like me."

"Like you how?"

"Is not old. Not boy. Like me. Yellow hair. I drive for him. Take stuffs to places."

"What kinds of stuff?" Hugh had his notebook out again and was quickly filling pages with scrawl.

"Stuffs for buildings. Stuffs in buildings."

"Stuff like a giant hand?" I asked. Ernesto nodded.

"Where were you going with the giant hand?" I asked.

"To place for keep stuffs. Is other town, not Winslow Falls. Not far. Boss say to me to put hand with other stuffs, but I am never drive in snow and have much problems."

"Can you tell us anything else about your boss? How did you meet him?"

"Luisa cleans house for a lady. Lady say to Luisa she knows a job for someone to work without papers. Does Luisa have a friend for this job? Luisa says yes, and I go to the place lady says to find Boss."

"Do you know who the lady was?" I asked.

"The dead lady with cat." Ethel.

"So you hated the job. That's why you killed her." Ray leaned over Ernesto, who shrank even lower into his chair.

"Ray, don't try to help." I turned back to Ernesto. "Where did you meet your boss?"

"At Museum. Behind building."

"When was this?" I asked.

"Three weeks. Maybe little more."

"Do you know anything else about this man? His name? Any place you went together? Did you ever see his house?" Ernesto nodded his head with gusto.

"I helping him with stuffs on his garden. Big toys, like you are looking. And Jesus baby. Lots stuffs. He say for his childrens for Christmas." I glanced at Hugh and then at Ray.

"A big Santa? In his yard?" I asked, pointing to my suit. Ernesto nodded again.

"First the truck, now a job for Ernesto. Why does Chris's name keep coming up with Ethel's?" Ray asked.

"I don't know," Hugh said, "but I don't think he'll like his visit from Santa this year. Let's go."

"You two go on without us. Ernie here and I aren't going anywhere. I'm arresting him for trespassing." Ray swaggered to his banged-up metal desk and switched on his computer.

"Trespassing where?" Hugh asked before I could say something rude.

"Anywhere. Everywhere. An illegal alien is trespassing everywhere he or she goes. I intend to press charges against this guy even if you and Gwen lie about the accident." Ray hunted and pecked his way across the computer keyboard, swatting his false beard out of the way every few seconds. Thank God Augusta never fell for him. They might have had kids.

"I got some interesting information from Luisa this evening." I used the drive to Chris' house to fill Hugh in on Luisa's story.

"That explains how Beulah managed to get to the Museum that night. Do you think she's telling the truth about leaving her there alive?"

"I can't think of any reason for her to lie about it, can you?"

Hugh drummed his fingers on the steering wheel. "She could have been the one stealing from the museum. Maybe Beulah surprised her at it, and Luisa killed her, then set the fire."

"Then why would she have admitted she was there?"

"Maybe she's covering for Ernesto."

"You mean, she thinks he was involved with the deaths or with the fires?"

"Maybe both." He was right. Luisa had many reasons to protect Ernesto, and she could also be sheltering Diego. I knew how much I was willing to do for my own sons. Could Luisa be any different?

But I wanted to believe Luisa. I didn't want there to be a bad guy. I wanted a bolt of lightning or faulty wiring to be responsible for the fires. I wanted a slip and fall to be the cause of death for Beulah and even for Ethel, but that seemed less and less likely. I probably knew the person doing all this. I felt like someone had stolen from me.

We stopped in front of Chris and Trina's. It looked even worse than when the damage was fresh. The inflatable Santa had given up the ghost and lay crumpled at the edge of the drive. Mrs. Claus remained humiliated by the elf sprawled over her generous bust line like a felon in training. Mary and Joseph gazed mournfully into an empty manger. I wasn't Santa. I was the Grinch.

Hugh stopped the car, then fetched my crutches. After what happened here earlier, I was grateful to be allowed out of the car at all. I held firmly onto his arm, and we made it to the door. A low wattage bulb spilled light over Hugh as he thumped on the door with an overgrown bare fist.

"Don't you have any gloves or mittens?" I asked, looking at his red knuckles.

"Nope. Can't find any that fit." I reached out for his free hand, pressing my own palm flat against his as a standard of measure. He'd need something at least twice as large in all directions. Waiting for Chris to come to the door was not the best time for my thoughts to wander to what else he might have that was larger than normal, but wander they did. I blamed Augusta. If she hadn't been hanging around doing makeovers and boiling up pots of hormone stew, I'd be concentrating on the business at hand, not the feel of Hugh's hand.

Trina jerked open her front door and blinked at Hugh. I'd never seen her disheveled before. Her dirty blond hair stuck out like a poorly rinsed paintbrush.

Her bottom lip was missing its lipstick. A frazzled green bow had hitched a ride on her shirttail. "Last minute wrapping," she said, her eyes crazed and extra bright.

"Sorry to slow you down, ma'am." Hugh stuck out a protective arm between Trina and the door frame as her lolling eyes landed on me.

"What are you doing here? Krystal just stopped crying, and I'm too much of a lady to repeat what Chris said when he saw the yard."

"Is he here now, ma'am?" Hugh asked. My stomach fluttered, and I hoped she was going to say he'd abandoned the family and was never coming back.

"He's in the living room setting up the video game system he got for the kids. Until that thing is plugged in and under the tree ready to surprise the crap out them, he doesn't have time to talk to anyone. As a matter of fact, we're not even speaking to each other." She started to close the door, but Hugh's iceberg of a shoulder held it ajar. He held his badge at eye level. Trina shrank back and glared at me again.

"We need to talk to him now." Trina pulled the door open and stomped ahead of us into the living room. Presents avalanched toward us from all four sides of the room. I expect there was a couch in there somewhere, but I couldn't see it. Chris was on his knees in front of a glitzy artificial tree swearing and tugging at black and red cables.

"Those kids had better love this damn thing. I could wire a house faster than I can hook this up." He looked over his shoulder and dropped the gadget he was fiddling with when he saw us. "I thought Santa's helpers were elves, not giants." Chris hopped to his feet in one smooth motion.

"We're here to ask you some questions about one of your employees." Hugh pulled out his notebook and made a production of consulting it. "An Ernesto Tavares." Chris slid a glance at Trina, and she closed the living room door.

"A guy named Ernie worked for me two, maybe three years ago. You talking about him?" Chris crossed his arms over his chest and looked thoughtful.

"This is a current employee. Pretty easy to pick out of a crowd. Skinny, black hair, barely speaks English. Hired even though he's illegal."

"Can't say that he's ringing any bells." Chris widened his blue eyes at us and smirked some more. If I had to guess, I'd have said he was enjoying himself.

"So the fact that a man currently in police custody says he works for you and that you asked him to use a truck belonging to Ethel Smalley to haul materials surprises you, does it?" Hugh tapped on the notebook with his pencil.

"Indeed it does. He must be pretty desperate to be making up crap like that on Christmas. Did you say the guy's in jail?"

"Ray's holding him for now."

"Well, it sounds like you've got your criminal then. If he had Ethel's truck, he probably killed her and stole it. I'd say a murdering illegal alien would be thrashing around trying to pin blame on just about anybody to get out from under, wouldn't you?"

"He says he helped set up your lawn ornaments," Hugh said.

"Trina, did I or did I not spend all weekend two weeks ago, by myself, setting out a festive delight for our kids and all the rest of the neighborhood? It was a goddamned masterpiece until someone crashed through there like a nine-legged moose on roller skates."

"Every time I peeked out there you were all by your lonesome." Trina picked her way across the packages and slipped her arm through his. "You're such a good daddy." She swatted the air with her supercharged eyelashes. I wondered if all that mascara acted like dumbbells for her eyelid muscles.

"Is there anything else we can help you with? I wouldn't want to keep you since you must have a busy night ahead of you, Santa." Chris gave my suit another pointed look.

"There is one more thing," I said. "Trina told me you took the hand off the top of the clock tower and stuck it somewhere for safekeeping. Where exactly did you put it?" Chris dropped Trina's arm and looked momentarily off balance.

"I put it in the clock tower."

"You brought it all the way down the scaffolding, then went inside the building and up a steep flight of stairs to try and stuff it into the tiniest room in the Museum? That's what you're telling me?" I said.

"Hey, I'm a good guy. I wanted to keep it safe so

the clock tower seemed like the most out of the way place. If I'd known it was going to be burned up along with part of the Museum, I would have picked a different spot, but how could I have known?"

"That's a good question Chris. How could you have known?" I asked.

"That'll be all for now, folks. You have a pleasant holiday." Hugh stuck his hand under my elbow and twirled me toward the hall. Trina hurried after us and slammed the door, locked it, and extinguished the light over our heads.

TWENTY-FOUR

Pulling into the driveway, I noticed that Augusta had lit the Christmas tree. Its twinkling lights shone through the bay window. The porch light was on, too. It was a weird feeling to come home late and have the place look welcoming. It had been quite some time since any of the lights left on weren't ones I'd thought to leave on for myself.

"Not really the most festive Christmas Eve, was it?" Hugh switched off the engine like he was prepared to sit and talk a while.

"Christmas hasn't been the same for me since my husband died, and it's been harder since the boys moved out." I stared at my feet and tried to ignore the way Hugh's cologne mixed with the smell of wood smoke drifting from his clothes.

"Sounds like the perfect time to start something new." He reached over and touched my hand. I wished I wasn't wearing a thick wooly mitten.

"Like a New Year's resolution?" I gazed up into his face and thought about all the failed diets, unbalanced checkbooks and classic novels never read. He must have read my mind.

"That's not as auspicious as I'd like."

"Not auspicious is a pretty good way to describe my experiences in the romance department. Augusta's the expert at that sort of thing." My cheeks heated up, and I felt for the door handle with my free hand. Hugh squeezed on my mitten as if to keep me from running.

"I enjoy your company, Gwen. I'd like to enjoy more of it. I like that you think more about doing what's right than looking good while doing it. I liked you from the moment you said you dashed out to the Museum fire in your lingerie instead of taking the time to change."

"It wasn't lingerie." I couldn't believe it. The most romantic thing anyone had said to me in years, and it gets yoked together with my most public humiliation.

"Well, it is to me. I love flannel pajamas. Besides, I'm not saying you were running around town looking like a tart. I'm saying you put others first, and I like that about you. It's refreshing. Your whole damn attitude is refreshing. Look what you've got on right now, for Pete's sake. Who else does that sort of thing?"

"You sound like my sister. She always asks me if anyone else would be caught dead wearing the things I put on." I wondered if he thought oversized t-shirts with paint spatters and big holes were attractive, too. I had a whole collection of those serving as summer pajamas.

"I'm not Augusta." Hugh peered straight in my eyes. "I meant it as a compliment." Island music erupted from Hugh's belt. He let go of my hand and checked the screen on his cell phone. "I've got to take this. It's business." Hugh spent a few minutes on the phone and looked preoccupied as he hung up.

"That didn't sound good," I said.

"It isn't. House fire in Grantford. Looks like a Christmas tree caught on fire." Hugh glanced at the lights sparkling toward us from beyond my lace curtains.

"Anyone hurt?" I reminded myself to water the tree as soon as I got inside.

"That's why they called me. I've got to go." Hugh popped open his door and walked around to my side. His eyes looked tired as he held the door for me.

"Anything I can do?" I pulled off my mitten and reached out to touch his hand again. He held it in his own and lifted it to his lips. His mustache scratched against the back of my hand, and I felt the warmth of his mouth as he kissed it. My breath caught like it does when you think there's one more step than there is at the top of the stairs.

"See if you can get anywhere with Ernesto. Find out if he knows where Chris was having him take stuff. Maybe something will connect those two. And ask around the village. Find out if anyone saw them together or if Chris mentioned him." I climbed my front steps, glad of Hugh's steadying hand under my elbow as I noticed the ice built up again.

"I'm a lot more inclined to believe Ernesto than Chris." I pushed open the door and peered into the empty kitchen.

"I agree. I'll check in with you when I can. You

have a merry Christmas." He honked his horn as he pulled away. I stood watching his brake lights until they disappeared behind a stand of spruces.

Christmas morning passed quickly, unwrapping gifts and talking on the phone with our mother and Owen and Josh. It was eleven o'clock before either Augusta or I got dressed. Augusta had allowed me to peel potatoes for dinner when the phone rang again.

"Gwen, it's Bernadette. I hate bothering you on Christmas, but Harold's been pestering me to get you over here to speak to him." I'd known Bernadette most of my life, and she sounded closer to tears than I'd ever known her to sound.

"I'll be over just as soon as I can." Augusta stopped humming Christmas carols over a bowl of cake batter she had been stirring as soon as she heard me plan to leave.

"Where are you off to this time?" She propped one hand on her hip and talked with the other one, the one clutching a dripping wooden spoon. Cake batter flew around the kitchen and reminded me I needed to re-wallpaper.

"I need you to drive me to the hospital. Bernadette sounds like she's teetering on the edge, and Harold wants to talk to me about something. I couldn't refuse."

"Let me throw the roast in the oven to cook while we're gone." She whipped round grinding pepper over the prime rib and putting things back in the fridge while I found the coats and tried to remember where I put my purse.

Three-quarters of an hour later we were standing in Harold's room trying not to look shocked at how shriveled he seemed. Bernadette was shoehorned into a visitor's chair looking like she had seen the end times Pastor Norling mentioned every time the news from Washington disagreed with him.

"Darlin', why don't you and Augusta go on down to the cafeteria for coffee while I talk to Gwen?" Harold quavered. Bernadette struggled against the confines of the chair, using her ham-hock arms and beefy fists to pry herself up.

"We'll be back in a half hour." She thumped toward the door, then changed her mind and went to Harold's bed. Smoothing his brow with a flabby red hand, she bent with a grunt and kissed him. "I expect you to still be here when I get back." She and Augusta sailed out the door.

Harold once told me he joined the volunteer fire department to get away from Bernadette. He used to love her before he retired from forty-three years at the local sawmill. He said that he realized now that they had only managed to stay married for so long because he had almost never seen her. Since his retirement, they spent every moment of every day together except for his outings to the post office, the dump and the fire station. I wondered if he was glad of her company now that he was here in the hospital, waiting for a stranger to tear into parts of his body he was never going to see for himself.

"How's your Christmas been?" Harold asked.

"You didn't get me out here to ask about my holiday. What's going on?" I sat on the edge of his hospital bed and waited. Harold wasn't likely to be rushed into whatever was coming next, and I wasn't eager to hear it. It wasn't going make my day any merrier, whatever it was.

"Ray tells me Ethel's service is tomorrow."

"That's right. There'll be a memorial service since her body hasn't been released, and she can't be buried until the ground thaws."

"I'm sorry I'll be missing it. Tomorrow morning I'm having some kind of plumber's snake wound on up through my insides."

"You must be pretty worried."

"I told them they ought to just dose my prune juice with Drano and forget about all the fuss." Harold sank even deeper into his pillow. "Right about now I wish I hadn't survived the heart attack."

"Does this have something to do with the fires?" I scooched a bit closer on the bed. Harold closed his eyes and nodded. His chest expanded under the hospital sheet and then collapsed again as he let out a sigh.

"I didn't think it was going to get out of hand like this. I knew it was a bad idea, I'm not saying I didn't. I just didn't think anyone would end up dead."

"You know who's setting the fires, don't you? You've known all along. That's why you wouldn't call in the state." Harold nodded, his eyes still squeezed shut.

"I didn't want to hurt Bernadette. They said they'd tell her everything, and I couldn't face it. I never thought anyone would get hurt." I remembered the conversation I'd overheard Harold having on the phone a few days before.

"Who is it, Harold? You need to tell me before anyone else gets hurt." I reached out and laid a hand over his.

"Chris. It's Chris and Ethel. Chris was setting fires in buildings that were underinsured in order to buy them on the cheap and either renovate them or, like in the case of that camp on the river, to level whatever was left and build something more expensive on prime real estate. No one was ever supposed to be in the buildings when it happened. They promised me no one would get hurt and that they'd leave Bernadette alone."

"What were they going to tell Bernadette?"

"When I was a younger man, a few years after Bernadette and I were married, there was a rash of wild fires in California. Fire departments from all over the country sent guys to help out, including ours. Bernadette and I were having some problems. She wanted me to do something more impressive than working at the lumber mill. I liked it where I was. So when the opportunity came up to get away for a bit, I jumped at it."

"When was this?" I vaguely remembered something about the fires when I was a young teen. My parents had been upset about it and my grandmother was sure it was going to spread all the way to Winslow Falls. She slept with a fire extinguisher tucked up in bed with her for weeks.

"Thirty-five years ago. Hard to believe how long it can be for something to come round and bite you on your bony ass. Ethel was a waitress at a diner where a lot of us guys used to go and get something to eat after our shifts. Believe it or not, she was one fine-looking woman back then. And wild. The things she'd say flirting with you made you sweat. I've never been an adventurous man. I don't even like to try a new brand of toothpaste." Harold paused and let out another anemic sigh.

"But there I was, risking my life every day, hanging around with a lot of men who were unattached. Before I knew it I started flirting back. When she called my bluff, I'll admit I was scared and thrilled at the same time. I was only out there about three weeks, but it was long enough to get both myself and Ethel into trouble."

"Is Chris your son and Ethel's?" I couldn't believe it. It was impossible to imagine Ethel young and flirtatious and the sort of woman to lead a man like Harold off the straight and narrow.

"That's what she told me when she rolled into town eight years ago. I didn't recognize her, of course, but she knew enough about me from the time we were together to keep tabs on me from a distance. She may have used a private investigator to locate me."

"But she and Chris have never let on that they're related."

"I think they had a better working relationship

than a personal one. Can you imagine having Ethel for your mother?" I couldn't.

"The fires only started a few weeks ago. Did they ask you for anything before?"

"Ethel started with small requests for money. By the time Chris got here several years later, I'd drained off a big chunk of my pension and dried up a couple of whole life insurance policies. Once there wasn't anything else to tap, Chris came up with the idea of using my position as chief to cover up the fires."

"Why didn't you just tell Bernadette the truth? It was a long time ago. A lot of wives forgive those sorts of things." I thought about my own marriage.

"Bernadette and I don't have any kids, Gwen, and not for lack of trying. I would have done just about anything to keep her from being hurt that way." A tear drizzled out from under Harold's sparse eyelashes and traced the large pores of his nose.

"Did you set any of the fires?" Harold's eyes flew open wide, and he shook his head.

"I turned a blind eye, and I even gave a couple of tips for what not to do in order to avoid suspicion. But set them, no, I did not." I wanted to believe him but the truth is I was so surprised, I couldn't be sure of anything he had to say.

"The autopsy results came back on Beulah." I was starting to feel white hot and prickly. "She was hit over the head with something, and then her body was lit on fire to hide that fact. Was it Chris and Ethel?"

"I don't know. They never told me ahead of time which places they were planning to burn. They just did it, and then I ruled out anything but an accidental fire." Harold's hand trembled.

"So you were as surprised as anyone to get a call out to the Museum and find Beulah lying there like that?" I realized I'd been raising my voice when a nurse in a hot pink scrub top poked her head through the doorway and scowled at me.

"Why do you think I had a heart attack? I never would have hurt Beulah. She was my Sunday school teacher, for Christ's sake." Apparently, they didn't get to the part about taking the Lord's name in vain.

"Does Bernadette know about all this business now?" I wasn't sure how much of this was going to need to come out, and I didn't want her hearing something like this through the police or the grapevine.

"Yes, I know," she said from the doorway. "The old fool told me everything." Bernadette looked a little better. Her shoulders were upright, and there was an angry spark in her eye like she had decided to deal with the situation head on.

"When did he tell you about it?" I asked.

"Just after the heart attack. They'd gotten him stabilized and into the room. He didn't want me to hear about it from a lawyer or, even worse, Ethel herself if he didn't make it." Bernadette came to stand next to her husband and laid her hand on his shoulder.

"So you've known about this for days and never said anything?" I stared at her, a new unhappy thought growing.

"I didn't say anything, and I convinced Harold to wait and think about it before he did anything else stupid. Does it matter? Now that Ethel is dead, nothing else has burned."

"Someone killed Ethel and tried setting her house on fire. Chris is the best suspect." I didn't bother to mention to Bernadette she made a pretty good suspect herself. I'd seriously considered hitting Ethel over the head myself when she told me about Peter and the bank teller. If I'd found out it was Ethel that was messing around with my husband, even thirty-five years prior, I don't know what I would have done. Bernadette had plenty of time between the time Harold told her what was going on and when Ethel was killed to work up a real head of steam.

"What's going to happen now?" Harold stared at me with so much worry I didn't have the heart to accuse his wife of killing Ethel. If he had another heart attack and died, I wouldn't be a lot less guilty than whoever killed Ethel.

"I really don't know. I'm just the assistant chief, remember. I expect you won't be the fire chief any longer. A lot of people are going to be angry. I'm angry."

"I'm sorry. I never meant to cause trouble. I'm just a coward." Bernadette squeezed his shoulder again.

"You'd better get over that quickly. Things are likely to get unpleasant." I stood and zipped up my coat. "I wish you the best with the surgery. Bernadette, give me a call as soon as the doctors are done with him tomorrow. I want to know how he makes out." Augusta gave a little wave as we left.

TWENTY-FIVE

Smells of roasting meat filled the house when we returned. My stomach grumbled, but I had no appetite. Augusta busied herself finishing up the potatoes and making a salad while I tried to track Hugh down by phone. His cell phone went directly to voice mail, and the dispatcher wasn't much help either.

"Try his home number." Augusta suggested.

"I don't feel comfortable bothering him at home. This is business."

"It's urgent. And he's cute."

"You've mentioned. But he's a co-worker. Even if I was interested, it wouldn't be appropriate."

"Once it's appropriate he won't be around all the time, and the whole thing will fizzle."

"If it was meant to be, it wouldn't fizzle."

"Trust me, fizzle is easier than sizzle. I can see sizzle available to you right now if you position yourself correctly."

"I don't even want to think about what you mean by that."

"We can talk details later." Augusta poured herself a glass of wine. I looked on the fridge for

Hugh's business card with the number on it.

"I programmed it into speed dial. Hugh's number two."

"Dinah's was number two."

"I think you need a man more than any more takeout pizza." I hate it when Augusta's right. I may have been ordering fast food too much lately. The number two button looked a lot more worn than the other buttons.

"Can I get a little privacy? You're making me nervous. You're like the back stage prompter at a high school play."

"You're just confirming my point. If it was nothing more than a business call, you wouldn't be nervous."

"Please, go."

"All right, but I expect a full report. Don't leave out any juicy details."

"There is nothing juicy here. I don't even like juice." Augusta snorted and carried her wine out of the room. I punched the number two button and paced as Hugh's phone rang.

"Hello?" a perky young female voice said into the phone after the fifth ring. Augusta was going to be disappointed.

"May I speak with Hugh Larsen, please?"

"Sorry. He never came home last night from his fire call. May I take a message?"

"Yes, please do. Just tell him Chief Fifield, called and there have been some developments he should be aware of." I hung up and sank into the rocker. I wasn't looking for someone, so why did I care if some friendly young thing knew about whether or not he'd come to bed last night. Damn Augusta for putting foolish notions in my head.

"Don't let the girl on the line get you down."

"I can't believe you were listening on the extension."

"I can't believe you didn't think I would be. How can I coach if I'm not watching the game?"

"There is nothing to coach. I wasn't interested anyway. This was all your idea. I just want to keep my life on an even keel."

"No, you don't. You're lonely and struggling. And horny."

"Am not."

"Well, you should be. The girl on the phone may or may not be a factor. Did you ask who she is?"

"Of course not. It really isn't my business."

"Call her back."

"No. I don't want to talk about this anymore. I've got more important things to think about, like arresting Chris and whether or not Bernadette killed Ethel."

"I would have killed her if she had been messing around with my husband and my bank account." Augusta nodded to herself. "I still can't believe Harold had it in him, stepping out on Bernadette."

"I'm going to see Ray. I hate to admit it, but since I can't get hold of Hugh, I may need Ray's help." I reached for my coat and scarf.

"Do you want me to drive you?" Augusta put down her wine glass, half of it still untasted.

"I think I'd better walk. Ray loves pulling people over for drunk driving tests, and I'm sure he would love to strip search you." Augusta got a thoughtful look on her face as if she was weighing her options. Ray must not have measured up, because she sat back down at the table and took another sip of her wine.

"I think I'll give Gene a call and see what he's up to this evening. I don't think he had plans."

"I'm glad. I'd hate to think of you waiting up for me with nothing to do. You should enjoy yourself while you're here."

"I've been thinking about that. I may not sell Beulah's house after all." Augusta beamed at me.

"Why not? You have a life of your own a long way from here." I was stunned. Daily life hadn't included Augusta in thirty years. I wasn't sure we could survive living so close to each other.

"Beulah's death has given me a lot to think about. I've always had somewhere to live, but Winslow Falls is my home. I have the opportunity to live here again. It feels like it was destined to happen."

"You think Beulah was destined to be hit over the head?"

"That's not what I meant. It just feels right to be back home. Besides, you could use someone keeping an eye on you."

"Everyone in the village has their eye on me at all times. Call the police station if you hear from Hugh. Don't bother to wait up or stay home if Gene is free." I shrugged on my jacket and headed out on my cumbersome crutches. Just as soon as I could, I was going to get off the darn things.

I dragged my way along the icy sidewalk and noticed how empty the streets were. Usually in late afternoon there would be people coming and going on their way to Dinah's or the post office but not on Christmas. Even Dinah needed to kick back with a glass of eggnog and find out if she had been naughty or nice once a year.

The sun still shone, but it was sinking fast. A stiff wind clawed its way into the down of my parka, the wool of my hat and right on through my sweater and turtleneck shirt. Even my foot wrapped up six layers deep in ace bandage and topped off with two wool socks was feeling like I might need to amputate some toes. I was glad when the police station came into sight. Looking through the plate glass window, I watched Ray deal out cards to Clive and Ernesto. They all glanced up when I came through the door, but the only one who looked happy was Ernesto.

"Where's your suit, Santa?" Clive grimaced over his cards.

"Ray, could you deputize Clive and leave him in charge of Ernesto while you go to the Davis's house with me?" I peeked over Ernesto's shoulder at his cards. He had a sweet hand. If I didn't have to hurry, I'd love to see the looks on Ray's and Clive's faces when he laid them down.

"I can't believe you'd consider going back there after what you did to their Baby Jesus." Ray looked genuinely distressed. He may not have kids of his own, but he sure did love Baby Jesus—not enough to go to church on a regular basis but enough to be traumatized by a crushed Christ Child. Every year he sets up a crèche in the median triangle at the center of the village. If it snows he goes out and brushes off the Baby Jesus with a car scraper. Getting him to go with me was going to require a little commandment breaking.

"I felt so bad, I went right out and bought them a replacement. I didn't think they'd let me in after what happened with the front yard." I knew God would understand. In my book, God is all about the big picture.

"All right. Clive, you're in charge. Don't let this guy out of your sight. I'll be back as soon as Gwen's made her apologies." Ray patted his holster and grabbed a jacket. "Don't eat all the beef jerky while I'm gone." Ray pulled a heavy ring of keys from his jacket pocket.

"Are you leaving me a gun?" Clive didn't take his eyes off the small dark man seated across from him. Ernesto squirmed in his seat at the word gun. I asked myself if his English was better than he let on.

"We've been over this before, Clive. What we have here is more of an understanding between friends than anything official. I can't let you have an actual police weapon. Besides, you could take him without any trouble," Ray said.

Clive nodded and shooed Ray towards the door with a wave of his cards. Icy air filled my lungs as we left the warmth of the police station. We'd be halfway to Chris's house before the heater would kick in sufficiently to feel any difference in the temperature of the car.

"Hey, where's the baby?"

"There is no baby. I needed you to go with me to the Davis' house and I didn't want to tell you why in front of the suspect." That would get him. Ray never could resist official jargon.

"Are you going back for more questioning?" Ray punched down on the gas.

"I think we're past questioning. You may have to arrest Chris based on what I heard from Harold today." I explained the details of my visit to Harold. Once he got used to the idea that Ethel could ever have been a temptress, his eyes bulged so far forward he could have scraped the inside of the windshield with his lashes.

We pulled onto the county road and were only a half a mile from Chris's house when we saw a car coming toward us in the opposite lane. Squinting through the dusk, I could make out Chris's face through the windshield.

"Turn around. That was Chris. Ray, turn around." I reached out and shook his arm. Ray flipped on the lights and siren and wheeled the car around. Chris gathered speed by the turn leading toward the river. Water that had run off from houses and snow banks during the day had frozen as the temperature dipped with the sun.

"I wish he'd slow down. I can't feel the road."

"I guess you can get him for speeding if nothing else will stick." Not that I thought nothing else would stick. Harold's accusations made too much sense out of the situation.

Ray slowed down as much as he was able while still keeping Chris's SUV in view. Chris kept pushing the limits of the town's salting and sanding job. Taking the curve like a drunken teenager, he slid off the road. Ray stopped where Chris had gone over the edge. Chris's vehicle had crashed down through the pucker brush edging the river and lodged in the snow. He tried to push the truck door open. The snow came most of the way up the side of the door and kept it from opening up enough to allow a grown man to exit, even one as slippery as Chris.

I stayed in the car and watched Ray as he dug Chris out with a shovel he always kept in the trunk of the cruiser. He was about halfway through the job when Hugh rolled toward us in his Bel Air. I lurched out of the cruiser and waved at him. Hugh unfolded himself from the car and joined me at the side of the road. I noticed the sweater I'd lent him peeking out from underneath his jacket, but his hands were still bare.

"You've missed a lot today." I pointed to Ray and then filled Hugh in on Harold's sickbed confession.

"That explains why Harold was reluctant to call us in when the fires were getting out of control. Do you think Chris killed both women?" Hugh asked.

"I don't know. I know he's been accused of very anti-social behavior, and I know he sped up on the way out of town as soon as he saw Ray and me."

"Maybe it's you. I think something about you drives men over the edge into ditches." Hugh's mustache twitched above a big smile. "Do you think I ought to give Ray a hand?"

"No. I'm enjoying watching Ray do some real work for a change." We stood watching him hoist shovelfuls of wet, heavy snow. Once all the snow had been cleared, Ray pulled his gun from his belt and popped open the door. Chris looked annoyed and defiant, Ray elated, as they scrambled back up the hill.

Ray ushered his fugitive into the cruiser, a giant grin on his face. He shifted his weight from one leg to the other like a child needing the bathroom. "Winslow Falls is turning into a hotbed of criminal activity."

"Are you taking Chris back to the station?" Hugh asked.

"I am. I've got to get back and make sure Clive's doing okay with the other prisoner. My guess is they were in this together."

"You may be right. I'll give Gwen a ride back to the station." Hugh waved him off and then opened his car door while I slid across the yellow and gray upholstered seat. Hugh hadn't joined me. He was back down at the foot of the hill stomping down the snow to free the tailgate on the SUV. I saw him pawing around in the back. He came trudging back up the hill with a stack of three boxes in his arms.

Opening the trunk, he stowed them in back.

"What's in them?" I asked as he slid behind the wheel and turned the car around.

"Remember the items missing from Beulah's?"

"Yes."

"I think I found them."

TWENTY-SIX

Hugh drove straight past the police station and stopped in my driveway. I noticed someone had sprinkled salt and sand on the front steps. I wondered if it had been Diego and whether or not he and his family had enjoyed Christmas just a little even though Ernesto had been arrested.

"Shouldn't we get right to the police station?" I was ready to jump all over Chris about the fires and the blackmail.

"I thought we'd give the boxes a good going over at your house before we join them," Hugh said. "I wasn't impressed by Chris and can't think of anyone I'd like Ray to spend an hour grilling more than him. Besides, it's Christmas. Let Ray enjoy himself."

"I would like to see what's in the boxes before we question Chris. Besides, you look like you could use a cup of coffee." I filled the coffee pot while Hugh spread the boxes out on the kitchen table.

"I'm no expert, but is it strictly legal to have removed those from Chris's car without some kind of documentation?" I asked. "A warrant? Something?"

"If these are what we think they are, there's more of a risk that he'll say he never had them than complain that we took them." Hugh pulled off his jacket and draped it over the back of the rocker. "I've been meaning to return this sweater to you. I feel guilty about wearing it over and over." He ran his hand over a sleeve, tracing the pattern of the cables with his fingertips.

"I'm glad somebody's wearing it. Josh wore it once to please me, but it never fit him properly. It looks like I made it for you." I pulled a couple of mugs down from the cupboard and then dug in the fridge for cream.

"You made it?" Hugh examined the Saxon Braid and honeycomb patterns winding their way across his chest.

"Yes, about three years ago." I was surprised to find I felt shy. I'm proud of my knitting, and it brings me a lot of pleasure, but I don't think of it as awe inspiring.

"How long did it take you?" Hugh reached out for the coffee cup I was handing him and shook his head at the cream and sugar.

"Too long to guess. Keep it. I love to knit, but it takes some of the pleasure away seeing my work hanging around with no one wearing it."

"Knowing how long it took, I should give it back to you, but I really like it … so if you insist."

"I do. Let's look in the boxes." Hugh nodded and opened the flap on one of them.

"Does this look familiar?" Hugh held up a copy of *Maria Monk's Awful Disclosures.*

"It looks like one of the books missing from

Beulah's." I limped closer to get a better look. "That whole box looks like one of the missing ones from Beulah's attic." Just then, I heard footsteps running along the upstairs hall. Then the bathroom door closed. A man's voice called out, and I heard stomping on the stairs. Gene swaggered into the kitchen wearing the green bathrobe Augusta had unwrapped from our mother earlier that morning.

"Gwen! I was unaware you would be home." Gene blushed to the roots of his hair, which covered a lot of territory, considering how many of his follicles had abandoned their posts.

"Is Augusta home, or are you just here visiting her bathrobe?"

"Is there some kind of sleepwear mania in this town I ought to know about before I contract it?" Hugh asked.

"I think it only affects people who actually live here," I said as Augusta came through the kitchen door wearing street clothes.

"If I had known you'd be home so early, I would have made dinner. Have you eaten?" Augusta didn't look one bit embarrassed.

"We're fine. Look what Hugh found in the back of Chris's SUV." I pointed to the boxes on the table.

"Is this stuff from Beulah's?" Augusta asked.

"I think it is. Here are some of those paper shapes, and this has got to be that scrapbook." I lifted the velvet-covered book chronicling the life of Eustace Freemont Hartwell.

"How did Chris get this stuff? Beulah was dead

before we found it in her attic." Augusta reached out to take the book from me and laid it on the table.

"Maybe Chris was the person Ernesto heard at Beulah's when he was hiding out in the laundry room. He could have let himself in and helped himself to whatever he wanted." Tissue paper rustled as Augusta dipped her hand into another box. "There's not much else in here."

"I thought there was something else when we looked in it before. Let me see." I removed crumpled newspaper and peered deeper into the box. In the bottom was a faded blue star and a yellowed, spotted crescent moon. I held them up to show Hugh and Gene. "Why would anyone keep these?"

"Maybe they were party decorations," Hugh said. Gene looked interested for a second, then shrugged.

I tipped the box upside-down and gave it a shake. A small piece of paper fluttered to the floor.

"What's that?" Hugh asked.

"It's a stamp. A one-cent stamp with Washington on it." I dropped it into Hugh's palm.

"Weren't there letters in this box when we saw it at Beulah's?" Augusta asked.

"That's what's missing, a bundle of them all tied together. Maybe this stamp fell off one of the envelopes. I bet Chris thought it was worth something." Working in the post office, I've seen a lot of rate hikes on stamps. I may know a lot more about canceling stamps than I do collecting them, but I was certain this one hadn't been mailed in my lifetime.

"Allow me." Gene took the tiny paper from Hugh

and peered at it closely. "I cannot claim to be an expert on stamps, but I do know that it's worth less if it's been cancelled or if it's in poor condition."

"It isn't worth much, then?" I asked, disappointed.

"Sadly, no. These penny stamps would have been used with so much frequency that they simply aren't rare. It pains me to disappoint you, Gwen, but I've seen these in countless amateur collections hopeful relatives bring to me after an elderly person dies." He handed it back to me. "Please excuse me while I attire myself more appropriately."

"Don't hurry. Gwen and Hugh will be leaving in just a minute. They've still got a couple of suspects to put through the wringer." Augusta winked at Gene and handed a box to Hugh.

"You know," I said, "you own Beulah's house, and no one's going to bother you over there. You could do any sort of entertaining you'd like."

"I know, but it still feels like Beulah's. I'm afraid she would haunt me if I entertained a gentleman in her house."

"I think what you mean to say is that she only has twin beds." I stacked another box on the one that Hugh was already holding and gave her the third. "If you're in such a hurry to get rid of us, at least you could help carry out the boxes."

"Just stack that last one right on the top, and we'll be out of your way. Coming, Gwen?"

When we got to the police station, Chris was sitting at

the table in the center of the room with his back to
Ernesto. A country western station blared Christmas
carols. Clive was working on a game of solitaire
spread out on the deli counter.

Chris started to say something when we entered,
but when he saw the boxes Hugh held, he clamped his
thin lips together and crossed his arms over his chest.
Ray sat with his boots propped on his desk gnawing a
piece of beef jerky. Watching him work his jaws
reminded me that I still hadn't had Christmas dinner.
I wondered if they had bothered to feed Ernesto. He
looked about one meal away from the morgue. I dug
round in the pocket of my coat and found a roll of
mints that weren't too fuzzy. I handed them to
Ernesto, who gulped them down with enough gusto
to answer my question.

"Can you explain how items stolen from Beulah
Price's house after she was killed ended up in a
vehicle you were driving out of town?" Hugh set the
boxes in front of Chris.

"I don't know what you're talking about." Chris
slouched down in his chair.

"These boxes contain items reported stolen by
Gwen earlier this week. They were part of the
inventory Gwen and her sister conducted while
executing Beulah's estate." Hugh pulled out his
notebook and dropped his long shadow over Chris
like a net over a fish.

"What makes you sure they were at Beulah's?
Whatever's in there could have come from anywhere."
Chris jiggled his knee up and down. The gouged

wood floor bounced under my feet like an earthquake in training.

"Some of these things are pretty distinctive." Hugh pulled out the scrapbook. "Like this, for example. Eustace Freemont Hartwell. Not really a common name, is it?" Chris pushed his chair back from the table a little.

"Or how about this?" Hugh held the stamp between his thumb and forefinger and waggled it in front of Chris's nose. "A stamp. An old, old stamp that appears to have detached from a letter that was in this box and is now missing. Now, I've been told there are a lot of those sorts of old stamps floating around the countryside, but the letters are still missing from the box. I assume you may have an idea of where they've gotten to. It would suit me just fine to assume you killed Beulah in order to go through her house and help yourself to whatever you wanted."

"I didn't break into her house." Chris wiped the sweat beads that had formed above his upper lip on his shirt sleeve.

"But you killed her, right? Or maybe you and your mother did it?" Hugh said. Chris twitched like he'd stuck a knife too deeply into the toaster retrieving a bagel.

"My mother?"

"You made a bad tactical error," I said. "At the bottom of things Harold is a decent man. He told us about the affair he had with Ethel and the blackmail, including the fires. He didn't want to go into surgery with a bad conscience. You should have stopped before you killed someone. Or two someones. Did you kill your own mother, too?"

"We didn't kill anybody. We did set some fires. If my chickenshit old man spilled his guts, I guess there ain't any way to keep that quiet anymore, but I absolutely didn't kill anybody." The jiggling under the table got stronger. I was glad I had my crutches to help keep me steady.

"I'm not inclined to believe you," Hugh said. "As a matter of fact, I'd prefer not to believe you. Of all the people I've met in Winslow Falls, I'd like it best if you were the one I was hauling away to face a judge. Unless you've got something you'd like to share to help me change my mind, I think I'll ask Ray if I can borrow his desk to start the paperwork. It looks to me like this case is wrapped up as pretty as a Christmas gift." Chris squirmed in his seat like a kid on a six-hour road trip.

"Ethel rented a storage unit in Hoyt's Mills. I've got the key on the ring Ray took from me. She stored things there that she was clearing out of the Museum a little at a time. She'd sell the items on line at auction sites or even to dealers whenever she traveled out of the area," Chris said.

"How did she take so much of the Museum's collection without anyone noticing?" I asked.

"How much attention do you think people paid to what was in that rat trap? She stuck to the most boring exhibits and the things in storage. Anything she worried about, she swapped with an item that looked similar but wasn't worth anything. She'd pick up old teapots and jewelry at garage sales and flea markets. Then she'd make the switch."

"What about the upcoming inventory? Wasn't she worried about that?" I asked.

"Beulah accepted Ethel's suggestion that they do the inventory together and not bother anyone else with it. Beulah already thought the trustees hated doing it and didn't like to be bothered." Ouch. That stung. I did hate doing the inventory. Every year Beulah would call up and remind me that it was scheduled for the third week in January. I'd been relieved when she said that she could handle it alone with Ethel.

"That gives you an even stronger motive for killing Beulah. If she noticed the substitutions, you and your mother would land in jail." Hugh sat down opposite Chris and parted the boxes to get a clear view. "Without an alibi you look better." Chris flicked his eyes towards Ernesto and back to Hugh.

"I have an alibi. Ernesto and I were making a delivery to the storage unit at the time of the fire. Ask him." Chris straightened and spun round to face the other man. Ernesto stared back, not saying a word. "Come on, you ignorant jerk, tell him."

"You know, Chris, you really take after your mother in the people skills department," Ray said.

"Ernesto," I said, "do you understand what Chris is saying about you?" Ernesto nodded his dark head. "It won't help you to say you were with Chris if you weren't."

"I go with Boss to little building for stuffs from

Museum. When we are back to Winslow Falls, much problems with fire. I go to my sister house and say to her there is fire. Diego go to see and returned for to tell us what is happened." Ernesto kept his eyes firmly locked on mine, never looking once at Chris.

"See, what'd I tell you? I wasn't even in town when the fire started." Chris leaned forward, palms flat on the table.

"It still doesn't mean you didn't kill her. For all we know you coshed her over the head and then called your mother to finish off the job while you snuck out of town." Hugh stood up again. "At the very least you've admitted to committing arson. No matter what, you're headed for the county lock-up."

TWENTY-SEVEN

Hugh offered to drop me at home on his way to the county jail, but the thought of encountering Augusta and Gene again made me uncomfortable. I wish I could say it was because I didn't care for my sister using my guest room like a cheap hotel. The reality is I was just the tiniest bit envious. So I asked Hugh to drop me at Beulah's instead, saying I needed to pick up some more of Pinkerton's things.

Feeling sorrier for myself than I had in a long time, I waved Hugh off and let myself in with the key. Dust had settled on the surfaces. Only a week after her death, the house was taking on an unlived-in look. I eased back in Beulah's favorite chair and propped my bad ankle up on the ottoman. Without Beulah there to distract me with her conversation, I peered around in an unhurried way I hadn't before.

The walls were covered with mild landscape paintings in faded colors. Unsmiling faces stared out from sepia photos and daguerreotypes. I picked up one of Eustace and his wife. Squinting at the image I noticed that Eustace was gripping a cane. The head of the cane was a hand with the index finger pointing straight up. Just like the ornament on the museum clock tower. Just like the cane Beulah had used after her hip replacement surgery.

I'd commented on it when I first saw her using it, and she said it was a family heirloom. At the time I hadn't been aware of the Know-Nothings. Could Eustace have been a member? Beulah never mentioned anything like that, but then, maybe she was embarrassed that her family was involved with terrorizing immigrants. The cane looked like a good idea. My crutches were more than I really needed to get around, and I hated how cumbersome they were.

I stood up and circled the room looking for a cane. If Beulah had been using it, she should have left it around somewhere. Then I remembered, she would have had it at the Museum when she died. But it wasn't there. If the cane wasn't there when we found her body, someone had to have been there with her when she died, someone who decided to take it.

Leaving the front room, I inspected the dining room. It had long since ceased to function as a place to eat. Beulah had turned it into an office. Old-fashioned registers were stacked on the floor. Paperwork fanned out across the table. A wingback chair with a padded seat had displaced a wooden dining chair. Walking home at night from work, I often saw lights in this room and Beulah hunched over the table.

I glanced over what had been the work in progress when Beulah died. Genealogy and the list for the Museum inventory lay in front of the wingback. A pad of paper covered in Beulah's pointy scratching lay next to the inventory. I settled in her seat and scanned through the final things that had been on her mind.

Beulah's notes read like her conversation, scattered and informal. Notes about a cemetery with family names topped the list. Without a segue, Beulah's thoughts had moved to the inventory. She had noted the increase in the insurance policy rates and whether the cost could be justified. She questioned the valuation of the embroidery sampler collection and the value of the toy train set gifted to the Museum by the Purington family. *Ask Gene to Double Check* was underlined twice with an arrow pointing at a number equaling the premium total.

I stood up and moved around the room to warm up. Fifty degrees might keep the pipes from freezing, but it wasn't comfortable for sitting. The kitchen wall clock read seven. The street was dark and quiet as I relocked the door behind me. I was too tired to care if Augusta still had a visitor. I tested my ankle a little as I limped down the street. If I could locate a cane to replace the crutches, it would be more convenient.

My porch light was lit, and a note was centered on the kitchen table letting me know Augusta had gone to Gene's for a drink and that I shouldn't wait up. I shucked my dripping boots and went upstairs to soak in a hot bath. Just as I eased myself under the hot surface of the water, the phone rang. I ignored it and went on soaking.

Christmas cards and belated packages flowed into the post office December twenty-sixth with almost as much strength as they had in the days running up to Christmas. Guilt oozed from boxes and envelopes sitting in bulging drawstring bags in the back room. Trina did not flow or ooze into the post office. In fact, she didn't appear at all. I hadn't expected her to after helping to arrest Chris on Christmas Day. I hoped that Kyle and Krystal had really enjoyed the video game system.

Winston came in looking sober. Clive had been at Dinah's bragging about holding down the fort for Ray while Winston had been busy watching television as the grandkids ripped up his living room. Ray didn't make him feel better being in on Chris's arrest firsthand. The most exciting thing that happened to Winston on Christmas was finding out that his new antacid medication really was as good as the advertisements said it would be.

"I need some stamps, but don't give me any with Christmas designs. Gimme some flags or an eagle or something." Winston leaned his bulk up against the counter.

"How many did you want?" I slid open the stamp drawer and pulled out a selection for him to choose from. Winston always picked flags or eagles so I don't know why I bothered.

"I don't know. I need a bunch, but they've gotten so damn expensive, I hate to buy a whole sheet at once."

"Don't be a cheapskate. You know it's a carefully regulated industry. We only raise prices to keep up with costs. I'd like to see you go first class for what it costs to send a letter across the country."

"I remember when stamps cost three cents."

"They were three cents each for over a century. Have you ever heard of anything staying the same price that long?"

"I think it's all them fancy stamps. I'll bet they're driving up the costs. What's the matter with good old presidential stamps? I remember Eisenhower and Roosevelt. Washington even. If they're good enough to be on our money, why did we stop putting them on the stamps?" He scowled at the door and rolled his eyes as Clive strutted in.

"Is Winston giving you a hard time this morning Gwen?" Clive gave me one of his snaggletooth grins. "Cause I'd be happy to take him on over to the police station and keep an eye on him 'til he simmers down."

"No, thank you, Clive. He's just sore about the cost of stamps and the fact that they aren't making them with presidents anymore."

"I've got a bunch with presidents in my collection. They had a lot of them at the Museum, too, not that I know if they survived the fire." Clive collected stamps along with coins, bird nests and teeth from all manner of creatures. He brought the teeth in to show me once. It was creepy. So I tried to encourage the stamp collecting. I usually kept back a couple of sheets I knew would interest him, tucked out of sight beneath the plainer choices.

"Do you have any one-cent Washington stamps?" I rang up a book of ten flags for Winston and handed him the change.

"I have one, but I'd like to get my hands on a nicer specimen. There were a lot of them issued so they aren't hard to find. Nice ones are not as easy."

"What would you say yours is worth?" I asked.

"Fourteen hundred probably."

"Dollars?" I asked. The thought of Clive having more than two months' Social Security to rub together was flabbergasting.

"Of course dollars. What would I want with any foreign money?" Clive disappeared out of sight, and I heard him turning the lock on his post office box.

"If that one isn't very good, how much would a valuable one be worth?" How could I have been working in the post office all these years and paid so little attention? I guess I was just so sick of postage by the end of the day, it never occurred to me to enjoy it during my leisure time.

"An uncanceled one in very fine condition sold at an auction house around ten times that a couple of years ago." Clive's voice echoed through his postal box. A bunch of stamps at fourteen thousand apiece gave Chris a fine reason for murder.

TWENTY-EIGHT

Just before lunch Gene arrived in the post office carrying a cane.

"I thought you might be doing well enough by now to replace your crutches with this. Consider it a hostess gift for my visit yesterday." Gene blushed and cleared his throat.

"I can't accept this. It could be valuable."

"It cost me almost nothing. Give it no more thought."

"I think your idea of valuable and mine don't always overlap. Clive tells me the stamp you said wasn't valuable sells for about fourteen hundred dollars each, even in fair condition. Is that what you mean by not worth much?"

"I believe I also said I wasn't a stamp expert. My interests lie more with period furniture, autographs and ephemera." Gene plucked a handkerchief from his breast pocket and buffed the silver head of the cane.

"Clive said the museum had a bunch of those stamps. Do you think the ones in the collection could have been underinsured?" Gene's hands sped up on the buffing.

"Beulah seemed to think the fact that I have an

antique shop makes me an expert on everything over twenty years old. Do you know she once asked me to give her an estimate on her Mason jars? She had enough of them in her attic to start a jam factory." Gene handed me the cane.

"Augusta said pickle factory when we saw them. So, were they valuable?"

"Not enough to justify dragging me out on a cold evening to climb rickety stairs, they weren't. Beulah would expect me to trot on over any time something she noticed lying around the house caught her attention. I felt like a trick dog." Gene rolled his eyes.

"I'd get calls about her mail or a dripping faucet," I sympathized. "Beulah was just lonely."

"Perhaps, but that didn't mean I delighted in being at her beck and call."

"Do you remember the cane she used after her hip surgery? It looked like the hand on the museum." Turning over the cane in my hand, I liked the heft of it. I leaned my weight on it and felt it hold.

"I don't even remember her having one. Does that one suit you?"

"It's perfect. Thanks again."

"Enjoy. And give my regards to your charming sister."

On my lunch break I tried out the cane. As I shuffled along Diego appeared at my side, a shovel perched on his shoulder.

"No crutches today?" he asked.

"No. Gene at The Hodge Podge gave me this to try

instead."

"It is easy to use?"

"I think so."

"Many people use these for walking?"

"Mostly older people."

"My grandfather has one in Brazil. It is yellow metal on the top."

"Brass, I think you mean."

"Yes, that is the word." Diego nodded. "I was at the police seeing my uncle."

"How is he doing?"

"He is afraid. My mother, too. Immigration will send him back, and we are better having him with us because my father does not help with money."

"Do you know if Ray has called Immigration yet?"

"I am thinking he did not. The police station is not like ones on television." We had gotten to the station and looked in the window. Ernesto sat at the table pointing at a hand of cards fanned out in front of him. Ray was gesturing animatedly and laying down his own hand. The post office was supposed to reopen in five minutes. Fortunately, we've never received a visit from the Post Master General, so I wasn't worried about anything other than a few grumbles.

"No, it isn't really like a police station at all." I climbed the steps to the station and pushed the door open. Ray glanced up and dropped his hand over a pile of animal crackers in the center of the table.

"Are you gambling?" I thumped my cane to punctuate my words. "In the police station?"

"It's only for animal crackers. There's nothing

wrong with that." Ray looked as sheepish as I'd seen him since the time the Sunday school teacher caught him helping himself to seconds from the communion wafer tray.

"What are the camels worth?" I ate one from Ray's pile. Camels are my favorites.

"You owe me five dollars." Ray stretched out his broad palm like he thought I'd pay up. I snagged an elephant.

"Elephants are ten dollars, yes?" Ernesto looked at Ray for confirmation. Ray nodded and dug into the circus box for a camel and an elephant.

"You knew Chris played poker with Winston, Bill, Harold, Clive and me Wednesday nights, didn't you?" Ray dealt new cards and tossed a lion into the pot. I peeked at his hand and decided that lions couldn't be worth more than a dollar.

"I'd heard about it." I wandered over to look at Ernesto's cards. His pile of crackers was large, and with the cards he was holding, he could afford an elephant.

"Well, with Chris locked up and Harold out of commission, we could use another player. And Ernie here is good, real good." Ray chewed his lower lip as he watched Ernesto toss in two elephants and a camel.

"So I see. Too bad he's trespassing. You could add gambling to the trespassing charges, or at least you could mention it when you call Immigration." I winked at Ernesto.

"He's taught me more in the last eighteen hours about poker than I've learned in the twenty-five years

I've been playing."

"Well, then, it'll be a shame to see him go. I'm sure he could have taught you enough to beat the pants off Clive and the rest of them if he only had enough time." I turned to leave. "Good luck with the deportation, Ernie. I'll tell your nephew you said goodbye." Ray's hand hovered over his chip pile.

"I've been too busy to call Immigration. As to the trespassing thing, I may have been a little hasty. I'm a big guy. I know when to say I was wrong." Ray threw in another lion.

"Are you dropping the charges?" I stopped, my hand on the door.

"Ernie's free to go so long as he agrees to keep up my poker lessons. Bill's cleaning me out every week."

"I don't think you can force him to play poker with you," I said.

"I know that and you know that, but his English isn't so good, so maybe he doesn't know. I'd appreciate if you wouldn't tell him." Ray took one look at Ernesto going all in with a circus full of animals and folded.

"Ernesto, Ray says you're free to go. He'd like to invite you to play poker with him sometimes if you don't have other plans."

"I will play. I am no working if Boss is gone."

"I think you should walk Diego home so your sister can stop worrying about you." Ernesto beamed and jumped up. He dashed for the door, and I watched him embrace Diego. I expected the boy to look embarrassed or to tug away but he hugged his uncle back. Sitting down across from Ray, I snitched another camel and popped it into my mouth.

"Do you remember a cane lying near Beulah's body when we were working the Museum fire?"

"A cane? No. The only thing I remember seeing is Beulah."

"She was using one because of her hip replacement. It should have been with her when we found her."

"Maybe it burned up."

"The head of the cane was brass. It should have survived the fire."

"Yeah, so?"

"So who took it? If Beulah was dead, and we were the next ones on the scene, someone else must have taken it." Ray stopped looking at his cards and gave me his full attention. It still wasn't impressive, but at least he was trying.

"Like who?"

"Like someone who either killed her or saw her lying helpless on the floor and did nothing to help her."

"Do you think it was Chris?" Ray asked.

"It could have been him. It could have been Ethel. Either of them seemed cold enough to leave her for dead, and if she had found them at the museum taking stuff, then they had even more reason to kill her. Can you get a search warrant for Chris's house to look for Beulah's cane and then let me know if you find anything?" Ray jumped out of his chair and got on the phone.

I took that as a yes and trudged back to work, wondering what had become of Hugh. Was he still filling out paperwork about Chris and Ethel, or had another Christmas tree fire blazed up somewhere in his district.

Hugh phoned the post office ten minutes after I'd stowed my new cane in the back room. He sounded tired and far away.

"I meant to call before this. I got called out to a warehouse fire."

"Sounds grim."

"I could use a distraction. Nothing going on in town since I hauled Chris away?"

I filled him in about the value of the stamp, Beulah's missing cane, Ernesto's release, and the potential search warrant.

"Sounds like you've been as busy as I have. I'll give Ray a call and meet him at Chris's to go over the place. If Beulah's cane is there, it'll be pretty damning." We hung up as Clive came back into the post office.

"I thought you'd like to see my Washington stamp since you sounded interested earlier." He plopped an album on the counter and cracked it open. Thumbing through, he stopped at a stamp that looked like the one from the box at Beulah's.

"Where did you get this, Clive?" I looked at Clive in a whole new way. He always seemed harmless enough, but that's what the neighbors of serial killers invariably said.

"I can't see how it's any of your business." He snapped the album shut.

"Did you take this from Beulah's after she died?" I slapped my hand down on the album to keep him from making off with evidence.

"Of course not. It was a gift."

"From Beulah?" That was something I couldn't believe. Beulah was a generous person, but anything she perceived as valuable got sent to the Museum so everyone could enjoy it.

"No, from someone else." Clive tugged at the album.

"I mentioned seeing one like this recently. It was in a box of things found in Chris's vehicle as he was fleeing town. The boxes had been in Beulah's attic, and Augusta and I saw them the day after she died. You'd better tell me where this came from." I stared at him until he slid his bony hand off the album.

"Ethel gave it to me."

"Why would she give you a valuable stamp? I thought you said the two of you had stopped seeing each other."

"We had, but she wanted a favor, so she gave it to me."

"That's an expensive thank you. Did she know how valuable the stamp was?"

"Sure she did. She asked me about it the day after the fire at the Museum. I was coming out of the post office when she was headed in. She invited me over for lunch and asked what I thought it was worth." So

Ethel hadn't wasted any time getting the stamp from Beulah's as soon as the fire occurred. Did she know about the stamp when Beulah died, or was she just snooping around and got lucky? Did she go to Beulah's to get it, or did Chris? What did Trina know?

"So was that the favor, to ask you to evaluate the stamp?"

"Nope. She wanted me to hang on to something for her."

"Which was?" It was like pulling teeth. Usually I couldn't get Clive to be quiet, and now that I wanted him to talk, I couldn't pry it out of him.

"A suitcase."

"A suitcase? She gave you a fourteen-hundred-dollar stamp to hold on to a suitcase? What was in it?"

"I don't know. I just wanted the stamp. Besides, I thought maybe it was an excuse to get back together with me. I'm hot stuff, you know." Clive pulled a handkerchief from his back pocket and wiped his nose, carefully inspecting the contents before stuffing it back in his pocket.

"You have no idea what was in the suitcase, no idea at all?" What kind of a person was more interested in what was in his nose than what was in a secret suitcase?

"Nope. I never looked in it. I saw a little red suitcase about the right size for an overnight visit sitting in Ethel's favorite chair in the front room. When I asked her if she wanted me to take it when I left, she said no, she had something she needed it for first."

"Did she say why?" I drummed my finger on the album, frustrated that Ethel couldn't speak for herself.

"She said something about an appointment for an opinion. She seemed happy about the whole thing. She gave me a second piece of lemon pie."

"So you never got it?" A missing cane and a suitcase. Missing letters, valuable stamps. I wasn't sure if things were clearing up or getting muddier.

"Well, she was dead before the next day came. I'd no reason to go back to her house, and she didn't need me to keep it for her anymore, so I left well enough alone."

"You didn't think this was important enough to mention? She could have been killed over what was in that suitcase."

"If it was that dangerous, I'm glad I never did get a hold of it."

"I think you should leave the stamp with me for now. Hugh will want to take a look at this." Clive nodded and shuffled out. I unlocked the safe and put the album in it.

Through the glass in the door I could see Diego pulling his two younger brothers behind him on a long plastic toboggan. He looked happy for the first time since I'd met him. Seeing me, he waved and turned in the direction of the post office.

"You boys look like you're having fun," I said, watching Ronaldo and Tulio pile snow onto their laps and into each other's faces.

"We love snow. We built a snow house and snow persons. My mother is asking for you to come tonight to dinner. Will you do this?" I was completely beat, but I didn't want to give Diego any reason to stop smiling.

"I'd love to. Is there anything I can bring?"

"No, just come. Seven o'clock." Diego lifted a woolly mitten at me and rejoined his brothers in the snow.

All the rest of the afternoon I thought about the search warrant and the suitcase. I couldn't exactly call Trina's and ask her how things were going. I still didn't know if Hugh or Ray had gotten the warrant or if they had found anything in the search. Patrons filed in and out, and business went on as usual. It was pitch dark outside by the time the phone rang.

"Nothing," Hugh said, "absolutely nothing. Ray and I went over Chris's house like we were searching for nuclear waste. Zip. If there was ever anything to do with the fires or the Museum thefts, it isn't there now."

"So you didn't find the cane."

"Nope, no canes, but Trina sent a message for you."

I glanced over my shoulder at the overflowing sacks of mail and pile of packages near the back door. The floor was filmed over with sandy grime, and my email inbox hadn't been cleared out in at least a week.

"Let me guess," I said. "She quit."

"She definitely quit. I don't think it'll do you any good for me to repeat the specifics."

"I may have something to check into." I quietly told him about Clive and the suitcase. "Maybe the cane is in the suitcase." Hugh agreed to meet me at Ethel's when I got out of the post office in about half an hour. I toddled through the dark towards her house, comfortable using the cane instead of the crutches.

Hugh stood in the kitchen looking at the spot where Ethel's body had sprawled on the floor only a few days before. His shoulders slumped a bit, and his nose was raw and almost as red as his moustache.

"You look like death warmed over."

"I received a cold in my Christmas stocking."

"Did you get a box of tissues to go with it?"

"My mother gives me a half-dozen handkerchiefs with my initials on them every year, so I'm all set." I wondered if she knew he used them for picking up evidence at crime scenes.

"My mother always gives me weight loss books and exercise videos."

"That's not what I'd give you." Hugh winked at me in a very unprofessional manner.

I blushed and said, "Let's look for Beulah's cane." Hugh stepped across the new white tile floor, dropping snow as he went. I followed him toward the living room.

"Did Clive tell you where he saw the suitcase?"

"He said it was in the front room."

Methodically, we searched the first floor, beginning with Ethel's favorite chair. There was no suitcase in the front room, the dining room, the kitchen or hidden in the tiny powder room. Hugh climbed the stairs two at a time. I thought he was just showing off. One step at a time was still a struggle for me. Hugh passed a room decorated with kittens and heaped up with piles of clothes and mounds of junk jewelry and went on to one so full of clutter it was hard to see the bed in the middle of the room.

"I thought Beulah's house was difficult to sort out. I'd hate to be Ethel's next of kin."

"I think that may be Trina with Chris in jail. Do you see a suitcase?"

"Not here in the center of the room I don't." I wiggled my way through the piles and opened the closet door. Summery dresses hung on the rod, and plastic storage tubs stuffed with shoes covered the floor. It didn't look like there was space for anything else, not even as small a thing as the suitcase Clive described.

We searched under the beds, behind all the doors, even up in the attic and down in the basement. We didn't have any better luck here than Hugh had at Chris's. After an hour and a half we gave up and collapsed on the sofa.

"It doesn't look like the suitcase is still here," I said, leaning back against a toss pillow.

"If it ever was. Are you sure Clive was telling you the truth?" Hugh asked.

"Clive isn't imaginative enough to make up a story like this. He'd lie to get out of trouble, but I can't see him inventing this."

"If he's telling the truth, the suitcase must have

been important."

"But was it important enough to get her killed?"

"That's exactly what we need to figure out."

TWENTY-NINE

Thanks to a ride from Hugh I arrived at the DaSilvas at exactly seven o'clock. I sat down and enjoyed being surrounded by cheerful faces and Portuguese as I tucked into the deep-fried chicken turnovers Luisa urged on all of us. Potato salad and tomato salad, rice and chicken covered the table.

"Everything is delicious. Thank you for inviting me. If I'd gone home for dinner, I would have eaten a bowl of cereal standing over the sink." I reached for another glossy green olive.

"Thank you for helping my brother. We are being so happy he is with us."

"It was my pleasure." I saw Luisa elbow Ernesto, and he gave me a long look before speaking.

"Chris is at prison?" he asked.

"He's at the county jail. If he's convicted he'll go to prison." I put down my fork and gave him my full attention.

"Is only the fires he is at jail for?" He drummed his fingers on the tabletop.

"Right now it is. He may have had something to do with the death of Beulah or Ethel. Do you have something you want to tell me about this?"

"I am worried to say things. I am thinking I do

wrong things and not know."

"Does this have something to do with Chris?"

"I say to you I go with Chris to small building for stuffs when fire is at Museum. I not say we stop at house of dead lady first."

"You stopped at Beulah's or at Ethel's?"

"At the house you are hitting me with sticks." Beulah's house.

"Why did you go there?" I leaned toward him and tried to look encouraging.

"Chris give me a stick like you are using. He say to me he find this, and it is of the lady. We take it for to help her."

"Was she there when you went to her house?"

"No. House is dark, and Chris say for us to go in. He say lady like him."

"Did the stick have a hand?" I held up my hand with an index finger sticking straight up. Ernesto nodded.

"Did you take the cane into Beulah's house?"

"I was taking and Chris was looking for other peoples who like to say we are not good taking the stick to the house."

"Where did you put it?"

"He is saying to me to take to small place for coats. I put there and we go to other town."

"So you put it in the coat closet and left?" Ernesto nodded. "Did Chris say anything else?"

"He say I am touching with hands, and he have gloves for cold, and if I am saying about this police will say I was in the house of the lady, not him." I noticed that no one was eating anymore, but all the children were silent, listening, even the smallest one. Luisa laid her hand on Ernesto's shoulder, and he continued.

"I no have license for drive. I go to Boss house. He say is bad to lose truck and to leave big hand in car. He say is bad that you see me. He say I go away, back to Brazil. I no like to leave Luisa so I go for to hide at house where you find me."

Ernesto took a breath and slumped back in his chair. His eyes looked too big for his pinched face. Luisa squeezed his shoulder.

"Your information is important. It helps us to prove that Chris didn't help Beulah when she was at the Museum. He may have even killed her. If he took her cane, there has to be a reason."

"Do you think Chris killed her with the cane and wanted to hide it?" Diego asked.

"I think I need to see that cane. If it was used to kill her, there should still be something on it to prove it was a weapon."

"Is my uncle in more trouble?" Diego asked.

"Hugh will need to talk to him again. He may need to go to court to tell what he knows about this." Ernesto stiffened at the word court. "I don't think it will matter that he is illegal. The court is not Immigration. All they want is the truth about Chris. It was best Ernesto told me. I was already looking for the cane, and with his fingerprints on it, things would have looked bad for him."

"What about staying at Beulah's?" Diego asked.

With his English being the best in the family I wondered how often he acted as a liaison in things that were above the heads of most kids his age.

"My sister owns that house now. She won't mind you were there. Thank you for telling me, Ernesto. I should go to Beulah's to look for the cane."

I said my goodbyes quickly, refused the offer of a doggie bag, and plunged into the cold. My ankle was still hurting, but I didn't have a choice. The DaSilvas didn't have a phone or a car. My only other option would have been to have Diego pull me in his sled.

Even though it was only a half-mile to Beulah's, I was chilled through by the time I arrived on her doorstep. The house felt warmer than the outdoors by at least thirty degrees, but I was surprised to see how quickly puddles formed on the kitchen floor. I flipped on the light and went to the hall closet. Parting the wool coats, I peered in. At the back of the closet I could see the glint of its brass, hand-shaped knob.

I reached for it carefully with my mittened hand. I wished I had one of Hugh's handkerchiefs to use. He made it look easy. Returning to the kitchen, I held the cane under the light. Something dark had dried in the carved creases of the knuckles and around the brass cuticles of the fingers. It looked like someone had simply wiped it in a hurry instead of washing it carefully.

Beulah always kept a set of high-strength reading glasses on the dining room table with her work. I carried the cane with me to the dining room. The whole house was dark, and I felt a little nervous as I fumbled for the switch for the chandelier. As I reached for Beulah's glasses a small red suitcase sitting in a chair caught my eye.

I laid the cane on the table, stepped toward the case and tugged on the zipper. Pushing open the lid, I saw a loose pile of envelopes. The paper was yellowed. The writing was antiquated but legible, and I was able to make out the addressee. It was Eustace Hartwell, the man in the photograph with the cane, Beulah's great-grandfather.

More interesting was the lack of a stamp. The letter had been cancelled in Buffalo, New York, so it had been sent through the post. With a surge of excitement I tugged off my mittens, noting the signature M. Fillmore where the stamp should have been.

Turning the letter over in my hand, I slid the letter from the envelope and unfolded the crackling pages. Adjusting my eyes to the old-fashioned script, I scanned for information. It read like a thank you note. Appreciation for hospitality and gratefulness for introductions in the community filled the first sheet. Moving to the second sheet, the signature caught my eye. There it lay, just like the images I saw on the computer while researching the Know-Nothing Party. Millard Fillmore. My heart thumping, I reached for another letter. Opening it and turning to the last page revealed that it, too, was from the former President.

I spread all the letters on the table and arranged

them by date. The first ones were impersonal and polite. The later ones sounded as though written to a friend. They spoke of the campaign trail and the strength of the competition. Mostly, though, they spoke of the poison spreading through the nation in the form of Catholic immigrants. Millard Fillmore thanked Eustace for his support and the support of those he had encountered at the meeting of true Americans in Winslow Falls. Fillmore thanked Eustace for being a patriot in troubled times and expressed a certainty he could be counted on to rally his fellow party members at voting time.

The Know-Nothing Party, that's what this was all about. It wasn't about stamps. It wasn't even about the autographs on the envelopes. While they would probably be worth quite a bit of money, if the Franklin Pierce autograph I'd seen in Gene's shop was any indication of presidential signature value, I was willing to bet the contents of the letter was where the real value lay.

"But did Ethel realize what she had?" I asked myself aloud. My voice sounded louder than normal in the empty house.

"No, she didn't." Gene's voice came from the doorway. I turned and saw him standing there, the beaded vest from the attic dangling from his hand.

"What are you doing here, Gene?" My throat felt dry, and my stomach churned like it had on the night of the Museum fire. He stepped toward me, and I felt an urgency to put something physically between us. "Were you looking for Know-Nothing paraphernalia?"

"You don't know how sorry I am to hear you say that, Gwen. I've always liked you, and it will grieve me to distress Augusta." He stepped toward me. I tightened my hold on the letters.

"Did you take this suitcase from Ethel's?"

"They aren't just any letters. You don't realize what kind of a historical find this is. Virtually no information has survived about the Know-Nothings. To have a former president's signature on a letter discussing his part in their meetings is unprecedented. Add on the fact that he was abusing his ability to post his letters for free by just signing the envelope, and you're sitting on a gold mine. But it really isn't about the money."

"What is it about, then, owning a piece of history?" I stepped back a little further. His voice rose, and he paced in front of the door, flinging his arms about.

"Anyone with enough money can do that. I want to be an expert. I will be the world's leading authority on a subject, one that has intrigued both myself and political historians for decades."

"Did you kill Ethel?" I asked, hearing my voice crack. Any second now I was either going to vomit or burst into tears. Neither Hugh nor Augusta knew where I was. Gene was blocking the door I'd come in through, the one closest to the kitchen. I inched toward the one that connected the dining and living rooms, keeping the table between us.

"Stupid, grasping cow. Ethel had no idea what she

had gotten her hands on this time."

"But you knew."

"Of course I knew. Would I be here otherwise? From the first time I drove into Winslow Falls to look at the building I bought for The Hodge Podge, I knew the potential was here for a very big find. Local bigwigs don't place a Know-Nothing symbol up on the highest point in the town without a reason. I was certain something was going to pay off. I just needed to keep looking until I found it."

"Did she offer to sell you the letters?" I leaned on my cane, thinking about its potential as a weapon. The one that had probably killed Beulah was just out of reach.

"She asked my opinion on the value of the signature. She met me in her kitchen and handed me a letter. At first she didn't mention that there were more, but her greed got the better of her. She returned to the front room and brought back a few more for me to evaluate."

"That doesn't explain how she died." I wasn't sure I wanted to hear the answer. Too many bad things happened to people who had something to do with any of this. Mostly, I just wanted to get to the door. My heart was knocking around so hard I was sure it was going to break one of my ribs.

"When her stupid cat meowed at the front door, I removed the letter from its envelope. The contents were sufficiently interesting for me to peruse the other ones she had brought in. By the time she had persuaded the cat to come in, I realized this was what

I'd spent years looking for. When she saw me reading them, she tried to grab them back." Gene's voice rose higher. He stopped his pacing and noticed me creeping towards the door. "Sorry, Gwen, I can't let you leave."

THIRTY

I bolted. I launched through the doorway with a speed that I hadn't possessed since I was ten.

Gene was standing in front of the kitchen door to the outside. I wasn't getting out that way. I thought about the layout of the house and made a dive for the basement stairs. I wrenched the door open and tripped on the first step. Running, tumbling and losing my footing all the way down, I prayed I'd make it to the bulkhead and out before Gene caught up with me. I couldn't stop long enough to feel for a light. Relying on memory, I raced through the clammy space running my hand along the rough stone foundation wall until I felt it disappear, and the bulkhead stairs stood before me.

Tears sprang from my eyes as relief washed over me. Ankle throbbing, knees trembling, I mounted the short flight of steps. Pushing upward on the double doors, I knew I was going to make it out after all.

The doors didn't budge. They couldn't be locked. When Bill Lambert installed the bulkhead for Beulah years before, he had suggested a lock. Beulah said she'd never been in the habit of locking her doors and wasn't about to start so late in the game.

"Snow." The lights flickered on, and Gene's voice floated towards me from the basement stairs. "There's a couple of feet piled on top of the door. You'll never push your way out." I shoved and pushed harder, becoming even more frantic with each footfall clattering over the concrete floor.

"I really am sorry," Gene said. I rattled the door desperately, looking back over my shoulder. A puff of cold air drifted toward my face, but the crack wouldn't widen enough to let me out. Gene's hands grabbed my waist. I struggled to pull away, but it wasn't helping. He was larger, stronger, and wasn't working with a sprained ankle.

"Please, Gene, you don't want to do this." Tears slid down my face. I felt myself start to hyperventilate.

"No, I really don't, but in order to get what I want, I must."

Gene dragged me toward him. My feet barely touched the stairs on the way down. He clamped down on one of my arms with his left hand and put the other on the back of my head. Before I knew what was happening, he thrust my head toward the rock wall of the foundation. My forehead took the bulk of the impact, and my vision blurred. Before I even registered the pain he was dragging me toward the laundry room. He shoved me in and slammed the door.

I heard a dragging noise beyond the door. The noise stopped, and I heard something heavy thump up against the laundry room door. Hauling myself to my feet, I threw my weight against the door and tried the knob. It turned smoothly in my hand, but the door opened barely a crack before it bumped against whatever Gene had lodged there. My best guess was the old water heater Beulah hadn't had hauled away because of the disposal cost when she had a new one installed.

I heard Gene stopping in front of the laundry room every few moments. As I tried peeping through the crack between the door and the jamb, blood trickled down through my eyebrow and into my eye. I wiped it away with my sleeve, but it kept flowing. I felt for the light and then searched for something to stop the bleeding.

I grabbed a yellow cotton blouse and held it against my head. Standing near the door I surveyed the room for a way to escape. Straining my ears, I heard Gene mount the wooden stairs to the first floor. A wave of relief washed over me. Maybe he thought he had killed me and was leaving with the letters.

The windowless room was small, no more than eight feet square. The walls were constructed of two-by-fours and plywood. The door hinges were on the outside. In front of me sat a washer and dryer and an old-fashioned soaking tub. Above them hung a bank of three cabinets. At the end was a full-length closet. A drying rack and a table for folding ran along the wall opposite the laundry machines. An ironing board was propped in the corner.

I heard Gene's footsteps on the stairs again. I pressed the side of my face against the crack in the door, but Gene remained just out of view. I heard sloshing and smelled sulfur. There was a glow and then a blaze. Through the crack I could just see a mound that looked like it was made of coats and an area rug. Sticking out from the bottom of the pile was a wooden leg and a bit of skirting from an upholstered chair. I could hear Gene's feet as he dashed up the stairs.

My eyes smarted as smoke and fumes first floated, then streamed, through the opening in the doorway. I slammed it shut and searched again for a way out. Smoke barreled under the door. The smell was vile, not the familiar smell of burning wood but a smoggy stench of synthetic fibers and upholstery foam. Grabbing at the laundry draped around the room I threw it into the sink and turned on the water. I stuffed the drenched clothes against the base of the door. More smoke crept in through the gap at the top and hovered along the ceiling.

I pulled open a cabinet door looking for something, anything that could either cover the smoke or help me hack my way out. Soap, bleach and old fashioned spray starch were lined up neatly on the shelves. The next two cabinets held an old iron, cast-off baskets, clothes pins and cleaning rags. A hamper full of sheets sat on the floor of the closet. I decided to soak those and try hanging them from the ceiling in front of the door. I grabbed them and tossed them in the sink before I realized why they had been there. The closet was empty except for the hamper because it was a laundry chute. Beulah had it included several years ago as part of the laundry room design.

I'd told her at the time laundry chutes were losing favor with new home builders because of their ability to act as an unobstructed tunnel for flames in the event of a fire. I'd never been so glad not to have been listened to in my life.

I yanked the hamper out of the closet and ducked inside to get a closer look at the opening at the top. I was going to need a boost—and to shrink my circumference by about a third. I tugged on the folding table and slid it end first into the closet. I climbed on top of it and reached for the little door at the top. I could just barely touch it with the tips of my fingers.

The air outside the closet was getting smokier, and it was harder to breathe as I climbed down. Fire roared just outside the laundry room door. It felt like being back at the fire scene at the Museum. I grabbed the ironing board and pulled it on top of the table. Swaying and praying I swung a leg up on the board and tested its ability to hold me. It creaked, but it held.

I straightened and felt for the small door. Pushing against it, I realized it was latched from the outside. Frustration and anger launched me into a string of cuss words that should have blistered my tongue on the way out. Tumbling down off the board and the table, I re-entered the room to look for a battering ram. The only thing that looked helpful was the iron. The laundry room door crackled, warped and darkened in color. I grabbed the iron and scrambled back to the top of the chute.

I bashed the door with the iron, teetering and

rocking with each blow. The concern over the safety of a laundry chute was becoming more of a reality. Heat and flames felt as though they were seeking me out. Sweat mingled with the blood still weeping from my forehead.

The door must have been made of hardwood, because it never splintered. The latch gave way, and the door popped open. Twisting and wriggling, I pulled my upper body through the small opening. My hips attempted to remain behind but I dug against the door frame with my elbows. Ignoring everything but the blistering heat behind me I pried and squeezed. Fleshy bits circling my hips cried out in pain as I popped free.

Slamming the door behind me to help contain the fire, I dashed for the dining room. The suitcase was gone, but Beulah's cane still lay on the table. I grabbed it and ran.

Bursting into the cold fresh air, I sucked in a deep breath. Skittering along the icy walk, I hauled up short. On the ground was a pile of arms, legs and fur. Gene lay stretched out flat on his stomach. Ernesto sat on his back. Clive had his heavy winter boot pressed against Gene's neck. In one hand Clive held Brandy's leash, in the other a little red suitcase. Brandy stood over Gene and growled every time he twitched.

"This is the suitcase I was telling you about." Clive held it out to me.

"How did you know to show up here?" I asked

Ernesto.

"Diego and me not like you going here with no person with you. We go behind you and wait," Ernesto said.

"I was walking Brandy and saw Ernesto and Diego standing around. Then Gene comes running out the house like he's seen a ghost, and he's carrying Ethel's suitcase, so maybe he had. There twern't any good reason I could see that he'd be running away from Beulah's or carrying that case, so I shouted to Ernie to stop him, and he just stuck out his foot. Gene went down ass over teakettle, and Ernie dropped on his back like a paperweight. I helped out a bit with my boot, and Brandy encouraged him to stay put.

"Where's Diego?"

"Gone to get Ray."

"We need the fire department, too," I said, but there was no need. The town's shiniest new engine jounced to a stop in front of the house, and Winston sprang from the cab like a man half his age. Ray and Diego pulled in behind and ran to stand over Gene.

"You don't look so good," Ray said.

"I look better than I would have if I'd been trapped in Beulah's laundry room for another two minutes."

"I meant your hair." Ray grimaced and pointed. I put my hand to my head to feel for my hat and touched the throbbing lump on my forehead instead. I must have lost my hat in the fray. Now that the fear had drained away, I felt dizzy and exhausted. And angrier than I'd ever been in my life. If there hadn't been any witnesses, I'm not sure what would have happened to Gene.

"Did you kill Ethel?" I shouted. Brandy growled and lunged forward.

"Don't interrupt, Dog." Clive gave her leash a gentle tug.

"She grabbed the letters out of my hand when she came back from letting in the cat. I couldn't let them go. She pulled on them and slipped in a puddle on the ceramic tile, hitting her head on the corner of the woodstove. I checked her pulse and could tell there was nothing I could do for her." Gene strained to lift his head a little to look at me.

"Heifer dust. The dent in Ethel's head didn't begin to match up with the corner of her woodstove." Gene slumped back to the ground as a high-pitched wail filled the air.

"There's the ambulance," Winston said.

"I need to call Hugh." Flames shot through the roof and lit the night sky.

"I'm already here." Hugh's voice called out as he loped toward me. I hurried to meet him and sank my grimy face into his chest. Coughing and crying, I felt the softness of the wool sweater I'd given him rub against my cheek. His chest felt sturdy beneath it and his arms capable as he wrapped them round me. His biceps muffled the sounds around us as he stood swaying a little, rocking me like an injured child.

THIRTY-ONE

Hours later as I sat at the table in the middle of the police station with a bag of animal crackers in my lap and a thick bandage stuck to my forehead, Hugh and Ray filled me in on what I'd missed while receiving medical attention. I wish I could honestly say I'd wanted to refuse help and be in on the last of the investigation, but truth to be told, I was rattled. The last little bit of brave I had got burned up in my anger at Gene. Just the thought of being anywhere near him again made me as queasy as I'd been the night of the Museum fire. So I skipped out and was grateful for a legitimate excuse.

"We searched Gene's shop and found the hand. He admitted to breaking into your house and taking it. He saw it once while he was picking Augusta up for a date."

"I wonder what he was planning to do with it?"

"I'm not sure he had a plan. I think he was just obsessed with any evidence pointing to the Know-Nothings."

"Speaking of evidence, other than him trying to burn me up at Beulah's, was there anything to prove he killed Ethel?"

"Faced with the facts from the medical examiner, it

didn't take Gene too long to start telling the truth."
Hugh sat next to me, his notebook opened up on the
table in front of us.

"It didn't sound much like what he tried telling
me, did it?" I asked.

"No, it didn't. Ethel asked him to evaluate an
autograph for her," Hugh said.

"Millard Fillmore?"

"Right. When he got a good look at it Gene
realized what she had and told her a figure that he
expected the signatures alone would fetch. He offered
to purchase them from her, but she refused, saying she
wanted to think about it."

"I bet he didn't like hearing that." I popped a
camel cracker into my mouth.

"He played along, telling her she was wise to shop
around for the best offer, and left. He knew she must
have gotten them from Beulah's or the Museum
because of the addressee on the envelope. Since he
was sure they were stolen, he convinced himself he
had at least as much right as she did to them and
determined to sneak in that night and steal them
himself."

"But she caught him at it, didn't she? I bet she was
up getting her pills." I fished a lion out of the bag and
then tossed it back, looking for another camel.

"How'd you know that?" Hugh asked.

"Haven't you heard? Postmistresses are nosy.
Actually she mentioned how cold it was when she got
up to take her pills at night since the window had

been broken."

"She came out just as he was leaving and startled him. He picked up the weight Chris had brought over to fix the window and struck her on the back of the head with it."

"That would explain the shape of the wound. What happened to the weight?"

"He tossed it down into the window well where the trim molding was pried off, figuring no one would think it out of place there if it was run into during a future renovation. Pretty good spot to dispose of it actually."

"Gene's a clever man."

"Not clever enough to dispose of you, I'm glad to say." Hugh reached over and cupped my cheek below the bandage. I leaned into it.

"I'm glad, too. What about Beulah? Do you think it's going to be possible to prove whether it was Chris or Ethel who killed her?"

"Between Ernesto's testimony about the cane and Chris's own admission about the arson, a good prosecutor will be able to build a decent case against Chris."

"But is he the one who killed Beulah?"

"Unless Chris pleads guilty to cut a deal, we probably won't know. Beulah's body was so badly charred we don't know if it was the head wound that killed her or smoke inhalation. Either way, he's responsible for her death."

"So there will always be questions."

"Only one that still interests me." Hugh leaned forward and reached for my hand. "Now that the case is closed, will I be seeing any more of you or not?"

Standing in front of the cellar hole the next day where Beulah's house had stood, I still couldn't believe the place had burned to the ground. Just looking at the charred debris made me shaky and angry all over again. Augusta was remarkably upbeat about the whole thing.

"At least we don't need to inventory it anymore." She turned up her collar against the stiff breeze and draped her arm over my shoulder. "Too bad I've already given up the lease on my condo."

"You didn't tell me that," I said.

"I finalized everything while you were at work yesterday. Good thing I can stay with you." I wasn't sure I would have called it good, but I'd been grateful to have someone else in the house with me last night when I woke up with nightmares about being roasted alive.

"So you'll be staying a while," I said.

"Yes. The Museum needs a curator, and there might be an opportunity for a new antique store."

"Good. I need to borrow something from your wardrobe again. I've got a date tonight with Hugh."